Passion's
Bright Fury

Candi
07

What Reviewers Say About Radclyffe's Books

"...well-plotted...lovely romance...I couldn't turn the pages fast enough!"—**Ann Bannon**, author of *The Beebo Brinker Chronicles*

"The author's brisk mix of political intrigue, fast-paced action, and frequent interludes of lesbian sex and love...in *Honor Reclaimed*... sure does make for great escapist reading."—**Richard Labonte**, Q Syndicate

"If you're looking for a well-written police procedural make sure you get a copy of *Shield of Justice*. Most assuredly worth it."—**Lynne Jamneck**, author of *Down the Rabbit Hole* and reviewer for The L Life

"Radclyffe has once again pulled together all the ingredients of a genuine page-turner, this time adding some new spices into the mix. Whatever one's personal take on the subject matter, *shadowland* is sure to please—in part because Radclyffe never loses sight of the fact that she is telling a love story, and a compelling one at that."—**Cameron Abbott**, author of *To The Edge* and *An Inexpressible State of Grace*

"*Stolen Moments*...edited by Radclyffe & Stacia Seaman...is a collection of steamy stories about women who just couldn't wait. It's sex when desire overrides reason, and it's incredibly hot!"—**Suzanne Corson**, *On Our Backs*

"With ample angst, realistic and exciting medical emergencies, winsome secondary characters, and a sprinkling of humor, *Fated Love* turns out to be a terrific romance. It's one of the best I have read in the last three years. Run—do not walk—right out and get this one. You'll be hooked by yet another of Radclyffe's wonderful stories. Highly recommended."—Author **Lori L. Lake**, *Midwest Book Review*

"Radclyffe, through her moving text...in *Innocent Hearts*...illustrates that our struggles for acceptance of women loving women is as old as time—only the setting changes. The romance is sweet, sensual, and touching."—**Kathi Isserman**, reviewer for *Just About Write*

Visit us at www.boldstrokesbooks.com

PASSION'S
BRIGHT FURY

by

RADCLY*f*FE

2006

PASSION'S BRIGHT FURY

© 2003 By Radclyffe. All Rights Reserved.

ISBN 1-933110-54-6

This Trade Paperback Original Is Published By
Bold Strokes Books, Inc.,
New York, USA

First Edition: Renaissance Alliance 2003
Second Edition: Bold Strokes Books, Inc., September 2006

CREDITS
Editors: Jennifer Knight and Stacia Seaman
Production Design: Stacia Seaman
Cover Design By Sheri (GRAPHICARTIST2020@HOTMAIL.COM)

By the Author

Romances

Safe Harbor *order*   Love's Masquerade

Beyond the Breakwater *order*   shadowland – *order*

Innocent Hearts *order*   Fated Love – *order*

Love's Melody Lost *order* Distant Shores, Silent Thunder

Love's Tender Warriors *order*   Turn Back Time *order*

Tomorrow's Promise *order*   Promising Hearts *order*

Passion's Bright Fury *read*

Honor Series

order

Above All, Honor

Honor Bound

Love & Honor

Honor Guards

Honor Reclaimed

Justice Series

read A Matter of Trust (prequel)

Shield of Justice

In Pursuit of Justice

Justice in the Shadows

Justice Served

order

Change Of Pace: *Erotic Interludes*
(A Short Story Collection)

Stolen Moments: *Erotic Interludes 2*
Stacia Seaman and Radclyffe, eds.

Lessons in Love: *Erotic Interludes 3*
Stacia Seaman and Radclyffe, eds.

Acknowledgments

I resisted writing a medical novel for a long time because, despite the very sound adage of "write what you know," it has always been more fun to write about what I wished I could be. Cowboys and secret agents and artists have always fascinated me, and in writing those stories, for a short time, I could pretend. Medicine fascinates me, too, but it is always real and often far from romantic. I'm happy to have written this book because the characters, as they emerged with their own story to tell, made the experience rewarding, as always. I also discovered that I enjoy writing fiction with a medical setting, so the experiment was a success.

I am extremely grateful for the excellent editorial "polishing" performed by Jennifer Knight and Stacia Seaman on the second edition.

Sheri took my candid shots from the OR and turned them into a spectacular cover. As always, she finds the heart of the story and brings it to life with her unique style.

Lee deserves far more than my devotion, but that is the best I have to give. Thank you, love.

Radclyffe 2006

Dedication

For Lee
All my love

PROLOGUE

It was an ordinary Monday morning in July, and she scarcely noticed the people crowding her as she leaned against the metal pole in the center of the subway car. Her briefcase was secured in one hand; in the other she held the *Times* folded in half lengthwise in front of her face. It was 7:40 a.m., the height of rush hour. She had thirty blocks to ride underground to her destination.

Early-morning commuters filled every seat and pressed against her in the narrow aisle. She had given up trying to drink coffee during the trip; she had ruined one too many suits while attempting to manage a cup as she was jostled. This morning, had she stopped to purchase her usual espresso-spiked French roast, she would have taken a different train.

Sometimes, five minutes can change the course of a lifetime.

"Damn driver's gonna shake us all to death," someone grumbled.

"Excuse me, sorry," her pole-mate mumbled after losing his balance yet again and stumbling into her.

"No problem," she murmured.

Lowering her paper, she glanced through the thick, scratched glass of the sliding double doors opposite her to the dimly lit tunnel. Vertical concrete supports cast flitting shadows and the gaping mouths of dark recesses flew by quickly. Too quickly.

When the businessman next to her lurched into her once again, she tucked the newspaper under her arm, pressed the briefcase to her chest with an elbow, and grasped the pole with both hands. The car rocked heavily, and her pulse quickened as she fought to steady herself. She had to spread her feet to keep her balance. Everyone else was having difficulty staying upright, too.

The train went into a curve and seemed to tilt up on one side. Over the noise of her heart pounding erratically in her ears, she heard the reassuring squeal of the brakes being applied. *We're stopping. Nothing to worry about.*

That was her last clear thought before the world turned upside down amidst the sounds of rending metal and the screams of helpless humanity. Then there were only fragments of words and dizzying images that catapulted her in and out of consciousness, until finally reality coalesced into a blinding light in her eyes and a crimson roar of pain in her head.

She struggled to sit up, but the slight movement caused a new surge of agony in her right leg. Its terrible intensity forced the air from her lungs, and almost instantly, she realized that her arms were tied down. She fought to open her eyes and found herself staring into a huge silver disk suspended over her head, a hot white bulb in its center.

Through the piercing glare and a curtain of pain, she heard voices, strident tones forming half-sentences and clipped shorthand phrases.

Closed head injury...open tib-fib fracture...
Somebody call the OR...another one coming up...
Type and cross her...four units...
We need a CT of the chest and abdomen...STAT...

It took all her strength to speak. "Wha...oh, God...where..." She tried unsuccessfully to focus as a silhouette took shape in her field of vision, backlit by the bright light.

Gentle hands restrained her and a deep, calm voice spoke. "You were in an accident. You're at Bellevue. Can you tell me your name?"

She tried to shape the sounds of her name, but they floated away from her on a new wave of agony. She continued to gaze upward, dimly aware of fingers brushing over her face. Gradually, features began to emerge from the shadows above her, giving her something to cling to in the sea of confusion and pain. A face bending near—blue eyes so dark they were almost purple, intense and penetrating. Black hair, thick and unruly, escaped from beneath the band of a surgeon's cap that slashed across a strong, broad forehead. Prominent cheekbones and a bold, nearly masculine jaw swam into view.

"You're going to be fine."

She had no choice but to deliver herself into those confident unwavering eyes—and to believe.

CHAPTER ONE

Five years later

I don't have time for interviews," Saxon Sinclair said with barely contained irritation as she walked unannounced into the chief of surgery's office late in the last week of June. "And I'd appreciate it if you didn't schedule things for me without discussing them first."

The distinguished-looking fifty-year-old man behind the walnut desk smoothed his expensively styled, silvered hair, carefully placed his Waterman pen into the chest pocket of his spotless, starched white lab coat, and leaned back in his padded swivel chair to regard her. "I'm sorry," he said in his practiced bureaucratic voice. "I thought my secretary had cleared it with your office."

"Apparently not." She didn't believe him for a second and knew it showed in her tone. "I've got three fresh attendings, a first-year fellow, and a handful of brand-new residents starting in my trauma unit this week. I can't spare a minute to meet with some journalist. You'll have to get someone else to talk to him."

Preston Smith smiled, thinking how much he'd like to fire her arrogant ass. The intense, dark-haired woman in navy surgical scrubs was standing too close to the front of his desk to be respectful. She wore two beepers on her belt—the trauma pager that would summon her to the helipad or the trauma admitting area and the code beeper that would call her to the trauma intensive care unit in the event that a patient arrested. Rangy and lean, she was too athletic-appearing for his taste, and too aggressive for his liking. She probably wasn't even aware that she was leaning forward with her feet spread and her hands clenched at her sides.

Too bad the university was so concerned about the gender and minority profiles of their department chairs and division heads that his hands were tied. A clear bias might have a negative impact on future state and federal funding, especially now that every institution was feeling the financial crunch. The powers that be—more importantly, the powers that controlled his budget—would not take kindly to his firing one of the few female chiefs in the entire university hospital system. He conveniently ignored the fact that she was also one of the premier trauma surgeons in the state and had been the focus of several newspaper and magazine articles. Private and solitary, apparently wedded to her work, she was frustratingly competent and her reputation was unimpeachable. He couldn't find even the smallest thing, professional *or* personal, to hold over her head so he could force her into line. Seeking to conceal his aversion to her, he assumed a familiarity she had never invited. "You're the one they want to talk to, Sax," he said solicitously."You're the one with the name recognition."

"Then they can come back and talk to me in September." She started toward the door. *Pompous idiot. He hasn't actually been in the operating room in so long, he's forgotten how hairy the first few weeks of July can be.*

"I thought you'd want to meet with these folks and lay down the ground rules," he called after her, "but it's up to you, of course. You know how you want to run your unit."

These folks? She stopped and pivoted slowly, eyes narrowed. "Is there something *else* you haven't told me, Preston?"

"Image is everything in today's marketplace, and we're no exception. We're not the only level one trauma unit in Manhattan, or the only cancer center, *or* the only tertiary care facility," he said as if she weren't aware of these facts. "St. Michael's needs the exposure, and this is a perfect opportunity."

"What is this *opportunity*, exactly?"

He couldn't quite hide his triumphant smile. "One of the independent networks will be airing a documentary medical series, and the production company plans to film it here. It's an excellent vehicle for free advertising."

For a moment, she simply stared, rigidly still but for a muscle that jumped along the chiseled line of her jaw. Very quietly, in a voice edged in steel, she asked, "And what precisely does that have to do with me?"

"The producers felt that the series would have more impact if viewers could identify with a particular individual throughout the episodes, so they're going to present a year-long show based on the life of a surgical trainee."

"*Which* trainee?"

Smith made a show of moving some papers around on his desk, but Sax knew damn well that he didn't need to search for a name. This had all been decided without her input and had probably been set in motion weeks before.

"Ah...here we are. Deborah Stein."

"My new trauma fellow." It was a statement, not a question. Sax rubbed her eyes and contemplated homicide. "Does Stein know about this?"

"Of course. She agreed to it when she signed her contract." He didn't add that the final contract was contingent upon that agreement, and that he had led her to believe Saxon Sinclair was aware of the circumstances.

"Are you trying to tell me that I'm going to have civilians crawling around in my trauma unit with cameras and microphones and God knows what else while I'm trying to triage injured patients? You can't be serious."

Preston Smith stood up, his eyes suddenly hardening. "Actually, Dr. Sinclair, that's exactly what I'm telling you. The hospital needs this, and I've already agreed to it. You'll have to find a way to live with it, so I suggest that you meet with the film director as planned."

Saxon left without another word, because any longer and she wouldn't have been able to contain her temper. This was a fight she knew she couldn't win, and she had much more important battles to wage.

June 30, 6:00 a.m.

A figure, back turned, leaned against the wall outside Sax's on-call room, a newspaper held aloft in the traditional lengthwise, half-folded configuration of the habitual New York City subway rider. All Sax could make out was a mass of rich red curls fanning out over the collar of a khaki safari-style shirt and long legs encased in tailored trousers. She slowed as she approached, curious, because she was quite certain she was not expecting anyone. Her orientation meeting with new residents and staff was scheduled for 7:00.

At the sound of the footsteps in the deserted hallway behind her, Jude Castle turned and got her first look at the elusive Dr. Saxon Sinclair, chief of trauma at St. Michael's Hospital in lower Manhattan. The surgeon wasn't entirely what she expected of someone with that title—particularly not with a motorcycle helmet tucked under one arm, a well-worn black leather jacket, and faded blue jeans.

Jude stared, momentarily perplexed because the woman standing a few feet away, studying her with a raised eyebrow and a slight frown, looked familiar. And yet, she was sure they had never met. She would not have forgotten someone with such simmering good looks and the unapologetically self-assured attitude this woman exuded.

Probably a promo photo from somewhere, she thought, dismissing the uneasy feeling of déjà vu.

"Dr. Sinclair?" She found her voice and stepped forward with an outstretched hand. "Jude Castle, Horizon Productions."

Sax's frown deepened, but she accepted the proffered hand. The redhead's grip was firm and definite, her green eyes direct and self-possessed. Sax released her hand and pulled keys from the pocket of her leather jacket. Fitting the proper one into the lock in her door, she threw over her shoulder, "Do we have an appointment?"

"No." Jude edged closer to the door, planning to jam her foot in the opening if necessary. "We don't. I've been trying to set something up for weeks, but your secretary can't seem to pin you down to a convenient time."

"Probably because there isn't one." Sax blocked the path into the small room she used as an auxiliary office as well as an on-call sleeping area. She was startled to find herself almost nose to nose with the determined producer across the threshold. "This is a hectic time of year, and I don't have time for..." She ran a hand through her hair, disheveling the already wild tangle. She wanted to say, "uninvited media people," but restrained herself and finished with, "public relations."

"Understood." Jude held her ground. "I have an entire crew

arriving here tomorrow, and I'm short on time, too. Maybe we could do this over coffee?"

"Do what?" Sax pointedly stripped off her jacket and tossed it onto a narrow bed covered with medical journals and a pile of scrubs. Apparently, this woman wasn't leaving, and it wasn't really *her* foot she wanted to crush anyhow. It was Preston Smith's. She relented and motioned Jude to enter.

"Close the door," she said offhandedly as she reached for a pair of scrub pants and began to unbutton her jeans. "You can fill me in while I change."

Jude stared wordlessly for an interminable moment when it seemed Sinclair was going to step out of those sexy, nearly threadbare Levi's right in front of her. Catching herself gaping, she hurriedly faced the opposite wall where an old wooden desk labored under the weight of a modern computer system.

"I had hoped we could talk logistics." She cleared her throat, which was suddenly dry. "I don't want to get in your way, Dr. Sinclair—"

"You're *already* in my way." Sax pulled her T-shirt over her head and replaced it with a navy scrub top. She moved deftly around the redhead to her desk, found a pen, and stuck it in her chest pocket. Leaning her hip against the edge of the desk, she regarded her visitor warily. Jude Castle's stance and expression made her determination very clear. With a sigh of exasperation, Sax said, "I'm stuck with this, aren't I?"

Jude shrugged. "'Fraid so. I'll try to make it as painless as possible." She wasn't sure that levity would get her anywhere with the aggravated surgeon, but she needed to do something to take her mind off how damned attractive Sinclair was. It wasn't like her to be quite so affected by a pair of deep, brooding eyes and a mane of black hair that begged for fingers to run through it. She tried to ignore the faint flush of heat in her limbs. This was work, not social hour.

Sax pushed away from the desk, strode rapidly to the door, and jerked it open. She looked back over her shoulder and called, "Well, come on, then. You've got twenty minutes to fill me in."

"Thirty." Jude hurried after her. "Make it thirty, and I'll buy the coffee." She didn't get an answer, but she could have sworn she saw a hint of a grin. It was a small victory, but she'd take it for now.

CHAPTER TWO

June 30, 6:20 a.m.

Jude was used to running while on the job. She'd filmed almost everything there was to film at one time or another except actual combat—though she'd been close enough to the front in Kosovo that she'd needed to sprint to avoid being flattened by falling debris during bombing raids. She was practically racing now to keep up with Sinclair as they rushed through the halls. As she started to turn right at a corner clearly marked with a sign indicating the cafeteria, Sinclair grabbed her arm and pulled her in the opposite direction.

"Where—" Jude started to ask.

"Some things are essential in this business." Sax fished a handful of bills out of her shirt pocket and pushed through the doors that separated the main lobby from the clinical areas. "Good coffee is one of them."

She led Jude toward a tiny kiosk tucked into the corner of the large admissions area waiting room. The top of a brass and chrome espresso machine was visible behind a stack of cups and a plastic bin of pastries.

"Ah, I see," Jude noted. "A *real* coffee drinker."

Sax leaned over the counter and peered around the cash register down the narrow aisle beyond. "Terry! Coffee—quick!" Glancing at Jude, she inquired, "What'll you have? Terry's making me a red-eye."

"Perfect." With a grateful sigh, Jude accepted the cup of coffee with an added shot of espresso a minute later. When Sax started to pay, she caught her hand. "I've got it, remember?"

For a second, they both stared at Jude's hand on Sax's wrist. Jude stared because her fingers were tingling, and that made no sense at all. She hadn't a clue what the surgeon was feeling, because her face was expressionless.

Sax pulled her hand away from Jude's. "Sure. Thanks."

Carrying their coffee, they walked across the lobby level public seating area toward the stairs.

"So," Jude began, anxious to take advantage of every minute with her reluctant subject, "I need to clarify a few details of the shoot with you."

"I gathered that," Sax responded dryly. She held the stairwell door open, a little surprised at how easily the director had maneuvered her into discussing something she wasn't at all sure she wanted to happen. She was usually not so susceptible to persuasion, but she had to admit that the redhead had a subtle charm that was hard to resist. To take her mind off *that* disconcerting thought, she said, "I have an orientation meeting with new staff in forty minutes. We can talk in the conference room before everyone arrives. That's probably the only time I'll have free all day."

"Fine." Jude sipped her coffee as they climbed the stairs. "Oh yeah. Nice."

Sax heard her faint groan and grinned in spite of herself. "Definitely."

When they were seated in the small meeting room adjoining the hospital cafeteria, Sax leaned back in her chair and regarded Jude seriously. "Preston Smith told me last night that you want to film a documentary in my trauma unit."

"Last night? You just found out *yesterday*?" Jude could not hide her surprise. She also felt a small shock of anger to find herself placed in the position of ambushing the one person she wanted on board from the start. "We've been negotiating with the hospital for months about this, and I was told that everyone involved was on board. Why didn't he tell you before?"

"Probably because he knew that I would refuse," Sax offered mildly, watching her companion over the top of her coffee cup. So far Jude had been unflappable—confident and capable, but surprisingly nonconfrontational. An iron hand in a velvet glove. Sax was impressed, and she didn't impress easily.

"Really?" Jude commented just as placidly. She thought she understood some of the surgeon's resistance now. She could hardly blame Sinclair for being aggravated if she'd just been informed about the project, and that also explained why she hadn't been able to get an appointment with her sooner. Sinclair's secretary had probably thought Jude was just another media hound looking for an interview and had put her request for an appointment on the bottom of the pile. But she sensed something else beneath the other woman's opposition— something more personal than bureaucratic conflicts. "Mind telling me why you're opposed to it?"

"Because you and your cameras don't belong in a trauma unit. It's an invasion of privacy to film what might be the most intimate and personal moments of someone's life." Her concern about patient confidentiality was true, even if it wasn't her only objection. She had no intention of disclosing her own aversion to publicity.

Jude was used to fielding these kinds of objections. "We'll get releases for anything that we air," she pointed out reasonably. "We can block the patients' faces electronically if we need to."

"And what about the ones who can't give consent—the comatose, or the moribund, or the children?"

Jude was about to give another stock answer, but something in Sinclair's voice made her stop. There was an edge of anger, of protectiveness, that intrigued her. She sat forward, meeting Sinclair's intimidating gaze head on. "What if I guarantee that every precaution will be taken to protect individual privacy? I'll be there myself the entire time that the cameras are rolling. I'll talk to the families personally if there's a need. No one will be filmed without consent."

"Your presence is going to interfere with Deb Stein's training. She's going to be more worried about looking good for you than about learning to make decisions and exercise good judgment."

"I thought the trauma fellows took call with a senior attending who supervises them," Jude stated.

"That's true. They do. Deb Stein will be on duty with me most of the time."

"And you're concerned that...what? She'll pay more attention to me than to you?" Jude's voice rose in a way that suggested she was trying not to laugh.

Sax was forced to grin again. The dynamic director was proving hard to resist. "She'll be distracted at least."

Jude regarded Sinclair intently, aware that this confrontation could spell success or failure for the project into which she had invested all her energy and considerable resources for six months. She *could* do it without the trauma chief's cooperation if she had to. The signed contract from the hospital would stand up in court if it came to that. But if she went that route, going over Sinclair's head to get the job done, it would make the work hellishly difficult. And she didn't want this woman as an enemy for a lot of reasons, not the least of which was that she found her obvious lack of concern for diplomacy refreshing.

"What is it that *really* bothers you about all of this?" she asked quietly.

"There are some things people don't need to know, maybe don't even want to know," Sax said, surprising herself. *I don't even know this woman, and she has me admitting things I wouldn't say to a single living soul before now.* "What happens in that unit—not always, but often enough—in those few seconds when life hangs in the balance are not events to be exposed for the sake of curiosity. These patients aren't just naked and defenseless—they're helpless. And sometimes what we do in there is not pretty."

"You've just described human drama, Dr. Sinclair—real life. Don't you think that the public can appreciate that and understand how special it is?"

The public's right to know—the relentless pursuit of the story in the name of truth—is often just a convenient excuse for invasion. Whatever happened to preserving a person's dignity and privacy when they can't speak for themselves? Sax merely shrugged and answered flatly, "I don't know. I'm not a sociologist—I'm a surgeon."

"Yes," Jude agreed, thinking that Sinclair was much more than that. "And it's your trauma unit. But can we agree to give it a try?"

"Do I have a choice?"

"I'm sorry," Jude said, to her surprise meaning it. "No."

Personal Project Log—Castle
June 30, 7:50 a.m.

Sinclair stood up at 7:00 a.m. on the dot, and every person in the room grew quiet. There were a dozen people present—six senior staff, the first-year trauma fellow, two general surgery residents, and two medical students. I was the only outsider—the only non-physician. She walked to the front of the room, leaned against the edge of the conference table, and folded her arms over her chest. She looked relaxed in just a scrub shirt and pants—as if she didn't have a care in the world. She never said a word until every eye was on her. I felt like I should jump up and salute. I thought one of the younger residents might. God, she looked tough.

I expected a speech. She didn't give one.

She laid out the ground rules instead. [Note: Title first episode "Rules of Engagement."] Twenty-four hours on, forty-eight hours off—except on high-volume holidays like the one coming up, when everyone works more frequent shifts. Rounds in the trauma unit at 8:00 a.m. and no one goes home until they're over. Which by my calculations turns out to be somewhere in the range of thirty hours straight without much sleep. I lost track of what she said after that, because I was trying to imagine that kind of schedule. I'm used to working hard, sometimes days at a time when a story is breaking. But I'll be the first to admit I don't function at my peak the whole time. And I'm not cutting into people.

She got my attention again with the very last thing she said—the only direct order I can remember her giving. She said, "Some will die in the field, and there's nothing you can do about it. Those, you let go. But if they come into my trauma unit warm and with a pulse, you'd better not lose them."

Jude caught up to Deborah Stein just outside the conference room. "Deb," she called, drawing even with her as they started down the hall.

"Hey, Jude," the blond, two-time basketball Olympian answered with her trademark effervescent grin and sparkling blue eyes. "Good to see you again."

"What happens now?" Jude asked as they double-timed down an intersecting corridor off the main hallway. *Doesn't anybody walk at a normal pace around here?*

"You heard the chief. Rounds in the trauma intensive care unit in five, and then we wait for a trauma call. I'm assigned to the admitting unit this month, so I don't have any floor responsibilities."

"Gotcha." Jude mentally reviewed what she remembered from the all-too-brief synopsis the surgical department had provided her. She had a feeling, however, that Sinclair didn't adhere to any script. "So once the patients are transferred from the trauma intensive care unit to a regular floor bed, you don't have any responsibility for them?"

"Well, I'll be involved in that aspect of things during the weeks I'm not taking trauma call. It's an either-or kinda deal because you can't really do both at once." Deb held open the heavy gray windowless door with the red rectangular sign announcing the TICU—Trauma Intensive Care Unit. "Grab a cover gown. I'll get you some scrubs later so you don't have to worry about your street clothes getting ruined, and you won't have to keep covering them up every time we go in and out of the units."

"Thanks," Jude replied absently.

Standing just inside the door, she scanned the length of the brightly lit rectangular room. A U-shaped counter area to her right was empty save for a few swivel chairs left askew in the middle of the space, a plethora of charts scattered over the countertops, and a misshapen box of fossilized donuts. What captured her attention were the ten beds lined up along the opposite wall, separated from each other by a few feet of space and featureless curtains on ceiling tracks that were all pushed back to expose the occupants to anyone who happened to be looking.

Almost every Spartan, steel-railed adjustable bed contained a genderless, nearly naked form dwarfed by the dispassionate machines of modern medicine. Free-standing ventilators the size of dishwashers flanked every bed, delivering a predetermined volume of gas, ten to fifteen times a minute, through the hard plastic breathing tubes jutting from the vicinity of every patient's mouth. Arms were strapped to extremity immobilizers or tied by soft cotton restraints to the bed rails. Tubes of all sizes ran from every orifice, delivering salvation in the form of antibiotics and liquid nutrition or removing the waste of injury and decay. Monitors occupied every available space, metering out lifetimes in a steady series of monotonous beeps and flashing pinpoints of light.

The trauma intensive care unit, one of the triumphs of medical technology, was a cold and impersonal place. Jude shivered.

"You okay?" Deb Stein asked.

"What? Oh...yes, I'm fine. Sorry." Jude dragged her gaze away from the silent tableau. She searched the room, trying to shake the eerie sensation of having stepped into a nightmare. Finally, she found something to occupy her attention.

Sinclair stood at the center of a group of rapt personnel in white coats or rumpled scrub suits who were crowded around the bottom of the first bed. Her foot was up on the seat of a rolling chair, one arm propped on her raised knee. She held a long sheet of paper in her hand and her attention was sharply focused on the figure in the bed as she listened to what a young man next to her reported.

"Let's go," Deb whispered urgently. "Sinclair's already started."

"Will I be able to film in here?" Jude interjected, because she wanted this on tape. Sinclair, with every eye on her and every expression expectant, looked like a commander surveying a battlefield.

"Probably," Deb said as they approached the people clustered around the trauma chief. "We'll figure it out later—after rounds."

Jude had no choice but to agree, because she could see that she couldn't interrupt what was underway. Besides, she wanted to watch this. No one seemed to object or even particularly notice that she was there.

Nurses moved efficiently between the beds, going about the business of administering meds, adjusting fluid pumps, and drawing blood. X-ray techs threaded their way through the residents and staff blocking the aisles, slid rectangular film plates under the patients, then shouted "clear" with complete disregard for what was happening nearby. At the sound of the technician's warning, everyone shuffled behind the nearest person wearing a lead apron to shield themselves as much as possible from the radiation, waited for the tech to shoot the X-ray, and then moved back to their places with barely an interruption in their cadences.

A deep commanding voice caught everyone's attention.

"How high is his intracranial pressure?" Sinclair asked the fair-haired young man standing just in front of Jude.

"Thirty-eight."

"Up ten in the last two hours?" There was a faint edge to the trauma chief's voice.

"Yes."

"And what does that indicate to you, Dr. Kinney?"

Jude craned her neck to see Sinclair, whose blue eyes were fixed, laser like, on the young man's face. He was a first-year surgery resident according to the ID badge clipped to his pocket. His voice was taut with strain as he replied.

"It means that something is causing the pressure to rise inside his skull."

"Such as?" The edge had progressed to razor sharp now.

Jude thought she could hear him swallow.

"Uh...cerebral edema, subdural hematoma, uh...epidural bleed."

Sinclair set down her foot from the chair and straightened to her full height, her fierce gaze still on the younger physician. She seemed taller than Jude remembered, but she knew that they were very nearly the same height. It had grown very quiet, although activity still teemed around them.

"Are any of those conditions surgical emergencies?"

The resident blanched. "The subdural and the epidural bleeding."

"Then why don't I see the neurosurgeons in here looking at him?"

"We called...they said they'd be by," he offered tentatively. He glanced right and left as if looking for assistance, but his fellow residents studiously avoided his gaze. He was on his own.

"And if he herniates his brain stem while we're waiting? Who will be responsible for that, Dr. Kinney?" Sinclair turned her head a fraction and met Deborah Stein's eyes. "Call neurosurg. Tell them I want them here now. Contact radiology and let them know we need an emergency head CT on this guy. Check the chart and find out who signs the consents for his procedures, but don't call the family until we know for certain he's going to the OR."

"Right," Deb answered briskly and moved off toward the nurse's station on the far side of the room.

"Okay, who's next?" Sinclair asked, already stepping to the neighboring bed. Someone pushed the rolling chair over to her. She absently propped one leg up on it again and leaned forward to study the patient in bed two while a different resident began to give his report.

CHAPTER THREE

Personal Project Log—Castle
June 30, 10:45 a.m.

My first morning of rounds in the trauma unit just ended. I'm exhausted, and all I had to do was move from bed to bed and watch the process. I didn't understand everything that was being said, especially when they began reeling off blood gas values and talking about Glasgow coma scores. [Note: get Deb to explain this rating scale for head injury on film, preferably with a patient in the background. Get Sinclair's okay to film in TICU. Get DP to check lighting in there with film compatibility.]

What I did understand loud and clear is that trauma rounds are where the real business of the day gets done. It's the only time during the day that the whole team is together, and it's the time when Sinclair fine-tunes the treatment plan for every patient in the Trauma ICU. Each patient's status is summarized for her by the resident covering that person, and whatever needs to be done—consults, studies, medication adjustments, etc.—is discussed and ordered. Sinclair signs off on all decisions.

Now, at midmorning, the doctors assigned to the less sick patients on the regular patient floors will go see to them, and those doctors responsible for incoming trauma emergencies—Sinclair and Stein today—will go down to the Trauma Admitting area. And I—

"Ms. Castle?"

Jude jumped and clicked off her recorder. She smiled at Sinclair, who was leaning with one shoulder against the wall just outside the TICU, watching her. "Sorry. I didn't know you were there. Do you need me for something?"

"I want to show you the admitting area. I'm on my way down there now."

"Great." Jude slipped the small recording device into her trouser pocket as they walked. "Thanks for letting me tag along on rounds this morning."

"Were you recording then, too?"

"No," Jude said as they entered the stairwell. "I usually record notes to myself—impressions, reactions, reminders. Things I might use for voiceovers later in the film. If I want to tape you or anyone else, I'll ask first."

Sinclair didn't say anything for a moment, then asked, "How did you come to pick Deb Stein as the focus of your project?"

They exited on the first floor and passed the emergency room waiting area, already crowded with walk-ins—mostly mothers with children and middle-aged people with minor injuries. Individuals with potentially serious medical conditions usually arrived by ambulance and were delivered directly to treatment rooms. Ahead, down the hallway, was yet another set of windowless doors with a keypad lock restricting entry.

"She and I met three years ago at the Olympics," Jude said. "I was doing a piece on female athletes, and we started talking about her plans after the Games were over. When I began working on this, I thought of her."

"And she agreed?" Sax pushed in the code on the door lock. "It's the same as the phone extension—two four two zero."

"Yes, she did. Why?"

Sax shrugged and led the way along another sterile beige corridor. "That's what I'm wondering. Why?"

"You'll have to ask her. I'd like to talk to you, though—on tape—about your own training. Background information, personal experiences, that kind of thing."

Sax stopped walking. "Everything you need is on my CV. My secretary can get that for you. You have her number."

There was a note of finality in her voice that left no room for discussion. Jude kept her surprise, and her curiosity, to herself. She'd pushed enough for the first day. "All right, thanks."

"This," her companion said, leading her through a small alcove that contained scrub sinks and cupboards with surgical hats and gowns into another unadorned room that appeared to be a hybrid operating theater and treatment area, "is the trauma admitting area. Every trauma patient is brought in here, stabilized, and triaged."

There were three operating tables lined up in the center of the space, each of which could be enclosed by curtains for privacy if necessary. Above each narrow, stainless steel table hung large, circular silver lights containing brilliant halogen bulbs capable of lighting the area adequately for surgery.

Jude stared at the silver domes and flushed with a sudden wave of heat and dizziness. Her vision narrowed and spots danced across the darkening landscape. Reflexively, she reached out a hand to steady herself and was dimly aware of an arm encircling her waist.

"Ms. Castle," a quiet, calm voice murmured. "Are you all right?"

Jude forced herself to take a deep breath, knowing that this would pass quickly if she just kept breathing. Her legs were unsteady, and she held on hard to the warm solid body next to hers. "Yes," she whispered faintly. "Just...I'm sorry...just a minute."

Sax stood perfectly still, letting the other woman lean on her, holding her so close it might have been an embrace. A fine sheen of perspiration filmed Jude's forehead, and she was very pale. "Let's get you lying down," Sax said softly. She could feel her tremble.

"No," Jude responded quickly, pressing one hand to Sax's shoulder, straightening up with obvious effort. "I'll be fine. I'm okay, really."

Sax studied her, still not releasing her hold as she rested two fingers on the pulse in Jude's wrist. Fast but strong. "I agree. You will be fine, but right now, you still need to at least sit down."

"I'm sorry," Jude said again, laughing self-consciously as she allowed herself to be walked to a chair in front of a long counter that edged the rear wall. Her vision had cleared, and she was acutely aware of the arm around her waist. She was also aware of the hard length of Saxon Sinclair's body against her side and the soft swell of the surgeon's breast against her own. Her legs trembled again, and it wasn't from dizziness. She stepped away quickly and settled into the chair.

One of the nurses asked Sax if she needed anything, but she shook her head. Pulling another chair over close to Jude's, she asked, "What happened?"

Embarrassed, Jude blushed. "Nothing. I just got a little light-headed. Guess I should have had breakfast."

"That could be," Sax acknowledged, but she didn't really think that it was hypoglycemia. That usually gave some warning—a racing pulse, tremors, the gradual onset of faintness. Jude Castle had seemed perfectly fine until she walked into trauma admitting. "Has this ever happened to you before?"

"No." Jude was uncomfortable under the scrutiny of those penetrating eyes. *At least, it's been so long that I thought it was over.*

"We should get an EKG. One of the nurses can do one right down here."

"Really, that's not necessary. I feel fine now." To prove it, Jude stood and walked a few feet away, wanting to escape Sinclair's searching gaze. She needed to walk off the anxiety that clung to her like a bad dream, and she needed to forget the swift surge of desire she had experienced in Sinclair's innocent embrace. *This is not a good start.* Steadying her voice, she asked, "How many patients do you see through here every year?"

"Fifteen hundred, approximately." Sax watched Jude pace. The abrupt change in subject hadn't escaped her notice, but she understood the need for privacy. She understood secrets. "When we have a trauma alert, there's not much room in here. There will be EMTs, nurses, radiology techs, respiratory therapists, anesthesiologists, at least three surgeons, and assorted consultants."

"The families?"

Sax shook her head. "Not in here. There's a waiting room just down the hall where they can stay. Families usually can't see the patient until after they're transferred to the ICU or finished in the OR, depending on the severity of the injuries. This is a modern day MASH unit—we evaluate and ship as fast as possible."

"But sometimes you operate down here?" Jude found she was starting to forget her own discomfort as they talked. She'd drifted back to where Sax still sat and sat down opposite her again.

"Only in the case of a life-threatening emergency."

"Which would be...what?" Jude asked. "May I record this, by the way?"

Sax realized that she had been deftly maneuvered into giving an interview, and assented with a grudging grin of defeat. "A number of things can constitute an emergency. Anything that impairs breathing— a fractured larynx, for example—could require a tracheostomy. Sometimes, in the face of major blood loss from the pelvis or ruptured internal organs, we cross-clamp the aorta to send what blood there is to the brain."

As she listened, Jude continued to study the physical layout of the room as well as its contents. This was her set; this room would be the backdrop for most of the action she filmed. She would be spending a great deal of time here in the next year.

"What do you do between trauma alerts?"

"I'm usually in my office, taking care of administrative things, or at committee meetings, or making rounds in the unit. On a busy day when things are jumping down here, I work in my on-call room down the hall."

"Or," a male voice observed from behind Jude, "she tries to sucker someone into playing chess with her."

Jude swung around on her chair and stared at a man in pale blue scrubs, a color she was sure he had chosen to match his eyes if his two-hundred-dollar haircut and startling good looks were any indication of the care he took with his appearance. He might have been a male model posing for a uniform catalog.

"Jude Castle, meet Aaron Townsend, the head trauma nurse," Sax said.

Aaron gave Jude a friendly smile and a frankly appraising look as he took her hand. "Nice to meet you. I've heard rumors that we are going to be immortalized on film."

"I certainly hope so," Jude replied with a laugh, aware that he was trying to charm her in an inoffensive way that was probably second nature to him. Nevertheless, she didn't prolong the eye contact.

"Excellent," the handsome nurse said enthusiastically. "And I was serious about the chess thing. When the good doctor gets bored, she likes to humiliate people at games."

Jude shrugged, hoping she appeared more nonchalant than she felt. "Don't worry, chess is not my game."

Sax regarded her silently, wondering why, for the second time in less than an hour, Jude Castle was lying.

CHAPTER FOUR

June 30, 12:42 p.m.

Y ou'll need to work with the bare minimum of people in here," Sax said after Aaron Townsend left to give lunch relief in the TICU, which was short a nurse on the day shift. "Space is at a premium."

"I'll want at least two camera people, a sound tech, and a script assistant with me," Jude responded immediately. She was still thinking about the nurse's comments about Sinclair being a chess player. *Great. One more complication.*

"Not a chance." The tone was uncompromising, almost dismissive. Saxon Sinclair could not have made her contempt for both the project and Jude's professionalism more apparent if she'd announced it over the intercom.

Stung, Jude glared at her from a foot away. Under other circumstances, she might have handled things a little more diplomatically, but she was still shaken by her near fainting spell and off her stride. Without thinking, she said, "I don't need your permission, you know. I'm just trying to be polite here."

"You don't need to be polite, Ms. Castle." Sax stood up, never raising her voice, her blue eyes glacially cold. "What you have to do is be certain not to interfere with the work that needs to be done down here, or I'll have you thrown out on your ass."

Of all the arrogant, dictatorial... Jude fumed as Sinclair strode swiftly from the room. She rubbed her temples and tried not to curse out loud. *Lovely, just lovely.*

June 30, 4:42 p.m.

"Why did you decide to do your fellowship with Dr. Sinclair?" Jude placed the small recorder on the table in the conference room.

"Because she's the best," Deb Stein answered with a look that said Jude should've known the answer to that silly question.

"Define *best*," Jude probed, wanting to get a feel for her *star* and to lay the foundation for what was to come in the weeks ahead. "What makes her different from any number of other trauma surgeons?"

"On the record?" Deb asked, nodding toward the recorder. "Because her unit has the best survival statistics in the state, and I've seen her in the operating room. I rotated here as a junior general surgery resident, and she's amazing. She's got hands like lightning. Awesome."

Jude had a feeling that there was something else, because Deb had a little grin on her face. She reached to push the stop button on her tape recorder. "What about off the record? Come on, Deb. I can tell you're holding back on me."

"Well," Deb conceded, her eyes twinkling, "she's so godawful hot. Every dyke resident I know wanted to work with her."

"Aha." Jude hoped she wasn't blushing. "Okay, we'll keep that off the record." *What in hell is the matter with me? It's not as if I didn't think practically the same thing the minute I saw her. So what if she's hot. She's a royal pain in the—*

Deb Stein jumped up as the pager at her waist beeped, and without another word, she charged from the room. Overhead, the intercom blared. *Trauma alert STAT, trauma admitting. Trauma alert STAT...*

Jude grabbed her tape recorder and ran.

Sax stood gowned and gloved as the double doors to the trauma admitting area slid open and a stretcher bearing a mound of equipment, blood-soaked clothing, and an EMT straddling a human body rolled in. The female EMT kneeling astride the man was counting aloud as she rhythmically compressed his chest. "One, two, three, four, five... one, two, three, four, five..." slowing at the end of each sequence so her partner could deliver a breath through the inflatable Ambu bag attached to the endotracheal tube protruding from the man's mouth.

"GSW to the left chest," her partner called to no one in particular, his voice shrill with the adrenaline rush as he ran beside the stretcher, squeezing air into the unresponsive patient's lungs. "Intubated in the field. He's had five liters of Ringer's solution. Initial BP eighty palpable. We lost the pulse and pressure about three minutes ago."

"Exit wound?" Sax called as she and Nancy Stevenson, one of the trauma nurses, slid the large man from the gurney onto the treatment table. She quickly assessed his pupils. *Unresponsive to light. If he isn't brain dead already, he will be in two minutes if we don't get some oxygen to his brain.*

"None that we saw, Doc. The bullet went in, but it didn't come out."

Swiftly, Sax moved her stethoscope from one side of his chest to the other, listening for air movement as she watched the paramedic ventilate the patient. Deb Stein, followed closely by Jude Castle, ran in as Sax straightened up. "No air flow on either side. Stein, put a chest tube in on the right. Nancy, open the thoracotomy tray."

The team worked efficiently, nearly silently, repeating a drill they had performed hundreds of times. One nurse cut off the remnants of the patient's clothing; another slipped a sterile catheter into his penis and attached it to a urine collection bag; still another drew half a dozen vials of blood for laboratory analysis. A surgical intern pulled a tall metal stand up to the bedside and began folding open the layers of sterile linen covering a vast array of surgical instruments. A radiology technician arrived pushing a huge portable X-ray machine and stood waiting, calmly labeling individual film plates with the date and the letters UWM, which is who the patient would remain until someone had time to identify him. *Unidentified White Male.*

All the while, Aaron Townsend continued chest compressions, having relieved the exhausted EMT. It was fatiguing work pushing the chest hard enough so that the force was transmitted to the heart, and harder still to get the heart to squeeze out blood with enough pressure to travel to the brain and other vital organs when it was almost empty. And this man's heart had to be almost empty. Most of his blood volume had poured out the two-inch hole in his chest.

Her back pressed to the wall, Jude maneuvered as close to the action as she could get. No one paid her the slightest attention. She glanced at the clock. Forty-five seconds had elapsed since the stretcher had been wheeled in.

Peering around the anesthesiologist at the head of the table, she watched Sinclair. The surgeon's gaze as she studied the patient was hard and unwavering, her eyes nearly purple with intensity. Everything about her was ferociously focused. Had Jude been more aware of her own body, she would have released the breath she was holding, but she was too absorbed by the trauma chief.

"Hang that blood and squeeze it in by hand," Sax said sharply. She glanced quickly across the man's body at Deb. "Have you got that tube in, Stein?"

"Almost." Deb forced an oversized clamp between the fifth and sixth ribs with one hand while holding a clear plastic tube a half inch in diameter in the other, ready to guide it through the tunnel she was creating into the chest cavity.

"Push it in—you're not going to hurt him," Sax said while pouring Betadiene directly from a bottle onto the man's torso. "As soon as you've got it in, get over here and give me a hand cracking his chest." Even as she spoke, she was slashing a ten-inch curve between the ribs on the left side. "Rib spreader," she said tersely as a flood of dark congealed blood cascaded out onto her.

She held out her right hand, and a nurse passed her a ratcheted double-bladed retractor. Sax forced it between the ribs and cranked it open, exposing a deflated lung and a flaccid heart. Deb stepped up next to her, breathing hard, but her hands were steady.

"Open the pericardium and massage the heart manually," Sax instructed. She leaned away slightly so Deb could move closer, bending a bit to watch as her fellow made a slit in the protective covering enclosing the heart. "Not too deep, now. Stay away from the coronaries. That's it...nice. Get your hand around it."

Without raising her head, Sax announced, "The heart's still empty. Come on, people, pump the blood." Quietly, she encouraged, "That's it, Stein. Hold it in the palm of your hand and keep the pressure even."

"We're getting something on the EKG," Aaron relayed.

"Rate?" Sax never looked away from the gaping hole in the man's body.

"Still only forty."

"Push some atropine," Sax instructed. She and Deb Stein were so close their bodies were practically fused. "Keep going, Deb. You've got it."

Jude tore her gaze from Sax's face and looked at the clock. Two minutes and ten seconds.

"I've got a blood pressure," one of the nurses called.

"The heart's beating," Deb murmured, almost as if she didn't believe it.

"Stop the compression and see if he flies," Sax ordered.

For a minute, no one breathed. The EKG beeped steadily, the arterial line read a blood pressure of one hundred, and the blood flow from the chest wound slowed to a trickle.

"Tell the OR we're coming up," Sax said, a victorious note in her voice. She glanced up then, her gaze meeting Jude's. A grin flickered at the corner of her expressive mouth.

Watching the triumph dance in her blue eyes, Jude thought Saxon Sinclair was, unquestionably, the sexiest woman she'd ever seen.

June 30, 7:35 p.m.

Sax raised an eyebrow in surprise as she walked through the surgeons' lounge toward the door leading into the women's locker room. The common space between the locker rooms and the operating room proper was empty save for Jude Castle, who sat writing in a notebook at the long wooden table that held remnants of a pizza and a white layer cake.

"You're here late." She stopped opposite the filmmaker, who glanced up and smiled.

"I was waiting for you." Jude pushed her work away and studied Sinclair, noting the dark patch on her thigh that could only be blood, and the sweat dampening the shirt between her breasts. *She looks tired.* The thought surprised Jude. She realized that she hadn't imagined the formidable trauma chief being vulnerable to something so common, and then wondered where that idea had come from. *She's human, after all.*

"Really," Sax remarked, curious. "Why?"

"Because I owe you an apology."

Sax rubbed her face briefly and moved a chair so she could sit opposite Jude. She recalled their heated exchange now, although it seemed more than just a few hours ago. She remembered being angry but certainly couldn't remember anything that required an apology. And somehow, the idea of this woman apologizing to her seemed wrong. They'd both been rather hot.

"Look, Ms. Castle—"

"No, let me finish," Jude interjected, amused to see a quick flash of annoyance in the other woman's eyes. *Not used to being interrupted, are you?* "You were right about limiting my crew in the admitting area. It's a zoo in there during a trauma alert. I should have waited to assess things myself before I told you what I needed. I'll work something out."

"Okay, I appreciate you making the adjustments. Thanks," Sax said. "I notice, though, you're not apologizing for threatening to pull rank on me."

"No, I'm not."

"Fair enough." Sax stood. "Deb Stein is on call tomorrow night. You'd better get some rest if you're going to start keeping surgeon's hours."

"Are you done for the day?" Jude called as Sax walked away.

"Soon." Sax pushed open the door to the locker room. She knew she'd probably spend the night on the narrow bed in her on-call quarters because it was somehow less impersonal there than the space she called home, but that wasn't something she wanted to share.

June 30, 8:50 p.m.

Jude sighed and tried to stop thinking about Saxon Sinclair. She couldn't decide whether the woman annoyed or fascinated her more. *She has to be one of the most infuriating people I've ever met. She's rigid and inflexible and arrogant, and if that weren't bad enough, she's...she's accomplished and talented and driven. And...oh, hell...so damned attractive.*

"Aren't you hungry?" Lori Brewster asked with concern.

"What?" Jude glanced at her plate and the half-eaten entrée and realized that she had forgotten about it. "Oh, no. I mean...I was, but I'm not now." Seeing the worried look on her attractive companion's face, she hurriedly added, "I'm just distracted. It probably wasn't very smart of me to make a date for the first day of this new project."

The dark-haired attorney frowned and reached across the immaculate linen tablecloth to take Jude's hand. "We didn't need to go out. I haven't seen you in two weeks." She brushed her thumb over

Jude's palm. "We could have just gotten takeout and spent the evening in bed."

"I'm sorry." Jude squeezed Lori's hand. "I'm lousy company tonight." She hoped the fact that she had sidestepped the overture to sex wasn't as obvious to her dinner companion as it felt to her. She wasn't even sure herself why she wasn't interested.

They'd been dating for more than six months, casually, whenever they could find time, which was how they'd both agreed they wanted it. Lori was busy establishing herself in a competitive law firm where she intended to make partner ahead of the rest of the pack, and she worked ninety-hour weeks to make it happen. Jude traveled frequently for shoots and promotional meetings and didn't feel she could give a serious relationship the attention it required. So far their arrangement had been mutually satisfying.

She regarded Lori fondly, appreciating the appraising look in her eyes and reminding herself how much she liked her trim, athletic body. *We've got similar interests, we want the same things professionally, and we're good together in bed. What more could I want?*

She shook off the odd sense of disquiet she'd had ever since leaving St. Michael's. She also tried not to think any more about Saxon Sinclair or why she even cared if the irritating trauma surgeon liked her or not.

Quietly, she said, "Let's skip dessert."

The glass door on the shower slid open, and Jude felt a soft, smooth body press close against her back. Arms slipped around her waist, lips trailed across her shoulder. A voice, husky and intimate, whispered in her ear.

"Hey, I missed you. The bed is cold without you."

"I tried not to wake you." Jude leaned back into the embrace, turning her head to brush her mouth over a damp cheek. "Sorry."

"You okay?" Lori asked.

"Yes."

But Jude didn't feel quite okay, and she wasn't sure why. Nothing had changed. They had shared themselves with each other as in the past, enjoyably and with an easy familiarity that came from mutual caring. It was nice to feel the heat of another body and to touch flesh other than her own. It was nice to be physically satisfied. It had been every bit as nice as it had been the first time they'd slept together. Nothing had changed.

"Do you really need to go?"

"Mmm, yeah. I've got an early meeting with my director of photography in the morning. And *early* by surgeons' standards means 6:30." Jude turned in the mist and water to face her companion.

"Jesus, that's inhuman."

"I need to get some sleep and prepare a few things," Jude said with a grin.

"Well then," Lori murmured, bending her face to Jude's neck and licking the trail of water from her skin, "you should probably leave. I can't promise how much sleep you'll get if you stay."

Jude kissed her once, quickly, and stepped from the shower, reaching for a towel. "My very thoughts."

They parted with the usual promise to call when their schedules allowed, and by the time Jude reached home in the taxi, her mind was already on her plans for the next day.

CHAPTER FIVE

July 1, 6:50 a.m.

S ax passed Aaron Townsend in the hall as he was leaving after a night on duty.

"Everything quiet?" she asked, although she knew that it must be. She'd returned to the hospital in the middle of the night, even though she wasn't on call, and she knew that someone would have notified her if anything big had come in. She was second call, on backup if more than one major trauma arrived at once. Technically she could have taken call from home, but she was just as happy to sleep in familiar surroundings.

"Depends on what you mean," he said with a grin. "The only admission we had was some guy who lost a battle with his fan belt at 2:00 a.m. Don't ask me why he was working on his engine in the middle of the night, but he's in the OR now getting his fingers reattached." His sly expression suggested there was something else brewing—a secret that he found amusing.

Sax stopped walking and fixed him with a piercing stare. "Would you like to tell me what *else* is going on?"

"There are four people in the trauma bay hanging cameras and microphones from the ceiling right now."

"Really," Sax remarked dryly, thinking that Jude Castle hadn't wasted any time getting to work. She had to admit she liked that about the filmmaker. As irritating as this entire project was likely to become, she admired Castle's persistence and perseverance. She was a professional, and that kind of determination was something Sax understood. "Guess I'll wander back and see what's happening."

"Uh-huh." The head nurse watched her walk away and wished he didn't have a breakfast date. He would have loved to watch the confrontation. The undercurrent of competition between the two women hadn't escaped his notice the previous day. *It's going to be a very interesting few months around here. And they say that alpha males are dangerous when you put them together.*

He'd worked with Saxon Sinclair for four and a half years, and he knew just how tough an alpha female could be. Sorry to miss the upcoming show, he pushed through the ER doors into the bright morning sun and waved to the brunette in the convertible waiting at the curb.

Down the hall, Sax leaned against the doorway at the entrance to the trauma bay, *her* trauma bay, and stared at the strangers fast at work. A woman in jeans and work shirt stood on the top of a stepladder adjusting a ceiling-mounted camera that was directly over the patient treatment tables. Her blond hair was half concealed by a baseball cap turned around backward with the word *Sundance* stenciled in bright orange letters. Her figure, at least from the back view, was neat and tidy.

Two young men were stringing cable from the camera to a bank of monitors and recording equipment stacked on rolling tables pushed up against the wall near the nurses' station. Jude Castle stood observing them, intermittently referring to her notebook and then looking up to follow the progress of the equipment installation. She looked fresh and energized in khaki pants and a tight black T-shirt that left her nicely muscled arms bare.

For a second, enjoying the view, Sax forgot how annoyed she was at the invasion of her domain.

"The primary shots are going to have to be with the handheld," Jude remarked to the blond on the ladder.

"The best quality is going to come from this one up here," the woman countered.

"There's too much action to follow with a stationary. I'll want to focus on the surgeons, especially Deb Stein, and they're moving all the time."

The blond climbed down and pivoted to survey the area she would need to cover with her cameras. She halted when she saw Sax watching, and a small smile flickered across her face. "Good morning," she called in Sax's direction, a hint of flirtatiousness in her voice.

"Morning," Sax responded neutrally. Pushing away from the wall, she moved into the room. Her glance slid past the attractive blond appraising her to Jude. "Ms. Castle," she murmured by way of greeting.

"Dr. Sinclair," Jude said smoothly, "this is my DP, Melissa Cooper."

"DP?" Sax extended her hand.

"Director of photography, at your service," Melissa furnished with a grin as she met Sax's firm grip.

"Ah, I see." Sax looked back to Jude. "Could I speak with you for a moment, please?"

"Of course. Mel, would you make sure they run a sound check once they get their lines connected?"

"Sure," Melissa replied. As the two women walked into the hall, she checked out Dr. Sinclair's denim-clad ass. *Now there is one hot item. This is going to be a* very *enjoyable shoot. Oh, yeah.*

"You're up early," Sax said as they walked through the still-quiet corridors. "Let's grab some coffee. I'll buy this time."

"Thanks. I thought it would be a good idea to take care of some of the construction details before things got busy in there," Jude said carefully. She sensed the surgeon had something on her mind, and she wondered if they would have another skirmish.

"Traumas don't tend to follow a schedule, unless it's lunar. There's something in that tale. Every full moon we're swamped." They reached the coffee kiosk and Sax ordered two red-eyes.

"I just took a chance that we could get most of the set-up done this morning," Jude said. "I know it's unpredictable when you'll get busy, but that hour right around the changeover from the night shift to the day shift always seems to be quiet."

"Usually." Sax studied Jude's face, watching for a reaction as she asked carefully, "You've had some experience in hospitals, then?"

"Some." Jude stared straight ahead and didn't elaborate. Those six weeks were nothing she cared to discuss. She'd forgotten it, buried it, left it behind. She shivered.

"Cold?" Sax handed her a coffee.

"No," Jude said abruptly. "I'm fine." She took the paper cup and held it before her in both hands.

Sax found the body language interesting. Recognizing the subtle barrier to further personal questions, she said, "Okay. Let's talk about this project of yours. Since I can't get rid of you, I'd better find out what I'm in for."

Jude propped her back against the wall a few feet from the coffee stand, prepared to defend her project. "Okay—"

"Wait," Sax interrupted as she moved out of the path of an orderly pushing a wheelchair. "Come with me."

The view from the helipad was incredible. Like most New Yorkers, Jude was used to the kind of breathtaking vistas afforded by restaurants on top of skyscrapers and windows of offices on the seventieth floor, but the sights of the water with white dots of sails flickering over the surface and the majestic rise of the Statue of Liberty were still awesome and gorgeous. And Saxon Sinclair in profile, the wind whipping her black hair around her starkly handsome face, was pretty captivating, too. Jude wished she had a camera.

"Nice up here," she observed, trying to concentrate on the skyline and not the woman next to her.

"One of the few places in the hospital where there's any privacy," Sax commented. She wasn't certain why she'd brought the filmmaker up to the roof. It was one of the places she came to be alone, when the chaos in the world downstairs became too much or the lonely hours between midnight and dawn stretched too long.

It was amazingly peaceful here at night, surrounded by nothing but the wind and the dark and the omnipresent lights from surrounding buildings that substituted for stars in the urban landscape. Far below, the streets teemed with life and people living it, some in desperate abandon and some in unconscious ignorance. Up here, she felt both a part of it and apart from it, a watcher who on occasion ventured forth to take part in the game.

She turned her back to the view, watching Jude study the rooftop with that same intent expression she'd noticed several times the day before. "Looking for a shot?"

"Something like that." Jude stared at Sinclair in surprise, amazed that she could tell. Then to her consternation, she blushed faintly, because at that moment she'd been thinking again how much she would like to photograph the trauma surgeon. To change the subject, she gestured with an arm as she asked, "Am I imagining it, or is that actually a basketball hoop on the side of the parking ramp over there?"

"That's what it is, all right," Sax confirmed, taking the lid off her coffee cup and tossing it into a nearby trashcan.

"Is that for Deb's benefit?"

"Nope." Sax grinned. "It's mine."

"Ah, that's right. Aaron said you liked games."

"Some of them," Sax replied casually.

For no good reason, Jude's heart skipped a beat. *Forget it. That is* not *what she meant. You have got to get your hormones under control around her.* But she couldn't prevent a brief image of the other woman in her motorcycle jacket from flickering into her mind. And that image did nothing to still the surge of blood into places she really didn't want it to be going. Not at seven o'clock in the morning at the beginning of a very long day.

"So, are you actually planning to take call with Deb?" Sax asked as they leaned against the waist-high cement wall that encircled the rooftop.

Grateful for a conversation to take her mind off her body's unwelcome responses, Jude said, "Yes. I want to be where she is when something happens, and you said yourself how unpredictable it can be."

"For twenty-four hour stretches?"

"Whenever she's here, yes." Jude took in the huge white X stenciled on the rooftop and the windsock snapping in the breeze nearby, almost salivating at the thought of filming the helicopter's descent while a crowd of gowned medical personnel waited, bent low to avoid the swirling rotors. It brought to mind all those old clips from the

'60s of choppers twisting wildly over the scorched earth of a faraway land, olive-garbed men racing madly forward with their wounded on makeshift litters. *God, what a shot.*

"What about your crew—the photographers and sound people? Them, too?"

"What?" Jude was still focused on the faint images in her mind— battlefields and blood and Sinclair in black leather. "Oh, Mel is the main camera operator, and she'll work nights when Deb's on call. I figure that's when we're most likely to get a hit. Since I'll be here around the clock, I'll handle the cameras if she's not available. I'm not as good as she is, but I can manage."

"For how long?"

"Indefinitely," Jude said with a shrug. "Until I get what I need."

"That's a significant commitment," Sax observed, wondering if the filmmaker had any idea how disruptive that kind of schedule was going to be. "In time *and* energy. Every third night, sometimes *all* night, can wear you down pretty fast. On holiday weekends like this one we may even do twelve-hour shifts, depending on call-outs and how busy we get in the OR. That's a lot of lost sleep."

"You do it," Jude pointed out.

"It's my job."

"Mine, too."

Sax studied her, then grinned. "Point taken. Forgive my professional chauvinism."

"It's hard to be angry at someone who so readily admits it when she's being a jerk."

For a moment, Sax simply stared at her. Green eyes, sparkling with challenge, met hers, and she wondered what it was about this woman that was so damn appealing. She decided it might be the fact that she had yet to back down over anything. "Aren't you afraid that you'll offend me, and I'll be uncooperative?"

Jude laughed. "I missed the part where you've been cooperating so far."

"I'll try to be more obvious, then," Sax replied dryly, but her tone was playful.

"Tell me something, Dr. Sinclair," Jude said, still thinking about the battlefield images. "Tell me about the enemy."

"Enemy?"

"Yes. The enemy you face when a patient is delivered into your trauma bay. What is it?"

"Time," Sax answered immediately, not even stopping to consider where the question had come from. "A true trauma emergency is a race against time—blood seeps away, organs die, damage becomes irreversible."

"How much time do you have? To make decisions, to make a difference?" Jude asked softly, watching something in Sinclair's face change. The surgeon was looking past her, her gaze slightly distant, as if she were reliving something in her mind. Jude did not want to distract her; she did not want to let her know how much her expression revealed.

"Seconds. Sometimes not even that. You act unconsciously, instinctively."

"And if you're wrong?" Her voice was softer still.

Sinclair's blue eyes snapped into sharp focus and met Jude's. "We have a saying in surgery, Ms. Castle—better wrong than uncertain. Hesitation, for a surgeon, can be deadly. If you can't live with your decisions, you need to find another line of work." She turned to leave, saying, "I have trauma rounds in thirty minutes."

"What about Deb Stein?" Jude called after her, not wanting to let the moment pass. She needed to understand what went on beneath the surface, so she could hunt it out and capture it with her lens. "How will you know if she can make those kinds of decisions?"

Sax stopped and faced her. "You're interviewing me again."

"Is this year some kind of test for her?" Jude persisted, ignoring the comment.

Mildly exasperated at the other woman's tenacity, Sax shook her head. "No. Deb has proven herself already. This is additional training for her, above and beyond the basic requirements for a general surgeon to become board certified. She's *already* completed six years of resident training—six years of a system designed to wear down and wear out anyone not physically and psychologically fit for the specialty. The attrition rate is high in the first two years of a surgery residency for a reason."

"Sounds abusive," Jude observed, still probing.

"Some people would call it that. But better to find out before someone is set loose with a knife in their hand whether they can take it or not."

"So what is the purpose of *this* year, if Deb is already a competent surgeon?"

"I need to teach her to think on her feet, to make the right decisions without all the information, to trust her judgment. If anyone is tested this year, it will be me." Sax stopped abruptly. *Where in hell did that come from? Why is it every time I talk to this woman I end up saying things I don't mean to? She's downright dangerous.* Curtly, she said, "I'm sorry. I'll be late." She left before Jude could penetrate her guard again.

For several seconds Jude stared after her, feeling short of breath. She tried to tell herself it wasn't because of the passion she had glimpsed in the depths of Saxon Sinclair's eyes, or how very attractive she found it. Surely it was only the woman's professional dedication that left her breathless.

CHAPTER SIX

Personal Project Log—Castle
July 1, 7:40 a.m.

I'm starting to get the picture now. Trauma surgery is the medical equivalent of the Special Forces or the Green Berets or something. At least that's the way Sinclair sees it. She's the commanding officer, the residents are her troops, and the war is against death. Jesus. I never thought about that before. It takes some kind of ego to take that on. She's got it, that's for sure, but I wonder how that happens. Where does that confidence, that absolute certainty, come from? [Note: Need more background on Sinclair. She and Deb are the brackets of this frame, the beginning and the end.]

That's the point of this year, I guess—to take Deb, the green recruit, and turn her into a leader, a warrior. [Note: Title second episode "Boot Camp."] This is the angle—the hook. This is the analogy that will get people excited, that will keep them coming back week after week. That and the human interest aspect of following Deb through the process. She's perfect for it because she's so girl-next-door. They loved her during the Olympics, and the up-close-and-personal interviews with her were a big hit. [Note: Call Sinclair's secretary for her CV. Arrange an on-camera interview with Sinclair regarding the necessary personality traits of a trauma surgeon. How did she choose Deb?]

July 1, 8:15 p.m.

"If I have to eat cafeteria food every third night or more often for the next six months, I want hazard pay," Melissa Cooper groused. "It's bad enough that my social life is going to go to hell, but with that fare, so will the rest of me."

"I told you to take a few hours off for dinner, or we could have ordered takeout," Jude pointed out, leafing through a surgical journal she had found under a stack of file folders on the counter. The article titles were mostly indecipherable to her, but the pictures were fascinating. She was sitting in the trauma bay in one of the ubiquitous swivel chairs, her feet propped up on the wastepaper basket. Nearby, Mel fiddled with her equipment.

"Problems?" Jude asked.

"No, I ran a video-sound synch check earlier, and it was fine. I just wanted to make sure we had the microphone settings optimized to capture everything we could. It would be better if we had off-camera mikes, too."

"I agree, but I don't think it's technically possible in the space that we have here. Besides, it will add to the immediacy and the atmosphere if our sound is a little rough. We want this to come across like a frontline, in-the-trenches kind of documentary."

Mel straightened and stretched. "That's what you're going to get if I have to rely on only two cameras and wear one of them." She pulled a chair out from under the long counter and regarded Jude contemplatively. "How are things with Lori?"

"Fine." Surprised, Jude had responded automatically. "Why?"

"Just wondering," Melissa said with a shrug. "You've been seeing her, what? Four or five months?"

"Six."

Melissa whistled. "Sounds serious."

"No," Jude said slowly, realizing that she rarely gave her relationship with Lori much thought. *It just is...what it is.* "Not really."

"Is she seeing anyone else?"

"Not that I know of, but she might be. We never made any exclusivity agreements."

"Are you?"

"No." Jude eyed her friend and colleague suspiciously. "I barely have time to keep up the one relationship I have as it is. So why the twenty questions, Mel? Are you planning on asking her out?"

"God, no." Melissa laughed. "She's hot, but she's way too establishment for me. Just curious as to what's going on with you. If I were going to ask anyone out, it would be Sinclair. She's got a look about her that says she could be interesting."

"Interesting?" Jude asked carefully, trying to ignore a sudden twist of jealousy. *You've got absolutely nothing to be jealous about. What's it to you if Melissa goes after Sinclair or anyone else, for that matter? You already have a girlfriend and even seeing her every few weeks is work. Besides, Sinclair is definitely not your type. She's secretive and edgy and just plain difficult.*

Oblivious, Mel continued blithely, "In case you haven't noticed, she's got a thing about control. I bet she's the same way in bed."

Jude definitely did not want to spend any time at all considering what Saxon Sinclair would be like in bed. She had to work around her for days at a time for the foreseeable future, and she needed to concentrate on work while they were together, nothing else. "Well, good luck finding out."

"Is she available, do you know?"

"No idea." Come to think of it, she didn't know much about her at all. *I really need to get her in an interview.*

"Should I give you a detailed report?" Melissa teased.

"No thanks," Jude responded more sharply then she intended. She hoped the photographer didn't notice.

Before Melissa could comment, Deb and Aaron walked in together. "Hey," they both said in greeting.

"Evening," Jude answered, disappointed to see that Sinclair was not with them. "What's happening?"

Deb joined them as Aaron began restocking the crash cart with drugs after unlocking the multidrawer rolling cart with his key.

"Nothing at the moment," Deb replied. "Sinclair told me to tell you she's arranging an on-call room for you. Maintenance is putting a couple of beds and a desk in a small office down the hall. You can sleep in there and set up some of your equipment if you need to." She handed Jude several keys. "You might as well try to get some rest while you're hanging around with us if nothing's happening at night."

"I don't want to miss anything," Jude said uncertainly.

"I'll bang on your door if anything comes in," Deb assured her. "We always have some warning when a trauma is on the way, because either the EMTs radio us or the chopper calls ahead."

"Sounds fine, then," Jude agreed. "If it gets to be late and it's still quiet, I'll definitely take you up on it."

"I'll second that," Melissa added. She considered briefly that it might be handy in the coming months to have a room nearby with a bed available. She'd learned from experience that a little romantic diversion on an extended shoot could help pass the time quite nicely, and from what she'd seen so far, there was more than one possibility she wouldn't mind exploring.

July 2, 2:29 a.m.

Jude felt as if she'd barely closed her eyes when a sharp rap on the door brought her upright in the narrow bed. Across the tiny space from her, Mel turned over with a mumble and buried her head under the pillow. Heart pounding, it took Jude a few moments to realize where she was and that someone was at the door. Crossing quickly to open it, she inquired, "Yes?"

Sinclair stood in the empty hallway looking wide-awake. "Five minutes, Ms. Castle. We have three coming by ambulance from a pileup on the bridge. There could be more—I don't know yet."

"Right, thanks."

Sinclair was already moving off down the hall toward the trauma admitting area as Jude called over her shoulder, "Let's go, Mel. We're on."

The next five minutes passed in what felt like seconds. By the time Jude and Melissa reached the trauma bay, Aaron and two other nurses Jude didn't recognize were already waiting, garbed in protective gowns and gloves and pulling out instrument packs from tall steel cabinets. Sinclair and Deb were in scrubs and latex gloves. On the long counter lay the remnants of someone's late dinner, scattered sections of the daily newspaper, and a chessboard, clearly abandoned in mid-game. Jude averted her eyes, but not before she had instantaneously absorbed the position of the pieces. White was about to be checkmated.

From across the room, near one of the treatment tables, Sax watched Jude Castle and her photographer prepare. In their own way, they were very much like her team, working together with practiced efficiency, almost wordlessly. Jude spoke rapidly into her tape recorder, apparently noting the date, time, and specific circumstances of the upcoming shoot. Melissa shrugged into a body harness that was clearly meant to support the heavy handheld video camera. As she helped to secure the DVCam, Jude affixed the microphone to it for simultaneous sound and video synchronization. Once that was accomplished, Melissa took up a position where she could record the entrance and the arrival of the patients and checked the angle of view on the built-in monitor. Jude stood just behind her, where, Sax presumed, she could direct the photographer to concentrate on whatever aspects of the upcoming resuscitation interested her. *Smooth. Impressive.*

Jude glanced over. "Are we okay here?" she asked Sax.

"I think so. Go for what you want. If you get in the way, I'll let you know."

"Sounds good." Jude grinned. She didn't doubt for a second that even in the midst of fury, Sinclair would have no problem making her wishes known. Her last act, before the doors slid open and the first of three stretchers careened into the room, was to wonder if the surgeon ever relinquished control to anyone...ever.

CHAPTER SEVEN

July 2, 2:43 a.m.

It started out as a fairly routine trauma situation, or so Jude surmised. EMTs and paramedics from two separate divisions had responded to a multivehicle crash. The first victims to arrive were a family of three.

"Try to get something on all of them, but concentrate on Deb and the little girl," Jude directed Melissa as medical personnel converged on the gurneys.

Efficiently, team members moved each patient to a treatment table with the effortless choreography of long practice. As far as Jude could tell, all three family members were conscious, although both the mother and father were strapped to backboards with restraining cervical collars around their necks.

A blond child who appeared to be about five lay on the third stretcher, looking small and vulnerable amidst the monitors clustered around her. A large laceration extended from her scalp onto her forehead, and from where she was standing, Jude could make out the stark gleaming surface of white bone. Miraculously, the child appeared comfortable and not particularly frightened. She didn't even seem to be crying, although tear tracks smudged her smooth cheeks.

Sinclair was directing the activity even as she began assessing the male member of the trio.

"Fisher, check the mother. Stein, get the girl." She bent over the man, automatically performing the standard initial evaluation to confirm that he was breathing properly and that his pulse and blood pressure were adequate. While she worked, she shot questions at the paramedics who had lingered to watch the resuscitation. "What was the status in the field? Extrication times? Any hemodynamic instability or loss of consciousness?"

It sounded to Jude as if the handful of emergency personnel answered all at once, and she couldn't fathom how the trauma chief could possibly sort out the plethora of facts and numbers bombarding her.

Sax never took her eyes off the patient, her face intent as her hands moved rapidly over his body. "Were they restrained?"

"Yep. Seat belts and car seat," one of the paramedics standing by the door finishing his paperwork called out.

Sax straightened and glanced to her right where Keith Fisher, an upper-level surgery resident, was performing the exact same maneuvers on the mother that she had just completed. "Dr. Fisher," she said, not loudly, but with a degree of authority that got his attention immediately. His hands stopped moving and he looked up expectantly. "This patient is complaining of abdominal pain and he's got guarding in the lower abdomen. What do you recommend we do?"

The young man, clearly charged with excitement by the tense atmosphere, answered with a note of hope in his voice, "Open peritoneal lavage?"

Jude couldn't watch anyone but Saxon Sinclair. Of all the figures in the room, she seemed to be the epicenter, the focal point. Despite the air of controlled pandemonium permeating the trauma bay, her expression was calm and her attitude collected. Her movements were precise and economical, and in just the few moments that Jude had been observing her, she had clearly appraised the condition of each patient and given directives to orchestrate their care.

As Jude listened to the young surgeon-in-training suggest what she presumed was some sort of operation, for a fleeting second, she thought she saw Sinclair grin. She made a note in the log she was quietly dictating to ask her why.

"I'd agree with you," Sax said as she moved to the woman Fisher was examining, "if he were hemodynamically unstable and I suspected a major intra-abdominal bleed. But his pulse and blood pressure are normal, so we have time to get a noninvasive test *before* we need to resort to a surgical procedure." Glancing over her shoulder, she ordered, "Aaron, get him down for a CT of the chest and abdomen.

Tell them he's a possible seat belt injury and to check his spleen and retroperitoneum carefully."

Surprisingly, she stopped at the foot of the stretcher where the female patient lay and turned to Jude. As if she had all the time in the world, she said conversationally, "It's not uncommon to sustain an internal injury in high-speed decelerations when a person is restrained by a seat belt. Internal organs, particularly those that are very vascular or fragile, can rupture and bleed. That's why it's important to check the liver and spleen for hemorrhage. Areas where the organs are attached or where the major blood vessels run—the retroperitoneum—are other sites of possible damage. We could make a small incision in his abdomen right now and look, but I think a CT scan is a better choice for him."

"Thanks," Jude said, but Sinclair had already turned her back and was leaning over the wife. She introduced herself and asked the woman if she were having any pain. Jude couldn't hear the faint reply, but she could hear the anxiety in her tone.

"We haven't finished examining the three of you yet," Sax said calmly, "but everyone seems stable. Your husband will need some tests, and I'll let you know about your little girl in a few seconds. Now I want to take care of you."

There was something familiar in the surgeon's compassionate tone that struck a chord in Jude, and as she struggled with the half-memory, her pulse accelerated and her ears buzzed faintly. *God, not now!* She forced her attention back to the scene before her and, thankfully, her head cleared.

"Pull back a little bit to catch both the mother and daughter," Jude instructed Melissa hoarsely. She just needed to focus on the work and she'd be fine.

The photographer, who had been moving back and forth between the three stretchers, trying to record the various stages of treatment, grunted her assent. Just as Jude had spoken, the little girl called for her mother, and mother and child each reached out a hand, joining their fingers across the narrow space between the two beds.

"Are you getting this?" Jude whispered, practically climbing onto Mel's shoulder to check her angle of view.

"Yeah, yeah, I've got it. Don't worry," Melissa said distractedly, trying to keep one eye on the scene at large so as not to miss some developing event and, at the same time, concentrating on the intimate details that made the proceedings so very human. "You could give me an inch or two to move, Jude," she muttered as she followed behind Deb, working to keep the heavy camera steady against her chest. Even with the body rig to help support the weight, her arms would be shaking before too much longer.

Next to them, Sinclair gave detailed instructions about lab tests and X-rays for the mother to one of the nurses and finally joined Deb beside the little girl. Both Jude and Melissa moved in close behind her, but she seemed not to notice them.

"Anything?" Sax asked, studying the small patient.

"Neurologic exam is intact. No evidence of airway or hemodynamic instability. She has the obvious laceration, but I can't palpate a skull fracture. No bruising on the chest or abdomen to suggest blunt trauma, and she's moving all four extremities to command. She'll need a head CT to rule out a fracture or any associated intracranial injury, and then she's going to need that laceration repaired."

As Deb reported, Sinclair bent close and murmured something that Jude couldn't quite make out, but she hoped the mike on the camera would pick it up. Then, the trauma chief began her own assessment— listening to the little girl's heart and lungs, probing her abdomen, running her hands over each extremity. She checked the child's pupils and ears, nodded agreement with Deb's evaluation, and murmured, "Nothing to suggest evidence of bleeding or increased intracranial pressure. Looks like her only significant injury is that fairly straightforward soft tissue injury on the scalp. Do you want to repair it yourself after the CT or call plastics?"

"It looks pretty routine," Deb remarked. "As long as nothing else is going on, I might as well do it."

Sinclair appeared about to answer when a heavyset policeman, flushed and breathing heavily, barged into the trauma admitting area. He skidded to a halt and stared at her, struggling to get his words out.

"There's an ambulance pulling in right now...with a guy who crashed his motorcycle in the pileup. He was underneath one of the cars...and we just found him." He held out a large black trash bag, which he had secured under one arm. "This...this is...his."

Jude wasn't certain what she was watching, but she tapped Melissa on the shoulder and said urgently, "Get this."

"Put it down on this," Sax said, rolling a steel cart forward. As the policeman deposited his package, she looked at Jude and Melissa pointedly. "This may be...difficult."

"It's okay." Jude tried to ignore the escalating roaring in her head. The shape of the package gave her a pretty good idea of what was inside, but she was certain she must be wrong. Her heart was hammering as she continued, "Go ahead."

Sax peeled back the edges of the black plastic.

"Oh fuck." Melissa struggled to hold the camera steady, and it wasn't because her arms were tired.

Jude put a hand on Melissa's shoulder and fought a dizzying wave of nausea.

"Stein," Sax said curtly as she surveyed the perfectly preserved leg lying in the bag surrounded by ice. It had been severed at the hip and a portion of the pelvic bone was visible, still attached to the cut end. The rest of it looked perfectly normal, including the lower leg and foot. "Call the OR and tell them we have a level one coming up. Notify vascular surgery and orthopedics that we have a possible limb replantation."

Even as she was speaking, the doors slid open yet again and four paramedics came crashing through with the owner of the severed limb. For the next few moments, it seemed to Jude that Sinclair was everywhere at once. Nurses and residents descended upon the motorcyclist, cutting off clothes, inserting tubes into his nose and into his arms and down his throat. Sinclair and Stein removed a large pressure bandage that covered his lower body, at which point Jude commanded hoarsely, "Stop the camera, Mel."

Melissa was about to protest, but when she got a clear look at the gaping wound she realized Jude was right. The terrible injury was far too personal and private to be revealed without the victim's permission. "Yeah."

July 2, 6:29 a.m.

"Do you want to look at the dailies now?" Melissa asked, trying valiantly to hide her weariness. She hadn't thought anything could bother her anymore. She'd filmed children starving in African nations so impoverished it was impossible to believe such conditions existed in the modern world, and she'd documented the last moments of young men and women dying of AIDS in the most technologically advanced society ever known. She'd witnessed the gamut of human emotions from grief and horror to joyous celebration, and with the filter of her camera between her and the events she recorded, she'd been able to maintain her psychological equilibrium. Last night, she'd almost lost it.

"Let's do it later," Jude said dully. She glanced at the round, institutional clock, amazed at how much time had passed. Four hours swallowed up in a blur of noise and motion and blood. She surveyed the littered floor, the aftermath of battle strewn everywhere—wads of gauze soaked with blood and other fluids, discarded surgical gloves, clear plastic wrappers that had encased sterile tubing and intravenous catheters, a portion of a pair of denim pants. "God."

"We're not going to be able to show much of that, are we?" Melissa commented. Her throat was so dry it almost hurt to speak. Without looking at Jude, she stowed her equipment methodically, needing to restore order and sanity by repeating familiar tasks.

Jude twisted in the swivel chair in front of the counter and stared at the chessboard. Miraculously, it had remained undisrupted throughout what felt to her now like a tornado of barely contained chaos. Absently, she replayed Black's last six moves. *Nicely done.*

"We can't show *him,*" she said at last. She didn't need to review the videotape to know what she wanted to use from what they had just witnessed. "The network censors would never let it pass. Besides, I don't want this to be about satisfying morbid curiosity. There's still a lot there. We've got great shots of Deb and Sinclair, though."

Mel mumbled something affirmative. The dazed lassitude of her every movement told Jude how drained she felt.

Gently, she said, "Go home, Mel."

Finally alone for what seemed the first time in hours, she pressed her fingers to her aching temples. Her heart was still racing with the aftermath of tension, but what left her nerve endings so raw and her skin so hot were the images seared into her memory. Saxon Sinclair. Doing all she did. Being who she was.

Jude wanted to think about almost anything else, but all she could see were Sax's blazing blue eyes, intent and focused in the midst of chaos, and her hands, so quick and sure and tender.

July 2, 9:54 a.m.

Sax walked into the trauma admitting area and stared in surprise at Jude Castle. "What are you still doing here? I saw your photographer leave just before I started making rounds a couple of hours ago."

"I sent her home," Jude replied. "I think she earned her salary last night."

"So did you." Sax pulled out a chair and sat down opposite the filmmaker. She had expected Jude to want to get away for a while after the previous night's events. An injury like that was tough on all of them, even the most seasoned trauma veteran, but it must be nearly impossible for a civilian to assimilate. She had to work at not thinking too much about it herself.

It hadn't escaped her notice that Jude had looked as if she were about to faint when the severed leg was uncovered, not that Sax could blame her. She had a feeling, though, that it wasn't because Jude was weak-willed or squeamish. Her reaction had seemed very much like the one she'd had when she'd first walked into the trauma admitting area—a purely involuntary, autonomic response to a stressful event. Or the memory of one. Even now, she still looked pale and shaky.

"Are you okay?" Sax asked. "It was a long night."

Jude flushed, embarrassed, wishing that the surgeon wasn't quite so astute. "Yes, thanks." She knew where the unwelcome physical reactions were coming from, and she knew that she actually *was* fine, but she was troubled nonetheless. It was uncomfortable, disconcerting, and damned inconvenient to be suddenly awash with terror—no, the *memory* of terror—when she least expected it. She forced herself onto another track, because thinking about it only made it more of an issue. "How is...the boy? God, I don't even know his name. I don't even remember what his face looks like. I don't think I ever looked at *him.*"

She leaned back and closed her eyes, wondering at the rapidity with which she'd distanced herself from the horrors of human frailty. If it could happen to her in barely two days, how could anyone seeing it day after day possibly feel anything and still remain sane?

"His name is Stephen Jones, and he's twenty years old. He has a lovely girlfriend and a very devoted family. At the moment, he is still alive—against all odds—and he's going to need all their support if he's going to make it in the long run."

"You met with the family?" *How did you find the time? How did you find the strength?*

"Briefly," Sax replied. "Deb is with them now explaining what they can expect over the next few days. A big part of her training is learning to coordinate the various specialties that are involved in a trauma patient's care. Just as important as orchestrating the medical care is keeping the family informed and putting them in touch with support staff who can help with finances, insurance, and things like that."

Jude sighed. "Damn. I should have gotten that." She smiled wanly. "To tell you the truth, I needed a break."

"Understandable." Sax meant it. She studied the other woman, concerned by the faint tremor she noted in Jude's hands. She leaned forward, and asked again, "Are you sure you're all right?"

"I'm not as fragile as you might think, Dr. Sinclair," Jude said more harshly than she intended. It bothered her that the seemingly undauntable surgeon might think she couldn't handle the intensity of the trauma unit.

"Would you like to tell me *now* what's causing the flashbacks?" Sax asked mildly. "Or would you rather I find out when you finally faint and end up with a laceration on your forehead that I have to close?"

Jude stood up suddenly, not the least bit dizzy any longer. She was too angry at Sinclair's presumption, and too unnerved by its accuracy, to have even a faint memory of how ill she had felt just moments before. "You needn't worry that I'll be requiring your services in any fashion, Dr. Sinclair. I assure you, I'll have no problem doing my job."

No, I'm sure you won't. But is there any reason that you have to suffer so much while you're doing it?

Sax did not attempt to stop Jude from leaving the room, but she was disturbed to think of her struggling in silence. And it disturbed her even more to realize that she was breaking one of her own rules by caring.

Chapter Eight

The quietly elegant woman in the expensively tailored slacks and plain cotton blouse stood on the porch in the bright summer sunlight and listened to the sound of the motorcycle approaching. The unpaved lane that wended its way through the quiet countryside in front of her nineteenth-century farmhouse was lined on either side by wildflowers, and the stone path leading from it to her front door was edged with a collection of vividly colored petunias and marigolds.

As she watched, a figure clad from head to toe in black—T-shirt, jeans, and boots—pulled up on a huge Harley-Davidson and dismounted by her front gate.

Sax removed her helmet and propped it on the seat of her Harley. She ran both hands through her dark hair and started up the walk, grinning faintly at the woman waiting for her.

"Hey, Maddy," she said by way of greeting, taking the stairs up to the wide wooden porch two at a time. She slipped her arms around the woman's waist and hugged her, bestowing a light kiss on her cheek. "You look splendid, as always."

It was said lightly, but it was true. Madeleine Lane was possessed of a timeless beauty born of good bones and fine skin, and a figure that artists had attempted to render on canvas and carve from stone for centuries. She would have been beautiful at any age, in any time.

"You might have called to tell me you were coming," she admonished Sax fondly, ignoring a compliment that had long since lost all meaning to her. "I would have gotten a list of chores together. Are you staying?"

"Until tomorrow." Sax kept her arm loosely around Maddy's waist. "I don't suppose there's breakfast?"

"It's noon, Saxon."

Sax grinned. "I came straight from the hospital, but you always tell me not to speed, so it took me a while."

Madeleine regarded her granddaughter with a critical eye. She knew very well that Saxon's unpredictable visits were usually prompted by a need to escape from something—too much work, too much horror, too many of life's disappointments. There were faint shadows under her eyes now, and she looked thinner and more drawn than the last time she'd been here.

That had been nearly two months ago, in the middle of the night. Her granddaughter had arrived in a driving rain, drenched and shaking from far more than the cold. As had so often been the case, they had talked until dawn about nothing of consequence, and when Saxon finally departed on her motorcycle, Maddy still had no idea what had made her come. Saxon's silences didn't matter to her. They never had. All that mattered was that she always returned.

"Have you been to bed?" Maddy asked as they walked arm in arm through the dimly lit living room. Lace curtains were pulled across the windows to filter the sunshine and keep the room cool. The house was not air-conditioned because Maddy had never liked the way that felt.

"I'm not tired." Sax avoided a direct answer. She was seething with too much restless energy to sleep, and she hadn't been able to face the thought of returning to her expensively appointed but undeniably cold apartment. It wasn't for lack of a good decorator that her apartment lacked warmth; it was just because there was nothing of her in the place.

She hadn't even thought about her destination when she'd climbed onto her bike and headed north out of the city. The humid air had blown cool around her face at sixty miles an hour, and she'd soon shed the lingering pall of sadness and death that had seeped past her defenses. In less than an hour and a half, she had reached home. She hadn't grown up on the out-of-the-way farm, but it was home nevertheless—because it was where Maddy lived.

"Did you work all night?" Maddy tried again.

"Hmm?" *God, what a night. I can't remember the last time we had one so bad.* Sax caught herself just as she began to think about Stephen Jones and his missing leg and his ruined life. She couldn't afford to remember the look on his parents' face when she told them of his injuries or to imagine what the future would hold for him. *Treat them. Don't live with them. Keep your sanity.*

But sometimes the utter madness of it all crept up on you, and you went a little mad yourself.

"Oh, yes, I did," she answered off-handedly. "We were a little busy."

They had reached the large kitchen that ran almost the entire length of the rear of the farmhouse. Two years earlier, Sax had replaced the small rear porch and adjoining mudroom with a large glass-enclosed solarium that connected to the kitchen through double French doors. She had built it after Maddy had admitted that the nagging arthritis in her right hip bothered her less when she could sit in the sun. *There*, Sax had declared, *you can sit in the sun all winter long and still be warm.*

"Sit down while I make you some breakfast. Waffles okay?"

"Waffles are always okay," Sax said as she stretched her legs out under the broad oak tabletop.

Maddy set a cup of coffee by her granddaughter's right hand. As she removed items from the refrigerator and cupboards, she asked casually, "How are things at the hospital?"

Sax cradled the coffee mug in her hands and shrugged. "As crazy as they always are in July. New residents to keep an eye on, more people on the streets to get shot or mugged, more cars on the road to run into each other. It's the busy season."

"Uh-huh," Maddy responded noncommittally as she mixed ingredients.

"There's a film crew doing a documentary in the trauma unit."

Maddy glanced over, trying to read Saxon's feelings from her expression because her voice rarely revealed anything, but she hadn't really expected to be able to. Her granddaughter, she knew, had learned as a child to hide her feelings. That distance probably served her well in the highly volatile environment of the trauma unit, but it was very frustrating for anyone who wanted to know her.

"That's rather unusual, isn't it?" She dropped a bit of batter on the griddle to test the temperature. "It seems like it would be a terribly difficult place to film. How on earth could you have any kind of order on the set?"

"It's not like what you were used to," Sax said with a laugh. "No elaborate scenes, no retakes, and no catering to spoiled starlets."

"I'll have you know that I was *never* spoiled," Maddy said haughtily. "I was always the epitome of refinement."

"That's not what it says about you in the stories *I've* read."

Placing a couple of steaming waffles in front of Sax, Maddy said curtly, but with a laugh in her voice, "Those reports were greatly exaggerated."

"At any rate," Sax turned her attention to the home-cooked meal, "this is more what you would call cinéma vérité."

Maddy carried a cup of coffee over and sat down opposite Sax. "Must make things pretty hectic if they're filming while you're working."

"I thought it would be, but the director has been good about keeping her crew out from underfoot, so far."

"A woman director?" Maddy remarked in surprise. "I've always wished I had been able to do that rather than act. Or maybe along with it."

"Really?" Sax felt the pressure in her chest easing with the familiar rhythm of their banter. "I never knew that."

"It just wasn't possible then—or maybe it was, and we just didn't know to try."

Sax reached across the table and touched her grandmother's hand. "I'm sorry."

Maddy laughed. "Oh, no need to be. I haven't been pining about it all these years. But I'll look forward to seeing what she does with you."

"It's not about me," Sax swiftly clarified. "She's focusing on my new trauma fellow, Deb Stein."

"Hmm, yes, and I imagine you just fade into the background."

Sax caught the end of a fleeting smile and chuckled. Her heart was suddenly lighter than it had been in weeks. No one had ever been able to make her laugh at herself the way Maddy did. Maybe because no one had ever made her feel so...loved. "I don't think Jude Castle would agree with that. I've given her a hard time, I guess."

"Why?" Maddy asked seriously, wondering if this was the reason Saxon had come. It had been her experience that eventually her solitary granddaughter would work her way around to what was bothering her, even if she didn't realize it herself.

Sax turned in her chair to look out the window, noting that one of double doors on the garage was hanging askew. "I'll have to replace that hinge," she remarked absently.

Maddy waited.

"Photography is a treacherous thing," Sax said softly, almost to herself. "It's merciless and unkind in the way it captures the moment, exposing—no, *revealing*—the truth without the benefit of pretense or masks. You can't hide from it, not forever."

"Yet, there is no judgment in simply recording events," Maddy pointed out. "It's a neutral process."

"No," Sax responded vehemently, shaking her head. "It would be neutral if it weren't selective, but it is. Jude Castle directs the camera—she determines what the film will reveal, what moments will be emphasized, what story will be told. She has all the power."

"Ah." Maddy thought of how many years it had taken Saxon to feel she was in control of her own life, and safe. "She frightens you."

It wasn't a question.

Sax looked at her in astonishment, ready to protest once again. She met those blue eyes so like her own and felt the words die on her tongue. It was true, and it wasn't just her fear of what Jude Castle might see when she looked at her through the unvarnished eye of Melissa Cooper's camera. It was realizing how badly she wanted to be seen.

"Saxon!" Maddy pulled the shawl tighter around her shoulders as she peered up at the shadow moving on her rooftop. "You have to stop. That lantern is not enough light. You're going to fall off and break your neck. Besides that, it's the middle of the night."

Sax pounded another nail into the flashing around the chimney and called down, "I'll be done in a minute."

She hadn't been able to sleep. Or rather, she'd fallen asleep soon after dinner and had awakened in a sweat around midnight. She'd been dreaming. It had been a very vivid dream. Her body was still tingling with a combination of arousal and fear as she sat up in bed, breathing hard, trembling. She'd dreamed of a woman leaning over her, holding her down with the barest of touches while she turned her blood to fire with a kiss. She'd awakened still aching with the memory of that kiss.

And when she couldn't get the image of the red-haired woman

with the emerald eyes from her mind, she'd vaulted from the bed, pulled on her jeans, and sought some chore to distract her from the insistent throbbing in her belly. It hadn't worked, but at least she didn't feel as if she were going to explode.

Resolutely, she climbed down the ladder and headed back upstairs to her bed. She hated to admit it, but part of her hoped that Jude Castle would visit her dreams again.

CHAPTER NINE

July 3, 2:40 p.m.

A re you sure you can't stay longer?"
"I need to get back." Sax straddled her motorcycle, her helmet cradled under one arm. "I'm on call again tomorrow."

"I know very well that you don't have to take call so often, not since you're the boss," Maddy pointed out, shading her eyes from the morning sun.

She'd heard her granddaughter prowling the house half the night and wondered now if she'd slept at all. It had been years since she'd seen her this restless and agitated—not since those first few months right after Saxon had come to live with her, back when she'd still had her Manhattan apartment. That period had been so difficult, she wasn't sure either of them would ever sleep again.

"You could let some of the others fill in for you."

"It's the fourth, and that's always a wild one," Sax explained, even though she knew Maddy was right. "Plus, there's more work if I'm *not* there, just piling up and waiting for me."

And you wouldn't know what to do with yourself if you weren't working. Maddy stepped forward and stroked Sax's arm. "Come back sooner next time."

"I will," Sax replied. "Call me if you need anything. And make that list of things that need repair." She leaned to kiss the other woman's cheek. "I love you," she murmured.

"And I you," Maddy replied. "I'll work on that list." She would, too, although she could easily afford to hire a handyman to keep the place in working order. But she knew that her granddaughter needed the excuse to pull herself away from the demands, and the repercussions, of her work.

"Why don't you bring that film director with you sometime? I'd like to hear what things are like in the industry these days," Maddy added. She didn't see the surprise in her granddaughter's eyes because Sax had already lowered the smoke gray visor over her face.

"Sure," Sax responded automatically, almost laughing at the absurdity of *that* thought. She couldn't imagine that a busy, cosmopolitan woman like Jude Castle would have any interest in spending an afternoon with her and a reclusive, aging movie queen out in the middle of nowhere, sitting on the porch watching the corn grow.

July 3, 8:53 p.m.

"It's good, Jude." Melissa leaned back in her chair with a sigh. The two of them had been sitting shoulder to shoulder in front of the desk in their on-call room for a good part of the afternoon and evening. They'd set up a computer to screen the videotapes from Melissa's cameras and had been reviewing the first footage from the trauma alert two nights before. "I was *there*, and I still held my breath in places watching it again today."

"Yeah." Jude consulted her log and then keyed in the digital markers to find a scene she wanted to view again. She muted the sound on the computer and watched Deborah Stein and Sinclair lean over the small blond child, comforting her while simultaneously examining her, quickly and proficiently.

"Do you see that?" she asked. "Watch the difference from here... to here."

Melissa moved closer, following Jude's instructions. "Yeah?"

"Everything changes when they start examining her—see there— even their expressions. Something clicks in...or off."

"They're working, Jude. What did you expect?" Melissa was not sure she understood what the director wanted her to grasp. "They're just focused."

"I know that," Jude said with a hint of frustration, "but that's the whole point. In order to *do* the work, they have to turn something off—shut something down inside. They have to sever the emotional connection, the...the *empathy* that most people would feel—are compelled to feel—just because that's what makes us human. What did *you* feel while you were watching?"

"I was working, too," Melissa pointed out adamantly. She didn't want to admit how relieved she'd been when Jude had told her to take off as soon as the trauma team had transported the motorcycle victim up to the OR the previous day. She'd needed some air, and that had shaken her.

"So was I." Jude fixed her with an unyielding stare. "And it was still hard to take. Stop avoiding the question."

"We've seen horror before," Melissa insisted, shifting uncomfortably in her chair. "Come on, tanks on fire, buildings crumbling on top of us—not to mention twenty-five-year-old guys who looked eighty, taping their final moments. What's the difference?"

"The difference is that in Eastern Europe there was physical distance between us and the events, and from the victims, too. When we did the AIDS feature, we knew going in what we would be filming. We had time to prepare."

"Right. So?"

"So, there's an immediacy, an uncertainty, to what happens in the trauma unit. You don't know what to expect, so you can't ever be ready."

"And I *got* that on tape," Melissa said. "Just look at the way we've got the wide angle arrival—boom, through the doors, a whole crowd of people and somewhere in there is the patient. Then we zoom in, cutting back and forth from patient to patient and from doctor to patient. It's all there—the motion, the energy, the frantic pace. For crying out loud, the camera movement alone tells the story."

It was clear from her tone that she was very happy with the tape and the way things had gone.

"Exactly," Jude agreed. "And next time I want you to slow it down."

"What?"

Jude grinned. They'd been at this place before, where what Melissa saw, and what she captured on film, wasn't precisely what Jude wanted to emphasize. The director's role, as Jude saw it, was to shape the bits and pieces of events into a cohesive whole with a clear message, thereby leading the viewer unconsciously to the same conclusion. That happened by virtue of what she included, and very often, by what she excluded from the hours and hours of footage they accumulated during the course of a long project. It would make her job easier if she and Melissa were looking for the same thing right from the start.

"Mel, what's the purpose of this project?"

"I can't do this on an empty stomach," Melissa growled, abruptly rising to pace in the twelve-foot-square space between their beds. She barely refrained from pulling her hair.

"Do what?"

"Do this goddamned mind-melding thing you always insist we do at the beginning of a shoot. I should have known that's why you got me over here this afternoon. Need I remind you that tomorrow Deb is on call again, and we're going to be here for another thirty hours or so?" She flopped onto the small bed, which she had a feeling she would not be spending much time in, and grumbled, "Besides, it's a big holiday, remember? I had hoped to get out of here in time to go home, shower, climb into something irresistibly hot, and go out cruising for someone wild and wanton."

"You can still do that. I just want to get us on the same page before we get too far into this and discover we're missing the shots we need."

"I *always* get the shots!"

"You do, I know," Jude responded soothingly. For almost four years, Melissa Cooper had been her DP on every major project she'd done, and she couldn't imagine doing something of this magnitude without her on board. The photographer's skill and vision were second to none. Plus she was a lesbian and her friend, and there had been a time, a long time past, when for a few fevered weeks she'd come close to being more. "But it will be simpler, don't you think, if you had some insight—"

"Oh, God, I hate that word. I *hate* it. You're going to make me process next, aren't you?" Melissa pulled the pillow over her head and shouted obscenities into it.

When her associate had finished her meltdown, Jude smiled her most charming smile and asked, "Is there any chance we can avoid the part where you say you can't work with me again, and where you tell me to find another fucking photographer because I'm too controlling? Also, by the way, how can you manage to stay in shape when you eat as many times a day as you do?"

"Sex. Sex burns calories, especially if you do it a lot," Melissa answered, turning on her side on the bed and facing Jude across the tiny space. "If I do this, will you buy me dinner?"

"Yes. Yes, anywhere."

"Will you go out clubbing with me?"

"Mel," Jude said hesitantly.

They'd had this debate for weeks. Mel wanted her to go bar hopping, and she had resisted. She'd used her relationship with Lori as an excuse, pointing out that she didn't need to go looking for other women, that she already had sufficient companionship. In reality, she was a little worried that if she accompanied Melissa to one of her favorite hangouts, she might just be tempted to experiment. And she simply didn't have the time.

For almost two years, she had been totally committed to working on one project or another. Her production company was young—*she* was young—and she needed to establish herself in a competitive market where, unfortunately, men still ruled. Lori was perfect for her for a lot of practical reasons, and she didn't want anything to upset that.

"I won't take you to anyplace grungy, just a little edgy, okay? I promise," Melissa said matter-of-factly. "Otherwise—no deal. I'm outta here."

Jude worked at looking affronted, but she was trying not to grin. Mel had always been irresistible. "I don't think the ink is even dry on your contract yet, and you're making me regret it."

"What contract?"

"All right. Deal," Jude relented with a sigh. "Now sit down over here and watch this. *Then* I'll buy you dinner."

Melissa pulled her chair close to the monitor again and waited while Jude found the section to view again. All business now, she narrowed her eyes and put herself back in the moment. Her vision tunneled to the view she'd had through her lens, and she murmured, "Go ahead."

"Watch Sinclair's face," Jude said softly.

The camera had caught Saxon Sinclair in a three-quarter profile as she leaned close to the innocent, vulnerable young girl peering up at her through tear-softened eyes. The surgeon's full lips moved silently as she spoke to the child, but no sound was needed to convey the tenderness in her expression. There was a world of feeling in the depth of her eyes.

"God, she's beautiful," Jude whispered, without realizing she had spoken aloud.

Melissa glanced over, stunned by her friend's tone, and even more astonished by her expression. The way Jude was looking at the image of Sinclair made her instantly hot. She'd always wanted to see that look directed at her, but even secondhand, it was doing the trick. She definitely needed to find a date later.

"Jude..." she began tentatively.

"There! Right there!" Jude pointed at the frame she had frozen on the screen. "She stands up to begin her exam and, bam—look at her now."

Melissa looked. The surgeon's face was cool, calm, completely composed. Sinclair was glacially removed from any part of the human drama raging around her. "Wow."

"Yes," Jude agreed softly. "Wow. Instant transformation—all emotion just...gone. Don't you see the contradiction in that? She's supposed to be the healer, only she also has to be—I don't know—detached and dispassionate. *That's* what makes her so good. But God, at what cost?"

Melissa thought about Sinclair—her obvious capability and her perfect control—and wondered what she was like when that restraint broke. "I bet there's a powder keg behind those cool blue eyes," she muttered.

Jude chose to ignore that remark, but something inside her twisted as she thought about the glimpses of fire she'd seen in Sinclair's gaze. Clearing her throat, she instructed, "Now, go back and find Deb somewhere."

Into it now, excited, Melissa searched the footage. "Okay, here's where I got her when she first evaluated the little girl."

"Watch for that change."

After a few minutes, Melissa remarked, "It never happens."

"No," Jude agreed, "I didn't think it would. But it will, sometime this year. That's what Sinclair is going to teach her—how to do what needs to be done no matter the cost, to herself or anyone else. That's the critical lesson."

"And that's the angle," Melissa said almost reverently.

"Find me that moment, Mel. *That's* the story."

CHAPTER TEN

July 3, 9:47 p.m.

W hat are you doing here?" Sax asked as she closed the door to her on-call room and turned to discover Jude in the deserted hallway. Finding her there so unexpectedly, she was reminded of Maddy's request that she bring *that director* along on her next trip north. And for one brief moment, she imagined Jude Castle behind her on the bike, body pressed to her back, arms around her waist, hands tucked into the curve of her thighs. She could feel the warmth of those hands cupping her. Her legs quivered unexpectedly, and she thrust her hands into her front pockets to hide the response.

"Waiting for Mel," Jude replied, flustered at running into the woman she had just spent the last few hours studying. Even the stark, powerful images of the surgeon on tape paled compared with how compelling she was in the flesh. Feeling the need to elaborate, she added, "She's in the OR locker room. Shower—she's taking a shower."

"Ah," Sax replied, raising a brow. "Something wrong with the plumbing in her apartment?"

Laughing, Jude explained, "I dragged her here from the gym earlier, and we ended up taking a lot longer than I expected. We were reviewing some film and time got away from us."

"I'm sorry there's no bathroom in your on-call room. I'll get you a key for mine. You can shower there if you need to."

"Thanks," Jude said, immediately unsettled by the prospect of inadvertently walking in on Sinclair in the shower, or vice versa. Needing to dispel the image of them both in a small steamy room with one of them naked, she asked quickly, "What are *you* doing here? I thought you weren't due to be on call until the morning."

Caught off-guard, Sax grinned a little sheepishly. "Just checking up on things. I was out of town overnight, and I wanted to make sure everything was stable here."

"So, we're both working." Jude added under her breath, "Why am I not surprised?" She wondered, though, if Sax really was working, considering what she was wearing. Totally in black, dusty and disheveled, she looked so *un*like a doctor and so much more like a Soho artist or a bartender at one of the bars Melissa loved to frequent that it was difficult to reconcile this vision with that of the woman she'd watched, just moments before, choreograph a masterpiece of high-tension drama.

One thing she *was* certain of, though. The surgeon was intriguing. *And sexy,* she thought, remembering the way Sinclair's hands had moved so surely over flesh and bone. Without her intending it, her gaze traveled from those hands, which now rested partway in the pockets of low-slung jeans, up the long stretch of torso to linger briefly on the tantalizing hint of breasts beneath a body-hugging silk T-shirt, along the sculpted column of Sinclair's neck, and finally over the angled architecture of her face. Deep blue eyes, laser sharp and penetrating, stared directly into hers.

Jude blushed, feeling unexpectedly exposed. *God, I'm standing here cruising her, and she knows it. I never do that.*

Completely unaware, both women took a step closer until they were only a few feet apart.

"You should get some rest," Sax said quietly, watching the smooth ripple of blood surge and throb beneath the ivory skin of Jude's throat. "Tomorrow's Friday, and there's going to be a full moon, *and* it's the Fourth. We're gonna get killed tomorrow night."

"You think?" Jude's voice was so oddly thick she almost didn't recognize it. The air between them was nearly vibrating, and her skin sang.

"Count on it," Sax murmured, captivated by the way Jude's lips darkened and swelled as her neck flushed a pale rose. A fist of fire forced the breath from her lungs, and she almost gasped out loud.

"I will then. Get some sleep. Tonight," Jude managed. She was having trouble forming sentences. In another second, she'd be incoherent. *Dear God.* She caught herself leaning forward, drawn by the intensity of Sinclair's gaze on her mouth. Startled, she almost jumped back. For a heart-stopping second, she thought Sinclair was going to take a step forward and close the distance between them, but, mercifully, a voice interrupted.

"Time for dinner?" Melissa asked lightly, not entirely certain what she was seeing. It appeared for all the world as if the two of them were about to jump each other. However, she knew that couldn't be true because drop-dead gorgeous Jude Castle just did not *do* that kind of thing. It wasn't because she was too uptight to do something risky or outrageous; she was just too preoccupied and too damn practical. A pity, that was for sure. "You coming with us, Doctor?"

Sax turned slowly to face the newcomer, her vision cloudy, as if she were underwater. Except she was anything but cool. Her entire body was hot; she was surprised she wasn't dripping sweat. The blood was roaring through her head, and she wondered if either of the women near her could sense the sex seeping from her pores. *Jesus Christ.*

"No," she replied. Her voice was low and gravelly, and she cleared her throat as she straightened and stepped back. "No, I need to...uh... I have some things I need to take care of." She took another step away and pulled herself together, back from the edge. "Good night, Ms. Castle, Ms. Cooper."

Sax barely noticed leaving the building. Outside, safe in the anonymity of night, she swung one leg over her Harley and tilted her head back to the sky, breathing deeply. Her T-shirt clung to her chest, soaked through in places with sweat that was rapidly turning cool. She shivered in the heavy, scorching air, running a shaky hand through her hair, astonished at the tremor. *Nothing* made her hands shake, not fatigue or caffeine or disaster. Not even the perfunctory physiologic release of orgasm did what standing three feet away from Jude Castle, feeling the redhead's eyes move over her body, had done to her. Even now, she was burning.

She glanced back at the hospital exit, half expecting to see Jude and Melissa emerge. She really didn't want to see the filmmaker again so soon, because it had taken all her restraint not to accept the offer to join the two of them for dinner. She didn't need any further stimulation; she needed to get her mind off those green eyes stripping her bare.

❖

After a silence that stretched for far too long, Melissa nudged Jude's shoulder and asked, "What was that all about?"

"Nothing." Jude was still slightly dazed. *What in God's name just happened?*

"Excuse me, but I could have sworn the two of you were about to start ripping each other's clothes off."

"We were just talking, Mel," Jude said a little more sharply than she'd intended. She was too unsettled by her unanticipated and completely uncharacteristic reaction to make a joke of it.

It was true that she found Sinclair fascinating, as well as compellingly attractive, but she had met other interesting, eye-catching women in her life, and they hadn't thrown her system into overdrive. It wasn't like her to respond so physically, so *mindlessly,* to anyone, but especially not to a near stranger. Her knees were still quaking, and arousal thudded persistently between her legs. What she wanted at the moment was not dinner. What she wanted was to have Sinclair's hands on her.

Determined to ignore the signals her body was emphatically sending, she said hoarsely, "Let's go."

"Anything you say." Melissa hurried to keep pace as Jude headed for the stairwell like the place was on fire. "But you've got to admit, she's fantasy material."

Jude didn't even want to consider that. She didn't have time for that kind of complication.

"Where are we going?" Melissa asked.

Like she cared. A distraction. That's what the situation called for. "Wherever you want," she replied.

An hour later, Jude knew she should have gone home to bed and settled for lying there awake. "This is really a bad idea."

"Why? We're not breaking any rules," Melissa pointed out. "And I promise to behave myself. I haven't tried to seduce you in at least three and half years."

"We have early call tomorrow, in case you've forgotten," Jude responded grumpily, even as she handed over her twenty-dollar cover charge. "And I know you're not going to try to seduce me."

How do you know that, when I don't even know it myself? Melissa thought, waving hello to one of the two bartenders working the length of a bar that extended all along one wall of the cavernous space. A heavy bass beat from speakers at either end of the room made the thick, hot atmosphere in the dimly lit room vibrate. She put her mouth close to Jude's ear and said, "We don't have to stay late. After all the work we did this afternoon, I think we've earned a couple of drinks. I promise I'll get you home in plenty of time to catch a few hours of sleep, unless you want me to drop you off at your lawyer friend's for a quickie."

Jude gave her a scathing look, but it was hard to be annoyed in the face of Melissa's irrepressible good humor. "All right, I agreed to come with you, and I'm going to stop complaining. But you might have warned me about this place first."

Feigning innocence, Melissa lifted both hands in mock supplication. "What are you talking about?"

Conversing in near shouts, they edged their way toward the bar through the milling crowd of women. Along the way, Jude couldn't help but notice that most of the women wore a combination of leather or denim. "This looks like some kind of leather bar. I would have preferred to at least dress the part if I had known that's where we were going."

"It's more of a biker bar, really." Melissa shouted to one of the bartenders for two beers. "Besides, you're wearing jeans. That's good enough." *And if you think it matters one iota what you're wearing, you have no idea how hot you are.*

Jude didn't comment on the fact that, in addition to the rough trade atmosphere, there was an unmistakable aura of sex in the air. At midnight, the place was packed with writhing revelers in a simulation of dancing that came very close to public sex. Under the strobing black lights, bodies seethed in a continuous fusion of arms and legs and searching hands.

"It doesn't bother you, does it?" Melissa asked, leaning close to be heard as she passed Jude a beer.

They cut a path through the crowd toward a post at one corner of an enormous dance floor. Jude pressed her back against the post to keep out of the stream of constantly passing people. She kept her eyes moving so she wouldn't accidentally witness something meant to be private. She didn't need a guide to know what was happening in the murky recesses of the shadowy room.

After a healthy swallow of her beer she answered Mel's question.

"Just because it isn't my particular style doesn't mean I mind." She watched Melissa, who was evidently cruising the crowd. "But aren't I going to cramp *your* style?"

"No." Melissa shook her head. "I don't have the energy for it tonight, anyway."

"My, my," Jude chided good-naturedly. "You were all primed earlier. Is our age showing?"

"Bite your tongue," Mel snapped, but she was smiling. "I'm going to need some sleep tonight, too, especially if we're going to be up until God knows when tomorrow. We'll just have a drink, think about what we're missing while we cruise all these gorgeous women, and toddle off home like good, responsible professionals."

"In that case, I'll have another beer." Jude wasn't much of a drinker, so two beers were just about the right amount to make her feel mellow without encouraging her to act stupid. After her intense afternoon and evening of work and the disquieting encounter with Sinclair, unwinding a little seemed like a very good idea.

"I'll get them." Mel placed a hand on her arm before she could move toward the bar. "I have to go to the john anyhow."

"Okay, but if you pick someone up along the way, let me know. I can always get a cab home if you get tied up." Mel gave her a wide grin, and Jude punched her on the arm. "That isn't what I meant."

"I know, I know. I'll be back in a few minutes."

As Mel was swallowed by the crowd, Jude turned back to the dance floor and idly observed the activities. Smoke hung like mist, and the strobes gave everyone an otherworldly appearance. Watching women moving against each other to the rhythm of the pulse-pounding beat, hands disappearing beneath T-shirts, hips straddling thighs, and mouths seeking sweat-dampened skin, she became aware of her own body responding.

She doubted she would have been as sensitive if she hadn't already been aroused when she arrived. The time it had taken her and Mel to grab a quick sandwich and walk the few blocks to the bar, however, had not been enough to dissipate the effects of the intensely erotic encounter she'd had in the hospital hallway with a woman she barely knew. That was not a thought she wanted to dwell on, and she tried to forget it as she glanced around.

The second time her gaze swept the shadows near the edge of

the room, she caught her breath in surprise and pressed harder against the column that supported her, unconsciously attempting to hide from view. Barely ten feet away, Saxon Sinclair leaned against the wall. Most of her body was shrouded in darkness, but her face was starkly highlighted in the flickering strobe light.

Irrationally, Jude didn't want the surgeon to know that she was there. Sinclair had obviously come straight to the club after leaving them earlier; she was still in her dusty black jeans and T-shirt. Standing with her head tilted back, one arm dangling by her side holding a longneck bottle loosely in her fingers, she appeared to be eerily removed from her surroundings. Jude was so close she could see sweat shining like jewels on her face. Her lids looked heavy, her eyes partially closed. In any other setting Jude would have thought her half asleep.

But that clearly wasn't the case. A woman, her back to Jude, was angled against Sinclair's side in such a way as to shield what she was doing from those nearby. From where Jude stood, however, she had an unimpeded view.

With a gasp of astonishment and an unwelcome rush of envy, she realized that the woman's hand was moving under Sinclair's shirt. And if the expression on Sinclair's face was any indication, the caress was more than casual. Jude knew she should look away, but the raw beauty of Sinclair's arousal had already mesmerized her.

Sax had no idea she was being observed. Her vision was unfocused as she stared unseeing above the heads of those around her. The thunderous vibration of the music hammered through the floor and up her legs, a furtive accompaniment to the echoing surge deep inside. She was dimly conscious of the heat from the woman leaning into her, but most of her awareness was focused on the cadenced movement of the woman's fingers on her bare skin. The muscles in her abdomen contracted involuntarily as the progressively firmer strokes trailed along her ribs and edged down toward the top of her jeans; the occasional rasp of a fingernail underscored the building pressure with a swift jolt of electricity that threatened to elicit a groan.

She had never lost the hard, heavy fullness that had started in the hallway outside her on-call room, and by the time this stranger had moved up beside her in the anonymous throng of the darkened bar, her arousal had moved from pleasure to the edge of pain. Stiffening as a practiced hand discreetly opened the buttons on her fly, she worked to maintain her composure. She was willing to acknowledge her physical needs and accepted the offered release, but emotionally, she was determined to remain detached.

Even as her hips involuntarily arched forward and her fingers tightened on the smooth cylinder of the beer bottle, she didn't look at the woman touching her. When skillful fingers unerringly found her, closing firmly along her length, her thighs shook with the effort to contain the explosion. She pressed her head hard against the wall, swallowing convulsively, struggling not to orgasm immediately.

She forced herself to concentrate on the faces swimming in the crowd in front of her, meaning to distract herself from the rhythmic torment of the fingers now stroking harder and faster over her clitoris, pushing her closer to her limits. With sudden clarity, she found herself staring into the same incendiary gaze that had nearly demolished her a few hours earlier.

She fell into Jude Castle's eyes and came instantly.

Jude almost felt the orgasm as it flew across Sinclair's face, and watching her shudder—jaws clamped shut, body rigid—imagined she could hear her moan. Her own stomach clenched, a molten trail of fire searing along her spine, and for one precarious second, she feared she might go over with her. It took every shred of willpower she possessed to contain the surging pulsations that gathered between her legs and threatened to peak as Sinclair's eyes fluttered closed with the last wrenching spasm.

Jesus. Jude forced herself to breathe. And finally, with an effort that tested much more than her mental resolve, she dragged her eyes away from Sinclair's face. She didn't need to view any more to know that she was going to be haunted by what she had seen.

When Sax opened her eyes, aftershocks still rippling through her, the woman who had delivered a brief wordless respite was gone, and so was Jude Castle.

CHAPTER ELEVEN

July 4, 6:02 a.m.

Howdid you sleep?" Melissa asked as she joined Jude at a table in the hospital cafeteria. She removed her coffee, a small carton of milk, and a cardboard box of cereal from a tray and then slid it onto the empty seat beside them. "Considering you didn't even want to stay to finish our second beer, I figured you must have been pretty beat."

Despite her casual tone, Melissa was desperate to know what had brought about the change in Jude's attitude in fifteen short minutes the night before. After maneuvering her way through the circuitous line to the bathroom and then clamoring over people in the bar line to secure two fresh beers, she had finally rejoined Jude only to discover that her friend wanted to leave immediately. Jude had kindly assured her she would grab a cab and had only waited to let her know she was leaving, but Melissa figured she might as well go, too. She hadn't planned on scoring and would've been too tired even if she had gotten lucky, so there was no point in hanging around.

Nevertheless, she couldn't help feeling that *something* had happened while she was gone. Jude looked positively spooked and hadn't said more than two words the entire time it had taken them to walk back to the hospital and pick up Melissa's car. No matter how hard she tried, Melissa couldn't get her to say anything on the ride uptown either. Eventually, she had just given up and left her to her preoccupied silence.

"I slept fine," Jude said without elaboration. She was working on her second cup of coffee and trying valiantly to finish a bagel. She knew it might be a very long time before she ate again, and she definitely didn't want any reason not to be sharp when she needed to be. The last thing she wanted was to get light-headed from hunger in front of Sinclair. "Honest, I feel great."

She had no intention of telling Mel something she didn't want to think about herself. When she had arrived home the night before, she had been too keyed up to sleep. The short walk to retrieve the car and the brief ride home had mercifully taken the edge off her acute state of stimulation. But she was afraid that if she got into bed wide-awake, all she would do was think about how incredibly erotic Sinclair's face had been as she climaxed. And then the low level of desire still humming along her nerve endings would flare into flame, and she would never get to sleep. Not without relief. She knew it wouldn't take much, considering how hot and how hard she had been less than an hour before. A few well-placed strokes and a little pressure, and she would lose it.

Just what I need, she'd snarled to herself. *Jerk-off fantasies about a woman I have to see every day. God.* Instead, she'd settled on a shower and shampoo to rid herself of the smoky, musky scent of the bar and her own pervasive excitement.

"Great." Melissa attacked her cornflakes with vigor. *So, don't tell me what's going on. Fine.*

Jude muttered noncommittally, her mind still on the previous night. The shower had relaxed her and helped her get to sleep, but unfortunately, it had done nothing to eradicate whatever unfinished business simmered in her imagination. An hour before dawn, she'd been jolted awake by her own sharp cry as the intensely sexual scenario she had been dreaming culminated in a violent orgasm. Gasping, heart racing, her palm pressed against the heat between her thighs, she had curled on her side and moaned into the darkness. Eyes wide open, searching the shadows, she had seen Saxon Sinclair's face.

"What?" Jude asked, vaguely aware that Mel had been speaking to her.

Nothing like that had ever happened before. She had always enjoyed sex, and orgasm was usually easy to attain with a considerate partner, but she couldn't ever recall climaxing while asleep. But then again, she couldn't ever recall her body taking over quite the way it had the night before during a simple conversation either.

For her, sex usually was a head thing, and her relationship with Lori was the perfect example of what she sought from a partner. When they had met at the home of a mutual acquaintance, she had found the bright, outgoing attorney attractive, but that wasn't really the primary motivating factor behind her acceptance when Lori had suggested they see one another again. After having talked with her for several hours at the party, comparing notes on professional goals and relationship philosophies, Jude had realized they would make a good pair. Dating Lori just made good sense.

However, nothing about what had happened the previous evening with Saxon Sinclair made sense. In fact, thinking about it made her head hurt. Even worse, thinking about it made her body pick up where it had left off in the early morning hours. She absolutely could not walk around for the next thirty hours in a state of arousal. Resolutely, she picked up her bagel and began to eat.

"Hello? Earth to Jude?"

Startled, Jude stopped in mid-bite and stared across the table. Melissa was regarding her with a quizzical expression.

"What?"

"You said that already," Melissa commented dryly. "I feel like I'm in the middle of an Abbott and Costello sketch. Pretty soon, I'm going to ask 'Who's on first?'"

"Sorry." Jude firmly banished all thoughts of sex and sexy surgeons from her consciousness. "Where were we?"

"Uh...I was asking about the game plan for today."

Thankfully back on familiar ground, Jude could concentrate. "Deb left a message on my machine that she's doing an 8:00 a.m. surgery, so I want to tape it. I asked Jerry to meet us here at 6:30 to set up the sound in the OR. While he's here, I want him to look at the situation in the trauma admitting area, too. Maybe we can fiddle with the mike placements down there and boost our sound quality a little bit. I think it's okay, but I don't want to miss anything critical during an alert."

"It won't hurt to check," Melissa agreed. "How do you want to play the taping during this live surgery thing?"

"Deb said that she'd be doing a lot of the case, so I think our focus should be on showing her level of responsibility now. Then we can contrast it to the changes at the end of the year."

"That makes sense if we're going to focus on her transition from trainee to full-fledged trauma surgeon." Melissa indicated the bagel on the plate Jude had pushed aside. "Are you going to eat that?"

"No, take it." Jude was still thinking about the upcoming shoot. "We also need to get the interaction between Sinclair and Deb this morning. Whenever they're together, that's where the action will be."

"Uh-huh." Melissa reached for the bagel. "I've got a feeling that wherever *Sinclair* is, that's where the action is."

"For Christ's sake, Mel, can't you keep it in your pants once in a while?" Jude snapped. "At least while we're working?"

Melissa gaped at her, astonished by her implacable friend's quick flare of temper. "Jude? Hello? Are you in there? Did the pod people visit your apartment last night?"

"Hell, I'm sorry," Jude said immediately. She shrugged her shoulders, trying to release some of the tension. "It's just that I've got a lot riding on this project."

"Sure," Melissa said easily, although she considered that explanation total bullshit. Whatever burr Jude had up her butt, it had to do with Saxon Sinclair, because every time the woman's name was mentioned, Jude went into orbit. However, poking a sore spot was not her intention. "Why don't we divide and conquer? I'll head over to the OR with my gear, and you can meet Jerry and check the sound system down in the trauma admitting area."

"Good deal. Thanks, Mel." Jude gave her friend's forearm a brief squeeze. "I'll meet you upstairs in thirty minutes, and I'll try to find my sense of humor along the way."

Watching her walk away, Melissa wondered what it was about Saxon Sinclair and Jude Castle that she was missing.

July 4, 8:11 a.m.

"Just make sure you don't touch anything that's green," the scrub nurse said with practiced nonchalance. "All the green sheets are sterile." It wasn't the first time she'd had to contend with visitors in the OR, and it usually fell to her to make sure they didn't contaminate the sterile surgical field. The surgeons were usually too busy working, or too busy talking to the media people, to pay attention to that kind of detail.

"Right," Jude said, moving out of the way as Deb entered the twenty-by-twenty-foot windowless space escorting her patient along with several nurses. The entire bed had been wheeled down the hall from the TICU to the operating suite, apparently to avoid the necessity of moving the patient and all the life-support equipment twice.

Jude looked over at Melissa to make sure her camera was rolling. It was unnecessary, but it was a habit she would never be able to break.

Once the patient was situated, Deb left to scrub her hands at the large, industrial size, stainless steel sinks just outside the door. Jude was surprised that Sinclair was nowhere in evidence. She'd assumed that the trauma chief would be participating in the operation with Deb. Occupying herself with dictating her log, noting the time and particulars of the taping session, she refused to acknowledge her disappointment. She'd already spent too much of her morning thinking about Dr. Sinclair.

A few minutes later, Deb returned, keeping her hands elevated above the level of her elbows so that the water would not stream down from the upper part of her arms to her hands, potentially contaminating them. The scrub nurse handed her a towel, then helped her into a sterile gown and gloved her. While this was happening, the circulating nurse exposed the patient and painted the twentysomething man's neck, chest, and abdomen with an antiseptic iodine solution.

"A tracheostomy is necessary because his lungs were damaged by all the fluid we needed to give him during resuscitation as well as by toxic breakdown products from injured tissue. He'll need ventilator support for quite a while," Deb explained. Twenty minutes later, she had finished surgically inserting a breathing tube into his trachea through an incision in his neck and had moved on to his abdomen.

As she made an incision that started at his breastbone and ended just below his umbilicus, she continued, "Plus, we don't expect him to be conscious and able to eat for at least a few weeks. That's why I'm going to put a feeding tube directly into his intestine so that he can be fed that way."

At that moment, the door opened and Saxon Sinclair entered. The atmosphere in the room altered perceptibly, or so it seemed to Jude. The light banter that had been flowing easily between the members of the operating team suddenly ceased, the unexpected silence echoing pointedly. Sinclair appeared not to notice but moved up close behind her fellow.

"Same case, Stein?" she asked with a hint of challenge in her deep voice. "You've been in here for forty minutes already. I've finished the newspaper, and I'm running out of things to read."

"I'm about half done," Deb said, apparently unperturbed by the mild heckling.

"Well, just don't make it your life's work," Sinclair commented sharply as she peered over Deb's shoulder into the wound. "Did you run the bowel yet?"

"Not yet. I just got into the belly."

"Make sure you do."

With that, Sax backed away from the operating table and crossed to Jude's side. "Good morning."

"Good morning." Jude hoped her voice sounded calm, because she felt anything but. She met Sinclair's eyes above the surgical mask that crossed the bridge of her nose and concealed the rest of her face. She hadn't been sure what to expect from their first face-to-face meeting following the previous evening's unintentional intimacy—an awkward embarrassment at the very least. Now, when Sinclair's eyes held hers unflinchingly, unapologetically, it wasn't discomfiture she felt but excitement. *She knows I saw her last night in the bar, and she doesn't care.*

"Everything going all right?" Sax asked, nodding toward Melissa, who was opposite them with her video equipment.

"Yes, fine," Jude replied. *Here we are discussing business like nothing ever happened. First, I watched you have sex, and then I spent half the night lusting after you. This is nuts.* She put her jumbled emotions firmly from her mind and concentrated on her work. "May I ask a question?"

Sax considered Jude silently for a moment, remembering the astonishing feeling of being driven to orgasm by the mere sight of her face. She couldn't ever remember anyone moving her so powerfully, even when they were actually in bed together. *I wonder if she has any idea what she did to me?*

"Go ahead." She matched Jude's casual tone.

"What does it mean to 'run the bowel'?" Jude wanted to know, but mostly she wanted to think about something—anything—other than how heart-stoppingly beautiful Sinclair had looked as she was about to come.

A mixture of amusement and regret made Sax grimace slightly behind her mask. *Well, that answers that question. Our exchange last night obviously had more of an effect on me than it did on her.*

"Stein needs to physically examine all of the internal organs to be sure there is no damage or disease. One of the easiest ways to do that is to gently pull the intestine through her fingers, so she can check for any tears or tumors or vascular damage. Then she'll hold the bowel aside to look at the liver and spleen and palpate the kidneys."

Jude could not resist watching Sinclair's eyes while she spoke. Something in her tone and the intensity of her gaze struck a chord. She had that disconcerting feeling of déjà vu again, and just as she was about to remember from where, Deb called, "Dr. Sinclair?" and Sax looked away.

"What's up?"

"I think the gallbladder's necrotic."

"Excuse me," Sax said, turning briskly to the OR table. "Suzanne, get some gloves for me. I'm scrubbing in."

July 4, 9:35 a.m.

After the case, Deb joined Jude in the OR lounge. She pushed change into the soda machine and, after retrieving her Coke, dropped onto the couch and propped her feet on the coffee table. "Did the boss leave?" she asked.

"Yes," Jude replied. "She said she had a chief's meeting."

They'd bumped into each other, almost literally, in the locker room. To Jude's surprise, even without the benefit of masks to cover any awkwardness, their exchange had been comfortable. She hadn't been embarrassed, nor did Sinclair seem to be. *Why should we be? It was hardly anything to be ashamed of. We're both adults and it might be assumed that we both have sex.* But it wasn't the fact of what she had witnessed, or even *where* she had seen it, but the fact that she couldn't forget how she'd felt *watching* it that was driving her crazy. She'd been as aroused as she'd ever felt when someone touched her for real.

"Great case, huh?" Deb continued, oblivious to Jude's distraction.

Happy for the diversion, Jude indicated her tape recorder. "May I tape?"

"Sure." Deb took a deep swallow of her soda. "God, I get so dehydrated when I operate."

"What *do* you do during long cases?"

"Ignore it," Deb said with a shrug.

"So, why was this a great case?"

Deb grinned. "Because I got to do an open gallbladder, which we don't get to do very much anymore since most of the time it's done through a laparoscope. You know, a small periscope that gets introduced into the abdomen through a tiny incision. Plus, besides getting to actually cut the gallbladder out, Sinclair assisted *me*."

"Is that unusual?" Jude had managed to get close enough to the table to observe Sinclair and Deb work, and she had been impressed that Sinclair didn't seem to be doing much except verbally leading Deb through the operation.

"It is for the first week of a trauma fellowship when she hasn't worked with me very often before. She pretty much let me do the whole thing."

"I was surprised," Jude acknowledged. "Why wasn't she there for the entire surgery?"

"This was a pretty straightforward case. She has to be around somewhere in the vicinity, in case there's a problem, but it's up to her how much I do on my own. So she was probably in the OR lounge most of the time."

"Is that..." Jude hesitated, searching for the word. "Legal?"

Deb glanced at the clock, drained her soda, and tossed it in a nearby wastebasket. "I don't think there's any legality involved. This is a training program. How much I do is up to her. I am a licensed physician, and in theory, I could walk out the door and start my own practice right now. I'm only here for more experience."

Jude chose her words carefully. "What if you weren't...competent? I mean, what if you weren't ready to be by yourself?"

"It's up to Sinclair to decide that." Deb grinned again. Then, with an expression that reminded Jude very much of Saxon Sinclair's, she said, "But you don't need to worry. Everyone's always said I've got good hands."

Jude laughed as she clicked off her recorder. *Surgeons. Then again, I suppose if you're going to have someone cutting into you, you want them to be confident about it.*

Personal Project Log—Castle
July 4, 10:01 a.m.
Digital Reference Marks 3025–4150

This is the kind of thing that will make or break us—this uncensored view of on-the-job training. Is the average viewer really ready to see how physicians are made? I read this book when I was a kid, The Making of a Surgeon, *and I remember being absolutely fascinated by how easily mistakes could happen even when everyone was trying their very best. I don't suppose that book could get written today, because in today's world, what doctor is going to admit that things go wrong on a daily basis? Not necessarily big things, or fatal errors, but definitely things that could turn out to be disastrous. [Note: ask Deb or Sinclair how the threat of litigation affects their decision-making process.]*

Maybe that's why Sinclair didn't want us filming in real time—she didn't want us to expose the potential dangers in the system...laugh. Yeah, right, Castle. She's definitely the type to be scared by publicity. Exposure does not seem to be a problem for her.

Jude clicked off the recorder and took a deep breath. That was a line of thought she did not want to pursue.

CHAPTER TWELVE

July 4, 11:30 a.m.

Jude stopped in the reception area immediately inside Saxon Sinclair's office suite and greeted the stylishly dressed, auburn-haired woman behind the desk. "I'm Jude Castle from Horizon Productions. Dr. Sinclair told me I could stop by for a copy of her CV."

She received a pleasant but reserved nod. "Of course. She mentioned you might come by. I'm Naomi Riley, Dr. Sinclair's personal secretary." Turning to a bank of file cabinets, she opened one of the drawers and within seconds handed Jude a surprisingly large document. "If you need any assistance with schedules or information about the training program, just call me."

"Thanks." Jude hesitated. "Actually, there is something I need. Perhaps you could help me arrange a time for a formal interview. I know she's busy..."

"I'll have to get back to you on that," Naomi replied in a practiced manner that suggested Jude might hear from her in the next millennium.

Laughing, Jude explained, "I didn't have much luck the last time I tried, but maybe she'll be a little more receptive now that we've met."

"I'm sure she'll make every effort," the secretary said smoothly, "but her schedule is always full."

"I understand. I'll check back with you." There was no point in making a fuss about it at this point. A two-front attack might gain better results anyhow. She'd speak to Sinclair, who would undoubtedly refer her back to her secretary, about an interview later. But at least then she could tell Naomi Riley that she and Sinclair had discussed it, and that might get her one step closer.

Despite the fact that she saw the surgeon frequently during the day, it was hard to pin her down long enough for questions and answers. She needed to have the formality of a scheduled appointment so she could discuss both Deb's training as well as Sinclair's own background. Jude still knew almost nothing about the trauma chief, and, considering what she *had* observed, the irony of that fact did not escape her.

"Okay. Thanks again," she said absently as she walked away, already skimming the first pages of the extensive curriculum vitae.

On the surface, it was pretty much what she had expected. Sinclair had been educated at a liberal arts college in the Northeast and had gone on to an Ivy League medical school. Her general surgical training had been at yet another top-ranked hospital, and she had completed her trauma fellowship right here in Manhattan at Bellevue, where apparently she'd then joined the staff.

Jude stopped suddenly, causing the person behind her to nearly collide with her. "Sorry," she mumbled, moving over to the wall out of the stream of foot traffic. She reread the words—Trauma Attending, Bellevue Hospital—and the dates. Abruptly, she stuffed the document into her briefcase and resumed walking.

Jude took a chance that nothing would happen for the next few hours. She stopped at a street vendor's cart, bought a cold soda and a bag of hot nuts, then walked until she found a patch of shade in a postage stamp–sized park. She didn't think about much of anything at all for a while but occupied her mind with the always-entertaining street parade of passersby that was New York City. When she'd finished her nuts and settled her mind, she got up and walked back to the hospital, determined that the past would not rule her present, or her future.

July 4, 3:22 p.m.

She found Aaron Townsend alone in the trauma admitting area, doing what he usually did when no patients were there—moving outdated drugs and instrument packs onto carts to be disposed of or recycled and taking inventory of what he needed to order or replenish. He glanced over with a welcoming smile when she walked in.

"Hi. Have you seen Melissa?" Jude asked, smiling back.

"About an hour ago. She said something about taking a nap. Actually, I think she referred to it as stockpiling zees. She's probably in your on-call room."

"How about Deb?" This seemed like a good time to get some more background.

"I think she's up on the roof with Sinclair."

Damn. I never should've left. Anxiously, she asked, "At the helipad? Is there a trauma alert?"

"If there is, nobody told me. They're just up there passing the time until we get some action. I'm sure they won't mind if you join them."

Jude hesitated for a moment, and then thought, *Why not?* She grabbed a small DVCam from the equipment locker left by her crew and waved goodbye to Aaron. This would be a good opportunity to get the footage she'd wanted of Deb during the downtime—the inevitable periods of inactivity between trauma alerts.

After nearly a week, she was getting used to the routine. The morning was usually taken up with rounds in the trauma unit followed in the afternoon by the completion of any work that needed to be done for the patients—changing intravenous lines, replacing or inserting chest tubes, minor bedside surgeries, review of X-rays, and other aspects of daily care. Unlike most specialists, however, trauma surgeons were not free to leave once the work was done. State law required that every level one trauma unit have qualified surgeons on site in the hospital twenty-four hours a day, as well as stipulating which specialists needed to be available for immediate backup call. All of which meant that there were sometimes lengthy periods during a twenty-four-hour shift when the entire team was just waiting.

Jude exited the elevator on the roof and walked up the ramp toward the helipad. Before she even turned the corner onto the flat rectangular landing section, she heard raised voices and an odd, repetitive pounding. She stopped abruptly when she got her first view of Sinclair and Stein. Then she leaned against the upright support of the elevated parking ramp and raised her video camera.

"You're slipping, Stein. You're out of shape," Sax taunted, dropping her right shoulder and driving past the blond. She pulled up twelve feet from the basket and sank the jump shot easily.

It was two o'clock in the afternoon, and the sun beat down furiously on the concrete surface of the roof. Sax was in scrubs and her shirt was plastered to her back with sweat. Rivulets of moisture ran down her face, and she had to continuously wipe her eyes with her bare forearm. Surprisingly, she was four points ahead. "Yeah, looks like I'm gonna whip your butt."

"You know, I *was* trying to be nice," Deb remarked conversationally as she caught the ball on its way through the basket. "Considering your age and the fact you're my boss and all."

"Yeah, sure, right," Sax grunted, unsuccessfully attempting to strip the ball from her fellow's hands as Deb dribbled hand to hand, a cocky grin on her face. "What a load of—"

"But now, I'm done being charitable."

Deb blew by her so quickly and so effortlessly that Sax was left standing with her mouth open. By the time she got her wits together, she managed to get her hands on the ball only to have Deb immediately steal it away. For the next five minutes, Sax was treated to a display of athletic prowess that was infinitely more satisfying than anything she had ever seen in competition, because there was nothing behind it now except joy.

Deb wasn't trying to beat anyone, not even her. She was just having fun. Sax made a valiant effort to get back in the game, but it soon became apparent that would only happen if Deb were feeling kindhearted.

Finally, she called, "That's it, Stein. Gimme my ball. I don't wanna play with you anymore."

Deb looked over and saw her chief smiling, although she was pretty sure she detected some frustration in her eyes as well. Surgeons were competitive about everything; it was just the nature of the beast. Ignoring caution and diplomacy, Deb didn't even try to hide her triumphant grin. She tossed Sinclair's ball back to her, and replied, "Thanks for the game, Chief."

"Yeah, sure, right." Sax turned, ball under her arm, and noticed Jude, fifteen feet away and still taping. "Turn that damn thing off unless you want me to toss it off the roof."

Jude stopped the video camera and actually held it protectively behind her back for a second before she saw the smile pulling at the corner of Sinclair's mouth. "What's the matter? Afraid to have a permanent record of you getting your ass kicked?"

"It's her first week," Sax said, coming to stand by Jude's side. "I was going easy on her."

"Yes, I noticed." Jude looked from one to the other. The two of them were flushed and sweating, but neither was breathing hard. Both were damned attractive women, but only one of them made her heart skip a beat. Looking away from Sinclair's dazzling smile, she added, "I *especially* noticed how you let her have a few shots there at the end."

Deb snorted disdainfully. "Tell you what. Next time, I'll take on both of you."

"Oh, no," Jude quickly countered. "Not me."

Deb muttered something that sounded like "chicken," then waved goodbye as she headed toward the elevators. Alone with Sinclair, Jude fell silent, not sure what to say. They were standing three feet apart, Sax with the basketball still under her arm, Jude with her camera tucked under hers. They stared intently at one another while a faint breeze lifted the hair at the backs of their necks but did little to cool the shimmering heat reflected from the cement surface.

"We should get out of the sun," Jude said softly.

"You're right," Sax agreed. She was hot and she wanted a drink, but mostly she wanted to touch her fingertips to the fine mist of sweat on Jude Castle's cheek. *Not a good idea. The last time you had thoughts like this you ended up with your back against the wall and a stranger's hand in your pants. Time to get a grip here.* "Do you play?"

For a second, Jude couldn't make sense of the question. "Basketball?" she asked, cringing when she realized how inane she must sound.

What else? Grinning, Sax nodded. "Yes."

"Not well enough to put myself up against the two of you. I'd like to keep my body parts intact for a while longer."

"It's all in fun," Sax said as she took a few steps closer to the waist-high concrete wall that edged the rooftop parking lot and helipad.

Jude came up beside her and looked down to the street, twenty stories below. "I could see that. It's a great segment."

Sax laughed. "Do you look at everything through your camera first?"

"I wasn't looking through my camera last night," Jude said before she could stop herself.

"Ah, that's true," Sax responded evenly. She was momentarily surprised that Jude had brought it up, but realized she probably shouldn't be. From their first encounter, Jude had been direct and straightforward in her dealings. Resting the ball by her feet, Sax leaned both hands on top of the wall. Still looking out over the city, she asked, "Is there something I should apologize for? I didn't mean for what happened to happen." *I didn't mean for you to see. And I sure didn't mean to go off just from knowing you were watching.* Frustrated at not being able to explain it to herself, let alone to Jude, she shrugged helplessly. "I'm sorry..."

"No, *I'm* sorry," Jude acknowledged, belatedly aware that Sinclair had not meant anything critical by the camera remark. It wasn't the first time someone had accused her of using her lens to put a barrier between herself and the world, and she had reacted defensively. The best defense being a good offense, she had attacked. "Absolutely nothing happened last night for which you need to apologize. My remark was way out of line."

"No harm, no foul," Sax said, looking at her now. "Shall we simply chalk it up to unusual circumstances, then?"

"I think that would be wise." Jude smiled slightly. *Because otherwise, we'll have to blame it on some kind of mutual insanity, and I'm not quite ready for that.*

"Agreed."

Reluctantly, Jude started to turn away. "I should probably find my photographer and review this morning's tape while things are quiet. If we get a first look now, it will save us time in the long run."

"You might want to catch some rest while you can. You never know what the night will bring."

"Is that what you're going to do?" Jude asked, and then thought perhaps she was getting too personal.

"No, I think I'm going to find Aaron and play a little chess. Unless you'd like a game?"

"No, thanks," Jude said hastily.

"Are you afraid I won't be able to tolerate getting blown out of the water twice in one day?" Her delivery was light, but her expression was probing.

Jude averted her gaze and backed up several steps. "I have no doubt you could hold your own."

"Not against you I couldn't," Sax said matter-of-factly. "But I don't mind trying. I'm curious, though, as to why you don't want anyone to know."

"Probably because I spent ten years having people watch me play," Jude said with a tired sigh. "How in hell did you know? I doubt there's another person in this entire city who could even tell you that there's such a thing as a world chess team."

Sax shrugged. "Once upon a time, chess was about the only thing I enjoyed. I'm just a good amateur, but whenever I'm interested in something, I read everything I can get my hands on about it. When I first started playing, you were still touring the world circuit. Who could forget a champion chess player named Castle?"

"Believe me, I got ribbed a lot about that." Jude smiled for real this time.

"Why did you quit?"

"I was seventeen years old, and I'd been playing since I was five. I was tired of all the attention, I was tired of traveling, and I was tired of not being a normal kid." Jude was surprised at how easily she could talk about it. She had never talked about it with anyone. Melissa was probably her closest friend at the moment, and even she didn't know. Jude had never discussed it with Lori. Her family was still too stunned, and on some level, still too angry at her for turning away from what was so clearly an enormous talent to even talk about it. "In the end, on one of the tours, I got to know some of the people who were doing a documentary about...unusual kids, and I became enchanted with the idea of filmmaking. I quit the circuit and started studying film."

From in front of the camera to behind it, Sax thought. "So, if I promise to keep your secret, will you play me?"

Jude laughed, suddenly feeling much more carefree than she could remember being in a long time. "Is everything a game to you?"

"Not everything." Sax smiled as she said it, although her eyes held something serious in their depths. "But almost. Are you going to answer my question?"

"All right, Dr. Sinclair. Let's play."

Chapter Thirteen

July 4, 4:48 p.m.

"What do you think they're doing?" Aaron whispered, pausing in his paperwork.

"I don't know." Melissa eased her feet down off the counter and straightened in her chair, stretching to get a clearer view of the board angled between Jude and Sinclair. "I *thought* they were playing, at first, but it takes longer than ten minutes to play a game, doesn't it?"

"Usually, unless you're not very good, and Sinclair is."

"Well, they've set the board up six times in the last hour, and they both look very...grim," Melissa noted. "Do you think this could lead to bloodshed?"

Observing the intent expression on the surgeon's face, Aaron shrugged. "Quite likely. Sinclair takes no prisoners."

While Melissa tried to decide if she should interrupt them, possibly saving her good friend from psychological trauma, Jude murmured for the sixth time, too softly for anyone else to hear, "Checkmate."

Sax stared at the board, playing the next half dozen moves in her mind to the inevitable outcome, seeing now where she had left herself open. Finally, she muttered, "Well, that's an improvement. I actually made seven moves this time before I blew it."

"We can stop," Jude offered. It didn't matter that she hadn't touched a board in years; there was no way she could *not* play the way she played. That was one reason she never played for entertainment.

"Why?" Sax raised her eyes to Jude's, a hint of challenge in her voice. "Afraid I might take you next time?"

For a moment, Jude wasn't sure how to respond. Deciding that diplomacy was probably best, she began, "Dr. Sinclair—"

"Sax," Sax interrupted.

"Sax," Jude said with a smile, "I just thought you might want a break."

"No, you didn't. You figured I must be tired of getting thrashed and you don't think I have a chance in hell of beating you. Right?"

"Uh..."

"But it *could* happen, right?" Sax persisted. "Maybe not the next game, or the tenth game, or the hundredth game...but it *could* happen."

"Possibly." Laughing, Jude nodded. "Why not? But are you planning on making this *your* life's work?"

"Maybe." Sax liked the way Jude laughed, thinking she hadn't seen her look so relaxed before and liking that, too. "I know I'm a long way from giving up."

"Are you always so persistent?" Jude asked.

"Only when it matters."

There was something in Sax's tone and the way that her gaze played over Jude's face that made Jude's heart race. She flushed, then cursed herself for being so damn susceptible to the surgeon's intense good looks and inescapable charm. *She's probably like this with everyone. And why does everything she says go right to my...damn...I'm the one who needs a break.*

"Do you want to stop?" Sax asked quietly, very aware of their thighs touching lightly as they each pressed close over the game board.

"Oh, no," Jude said just as quietly. "Not if you don't."

"Good," Sax responded as she began to reset her pieces on the board.

Personal Project Log—Castle
July 5, 2:27a.m.
DRM 4507–7010

>   *This is the first break we've had since a little after 6:00*
> *p.m. Stein and Sinclair are in the OR now, and we're not taping*
> *because I don't think Mel can hold the camera anymore. It's*
> *been nonstop downstairs in the trauma admitting area for*

eight hours. It started with a pileup on the bridge involving three cars, a tractor-trailer, and a row of yellow hazard cones. I don't know the total number of injured, even now, but I know some came here and some went to Bellevue and some to a couple of the other level one trauma centers.

Sax had to call in the backup team when three people needed immediate surgery for internal injuries and she needed to be available for more incoming. Several got transferred directly from here to the burn unit at NYU. Deb had to stabilize those people before they could be moved, and there's some incredible footage on that...I never realized before how lucid burn victims are right after their injury and how very little pain they may actually have.

Deb explained that with major burns the nerve endings are destroyed so there isn't much acute discomfort. I have to say it made it a lot easier knowing that. [Note: Check DRM 5500—there's a segment of Deb explaining to one of the patients what happened to him and what his injuries were. He asked her if he was going to die. He was very calm. I couldn't see her eyes, because they never moved from his. She didn't hesitate when she answered him, and there was something in the tone of her voice...an absolute certainty... that made you trust her when she told him he was going to be all right. I've heard that tone before, and I know the strength that was in her eyes. She's got it, whatever that thing is that makes some people able to connect with you so powerfully... so quickly...that you believe.]

Mel's already crashed. I'm going to stay up and wait for the surgeons to finish. Oh...[Note: Episode Title: "In the Trenches."]

July 5, 3:40 a.m.

Jude was awakened by a knock on the door. Sitting up in confusion, she glanced around, trying to get oriented. Melissa was snoring lightly on the other bed, fully clothed, one arm dangling over the side. *Hospital. On-call room. Damn, I fell asleep.*

Jude rose hastily, crossed to the door, and shielded her eyes from the light in the hallway as she stepped out of her room. The overhead fluorescents had been turned off; they usually were at night. Only the running lights along the wall provided faint illumination. The change was still enough to make her blink as her eyes adjusted.

"Hey." Sax could see from Jude's perplexed expression that she'd been asleep. But even with a pillow crease on her cheek and her hair tangled, she was beautiful. "Sorry to wake you, but we have another one coming. I didn't know if you wanted to be called..."

"No...yes. I mean, don't be sorry, I do want to be there, thanks. What is it, do you know?"

"Reports are that it's a taxi versus bicycle collision. The cyclist lost."

"At three o'clock in the morning?"

Sax smiled. "It's the city that never sleeps."

"Apparently." Jude watched Sax walk off down the hall. Turning to her roommate, she called, "Wake up, sunshine. We've got work."

July 5, 3:48 a.m.

In the trauma bay, Jude was jolted into a state of hyperalertness by the arrival of the EMTs, all thought of her previous exhaustion gone. The harsh, glaring lights, the clatter of wheels over uneven tiles, the hubbub of voices—the general sense of excitement mixed with anxiety—produced a bizarre kind of high that was oddly exhilarating.

The now-familiar routine began again. A male EMT called, "Vehicle versus cyclist, unresponsive in the field...multiple facial fractures, probable pneumothorax, open left femur fracture...BP 100 over 60."

Melissa, with Jude practically glued to her back, maneuvered closer with her camera as Deb and Sax, along with Aaron and several other nurses, moved the young man onto the treatment table.

"Anybody got a name?" Sax asked as Deb began the initial assessment.

"There's a wallet in his pants," Aaron replied as he slit the garment up the sides with large utility scissors. "Uh...Mark Houseman."

"Mark," Sax said forcefully as she leaned close to his face, gently lifting one swollen lid. "You've been in an accident. You're at..."

Bellevue...Can you tell me your name...

Jude shook herself mentally, forcing her focus to the man on the table. *The voice is the same, the words are the same, but it is not you. Not this time.* Her vision cleared, and the first surge of nausea disappeared. The relief that followed was like a stone lifted from her soul.

"Left pupil's fixed and dilated," Sax stated. "Aaron, call neurosurg and get them in here. He needs to be decompressed."

"Chest tube's in," Deb announced as she connected the thick plastic tube to a negative pressure collection chamber that would reinflate his lung and evacuate blood and fluid from his chest. Continuing her exam, she noted, "His mid-face is unstable...feels like there's an open fracture of the mandible, too."

"How's his airway?" Sax asked, although she had already checked.

"He'll need to be trached," Deb replied. "There's a lot of swelling in the posterior pharynx, and with all the facial fractures—"

Pleased that Deb had made a quick, accurate assessment, Sax said, "Let's do it now, then. Aaron, get the trach tray open."

"Roger."

"Have we heard from neurosurg?" Sax asked the room in general as she stepped back from the table.

"Pam Arnold's on her way in. She said half an hour," another nurse answered.

Jude edged closer to Sax, waiting for a break in the action. "Can you talk?" she asked when the surgeon seemed to be free.

"Go ahead," Sax responded, watching Deb prep the man's neck for the tracheostomy.

"Why isn't the neurosurgeon here in the hospital like you are?"

"Because state law only requires that subspecialists be available within a reasonable period of time, and if I insisted that the neurosurgeons, orthopedists, and plastic surgeons take call like we do, they'd all quit. We have a bigger staff than those divisions, plus they have much heavier day-to-day elective schedules. They can't work all night and then all the next day very often without burning out."

"Okay," Jude said, acknowledging that detail clarified. "One more question—what about consent for the procedures you're doing on this guy? How do you handle that with no family here and him unconscious?"

"Deb, make sure you keep the incision right in the midline... there's a lot of swelling in his neck, so watch your landmarks." Sax looked at Jude directly for the first time. "In an emergency situation, we can legally perform any life-saving procedure indicated. Once he's stabilized and upstairs in the TICU, though, we'll need family or a court order to give permission before we do anything else."

"Tonight, then, what you say goes?"

"Pretty much," Sax agreed. "So, how are *you* doing?"

Jude wasn't sure what the surgeon was asking, or why, and for an instant, she bristled at the intrusion. The look in Sax's eyes, though, was too unwavering, and too warm, to be objectionable. "I'm fine—not even tired. And I think I'm past the...personal stuff."

"Immersion therapy?" Sax gave a wry smile. "Every trauma has a lot of similarities. It's the little details that make the difference."

"Yes." Jude realized that viewing it over and over was helping her distance herself in a way that actually healed. "But you're good with the details, aren't you?"

Before Sax could ponder what was behind the statement, a stately blond in a silk blazer and slacks walked in, looking as if she'd just left the country club. She promptly set about pulling a cover gown over her clothes.

Excusing herself, Sax approached the neurosurgeon. "Pam."

"Hello, Saxon," the blond replied in a throaty tone that reminded Jude of Lauren Bacall. "What do you have?"

Deb answered as she finished tying in the trach tube. "Closed head injury, panfacial fractures, blown pupil."

"CT scan?"

"Not done yet," Sax said as Pam assessed Mark Houseman's reflexes and general muscle tone.

"Can we send him down now?" Pam Arnold was nothing if not efficient. "I'd like to get him upstairs and get this done. I've got a lumbar laminectomy scheduled for 8:00, and that patient's already waited two months. I don't want that case to be bounced."

"Deb?" Sax asked.

"He's good to go," Deb affirmed with a nod. "Airway's clear... vital signs are good."

"Excellent." Pam shed her cover gown. "You still owe me dinner," she tossed over her shoulder to Sax as her patient was transferred to a stretcher for the trip to radiology.

Jude couldn't hear Sax's reply, but she didn't need to. The satisfied smile on the blond's model-perfect face told the story. *You didn't really expect that someone like Sinclair would be unattached, did you? And why should it matter anyway?*

CHAPTER FOURTEEN

Personal Project Log—Castle
July 24, 10:45 a.m.

I'm finally going to get my official interview with Sinclair this morning. Even though I've seen her on and off every couple of days for the last three weeks, there hasn't been a good time for us to talk at any length. If she isn't in the middle of a trauma and up to her ears in blood, she's running to a meeting or unwinding with Deb or Aaron. The term trauma team *is apt. When they're not actually working, they're playing together. It defuses the tension, I think—the basketball, the chess, hanging around in the OR lounge kibitzing. [Note: Need a segment, or a series of sidebars, on their intense personal relationships—the bonding is very reminiscent of groups under severe stress, like police or firefighters, or soldiers. Title it "Officer's Club," maybe.]*
I just couldn't cut into that time with more questions for them. Sinclair's been good about answering technical details. I haven't been able to get her to fill in the blanks in her CV for me, though...in fact, looking back over interviews she's given, she manages to sidestep personal questions entirely. There's something off and I can't put my finger on it—

"Ms. Castle?" Naomi Riley interrupted Jude's murmured dictation. "Dr. Sinclair is ready for you."

"Yes, okay." Jude hastily pocketed her recorder. "Thanks."

When she walked into Sax's office, she was surprised to see how spacious it was, with windows on two walls that commanded a breathtaking view, a small Oriental carpet in front of a decidedly noninstitutional antique mahogany desk, and a matching leather sofa and chair set. Saxon Sinclair, in an elegantly cut dark silk suit, looked perfectly at home in the stylish surroundings. Jude had gotten used to her in scrubs or in the causal jeans she usually arrived in for work. Although she'd always found the doctor attractive, for a moment she was stunned by how striking she appeared now.

Sax glanced up from her paperwork, pushed a pile of folders aside, and smiled a greeting. "Good morning."

"Thanks for seeing me." Jude crossed the room and settled into one of the chairs in front of Sax's desk.

Despite almost daily interaction with Sax, here in these formal surroundings Jude was even more aware of the other woman's personal magnetism. Though she'd seen her working, had watched her play, and had witnessed her in unguarded intimate moments with patients, she appreciated now how little of Sax she really knew. Virtually every impression she had of her was visceral—emotional—images and reactions formed by being near her, observing her, listening to her.

Jude had never before formed a connection, certainly not an intimate one, in this way. Relationships had always been something that developed from a friendship, or from an intellectual exchange, or from an awareness of shared interests—as it had been with Lori. She had never been touched so primally by anyone, without any reason or rationale, and the enormity of that realization was shocking.

Jude was suddenly aware of the silence in the room, and the fact that she had very probably been staring. What she found strange was that when she focused on Sax's face, she discovered that the surgeon was regarding her intently as well. Clearing her throat, she said, "I didn't expect to be able to meet with you today. Aren't we on call again tomorrow?"

"Yes, we are." Sax hid a smile at the "we." Despite her initial misgivings, she had to admit that Melissa and Jude were becoming part of the team. Jude had been true to her word. She took care to preserve patient confidentiality, respecting the privacy of patients who declined to be filmed, and acknowledged the wishes of families who did not want some footage to be used.

And, being honest, Sax enjoyed seeing Jude on a regular basis, even if it was under less than intimate circumstances. She liked her drive, her passion, and her sense of humor. She liked...her.

Sax caught her mind wandering down avenues she did not want to travel and reminded herself of the purpose of their meeting. Striving for a businesslike tone, she continued, "But I don't particularly like to make appointments when I'm on call for the trauma unit. Half the time I end up in the operating room with a patient, and the meeting has to be canceled. It just clogs up my schedule down the line."

"Why aren't you off today?" Jude asked. "I thought when you were on call in the unit you went home the next day."

"Actually, only Deb's off the next day. New York state limits the number of hours a resident can work during the week or at any one time without a break." She smiled a little wryly. "There aren't any such regulations for staff. If I didn't come in today, I'd end up buried in paperwork, and Riley would probably leave me. And then I'd have to quit myself, because she's the only one capable of keeping me organized. Besides, I have to be in Albany this afternoon for a state review of funding allocations for level one trauma centers. I need to present our numbers for the last year and do the appropriate amount of glad-handing to see that we continue to get financial support."

"I never realized how much nonmedical work there was in being the division chief," Jude said. Aware that time was at a premium, she lifted her recorder. "Do you mind if I tape this?"

For a moment, Sax debated. She had agreed to meet formally with Jude simply because Jude had requested it. It wasn't something she would ordinarily have done, and she wasn't entirely comfortable with an uncensored conversation being recorded. Even though Jude had proven to be respectful and sensitive to the needs of the patients when filming, there were still some things about the institution, and herself, that the public did not need to know. She'd worked too hard to protect her privacy.

"You can tape any part of the conversation that deals with Deb's training."

"All right," Jude agreed, although it hadn't escaped her notice that Sinclair had deftly limited the scope of their interview and effectively placed anything about herself off-limits. On the other hand, Jude's professional interests did not include the trauma chief other than for background highlights, and she should rightly focus on Deborah Stein. *You just wanted to talk about her because you want to know more about her.*

"And I can only give you a half hour," Sax added with a genuinely apologetic shrug. "We're driving upstate to the meeting."

"I understand. I'll make this as brief as possible."

Jude had prepared a list of issues that she wanted to clarify regarding the hierarchical structure of surgical training, the factors that affected eligibility for the trauma fellowship, and the nationwide impact of level one trauma units on health care delivery and hospital financing. She worked her way through them quickly and efficiently. For her part, Sax answered cogently, having testified multiple times at the state and national level about similar issues.

"Out of all the residents whom you interviewed," Jude asked after the full half hour had nearly elapsed, "why did you choose Dr. Stein?"

"Because she was the best qualified candidate," Sax answered immediately. "She performed well in medical school; she had excellent recommendations from one of the top ten general surgical training programs in the country; and she demonstrated a clear and focused intention to pursue a career in trauma surgery."

"What about personal qualifications? How do they influence your decision-making?"

"Obviously, we try to choose individuals with a philosophy and work ethic that will mesh well with that of our team. As you've seen, we work very closely for hours at a time together, and it is helpful to have individuals with similar visions and expectations."

"Does gender affect your choice?"

"No, and neither does any other personal characteristic."

"I understand that's not always the case, even today. Surely, it was different when you were training," Jude suggested. "There are still very few female surgeons in this country and definitely not very many division chiefs. Certainly, you must have encountered difficulties because of your gender in view of your choice of specialties."

"The face of medicine is constantly changing, and the place of women within this sphere is well established now," Sax responded neutrally and entirely noncommittally. Then she glanced pointedly at her watch.

"Just a couple more questions," Jude said quickly. "I was doing the back stories on both you and Dr. Stein, and I need you to fill in a few of the details for me." Actually, she needed a lot more than that. While doing the routine back searches on Sax, she'd literally run into a blank wall. All the information in the CV Naomi Riley had provided her was verifiable, but it seemed to dry up completely when she looked for anything before college. "It's helpful for viewers to form a connection to you. That way they can look forward to returning week after week, because they feel as if they know you. You know the kind of thing—what your life was like growing up, why you wanted to be a surgeon—the sidebar type of story that was done so effectively with Olympic coverage recently."

"I'm sure the viewers enjoy that sort of thing," Sax said blandly, but her shoulders stiffened with sudden tension. "And I'm sure Dr. Stein will be happy to provide you with that information. However, this project is not about me, and I don't see where these questions are pertinent."

"You're nearly as visible as Dr. Stein throughout this documentary, and you *need* to be, because you're her mentor and her...guide...for this year. Her relationship with you is probably the most important one she has during this period in her life. Who you are matters."

"Does it?" Sax stood and began to push folders into her briefcase. "I think we're done here."

Jude stood also, stunned by the change in Sax's tone and expression. The surgeon had very clearly closed a door, and the action was as swift and lethal as a scalpel cut. It left Jude nearly breathless. She had never felt so completely and brutally shut out. It shouldn't have bothered her, because she'd gotten most of the information that she needed. In the course of her career, she'd certainly worked with difficult individuals before, and she'd never taken their rudeness or lack of cooperation personally.

But it wasn't Sax's manner that affected her so deeply; it was the loss of their fledgling personal connection. It was impossible not to take something to heart when it actually hurt.

"Sax..." Jude wanted to apologize but had no idea about what.

"I'm late, Ms. Castle. Please excuse me."

And with that clear dismissal, Jude had no choice but to leave.

❖

Jude had the afternoon free, since the next day she would be back in the hospital for another twenty-four hours of trauma call. She'd promised to meet Lori outside the hospital at 11:45 so the two of them could go somewhere for an early lunch.

Glancing at her watch as she descended the elevator to the main lobby, she saw she still had a few minutes before Lori was due. She headed for the exit doors and was surprised to see Sax a few feet ahead of her, briefcase in hand, clearly on her way to her meeting in Albany. For a minute, Jude contemplated catching up to her and then realized it would just be an intrusion. What could she say that would seem like anything other than what it was—curiosity about Sax's past and an irrational need to put their personal relationship back on better footing. Reluctantly, she slowed down to avoid the surgeon, but when she exited, she found Sax on the sidewalk apparently waiting for a ride.

"Is this an important meeting—the one with the state this afternoon?" Jude asked when they found themselves standing side by side.

"Since a good deal of our funding is controlled by the state, yes." Sax shifted her briefcase to her other hand and regarded Jude silently. After a moment, she said softly, "Ms. Castle—"

"Jude, remember?"

"Jude," Sax acquiesced with a nod, "we'll probably get along better if we stick to business."

She'd noticed the look of confused hurt in Jude's eyes when she'd terminated their interview so abruptly. She hadn't intended to sound so brusque, but she hadn't expected Jude to question her so pointedly either. She'd responded reflexively, with defenses honed over a lifetime. The way they parted had then bothered her all the way down from her office, no matter how hard she tried to forget about it.

"I wasn't aware that you were concerned at all about how we got along," Jude said stiffly. She disliked being placed on the defensive and resented it even more that Sax appeared to be setting limits on their relationship for reasons which were anything but clear to her. *Not that that should even be an issue. Damn, why can't you just ignore her and do the job?*

"I find that I am concerned," Sax answered contemplatively, "despite the fact that you and your crew are a constant source of irritation."

Jude was about to make a caustic response when she caught the edge of a smile. "Believe me, Dr. Sinclair, we have a long way to go before we could possibly master the art of irritation that surgeons seem to possess."

"That's a point I can't argue." Sax laughed, but when she continued, her expression was intent. "Look, about this morning..."

Before Sax could finish, Jude heard someone call her name and turned to see Lori approaching, a broad smile of greeting on her face.

"Hey," Lori said as she drew near, "I got through the deposition early and thought I'd take a chance that you would, too." She brushed a quick kiss across Jude's lips. "Mmm...my day's looking better already."

Momentarily nonplussed, Jude said, "Hi," and turned to Sax to make introductions but the surgeon was no longer beside her. A sleek Jaguar convertible was idling curbside a few yeards away and Sax was sliding into the passenger seat. Jude instantly recognized the attractive blond at the wheel.

As Sax pulled the door shut and reached for her seat belt, she looked back at Jude. For a moment, their eyes held. Then the moment was gone. Glancing once at Lori's hand resting casually on Jude's back, Sax smiled wryly and turned away as the Jaguar slipped out into traffic.

"Who was that?" Lori asked, caught by the intensity of the dark-haired woman's gaze.

"That was Saxon Sinclair, the trauma chief," Jude said dryly.

"She is...impressive." Lori couldn't verbalize exactly what it was about the woman that had been so compelling. Or what it was about the way she'd looked at Jude that made her uncomfortable.

"Yes, she is." Jude struggled to banish off the image of Sax and Pam Arnold looking for all the world like a magazine cover couple. She met Lori's uncertain gaze and resolutely changed the subject. "Ready for lunch?"

"Sure." Lori forced a smile. She was probably just imagining the almost palpable connection she had sensed between the two women. After all, they had done nothing more than look at one another across the span of a crowded city sidewalk.

CHAPTER FIFTEEN

Pam Arnold took her eyes from the road long enough to glance sideways at her passenger, appreciating as always the austere appeal of Saxon's profile. Heading back downstate, she'd left the top down on the Jag because the evening was still warm, and the wind streamed through the other woman's dark hair like a lover's caress. With her face illuminated by moonlight, Sax looked wild and remote and compellingly erotic.

"Are you on call tomorrow?" Pam asked, reluctantly returning her eyes to the highway.

"Yes," Sax replied faintly, watching the ribbon of macadam sliding hypnotically beneath their wheels, her mind elsewhere.

"I can't believe that after an entire afternoon of arguing our case for continued funding, we had to sit through dinner with those bureaucratic bores and go through the whole thing again. I am sick to death of politics."

"There's no way to avoid it," Sax commented. She hadn't been thinking of the afternoon's business as they tore south on the New York State Thruway toward home. She'd been thinking about Jude Castle and the woman who had greeted her outside the hospital. *It shouldn't be a surprise that Jude has a lover. She's bright and dynamic and...quite beautiful. A woman like her would not be single.*

Sax shrugged against the shoulder restraint, trying to work the tension out of her neck and back, telling herself to forget it. The morning's interview with Jude had caught her off guard. She was just tired. Still, for a moment, she recalled vividly the sight of the attractive stranger quietly claiming Jude with the subtle intimacy of a familiar touch. The memory sparked an emotion that was not only foreign but also disconcerting—envy. Intimacy was not something she usually missed or consciously desired. Intimacy came with a price, and that price was often pain.

"I don't know about you," Pam continued, "but I could stand a few hours away from work, away from the very idea of it, and I'm not in that big a hurry to get home. I'd like to take my mind off the fact that I've spent half my life training to do this job, and now I have to ask permission from idiots to do it."

Grateful for the interruption to her troubled thoughts, Sax nodded. "I wouldn't mind forgetting the entire day either."

"We're less than an hour from my cabin," Pam suggested impetuously. "Let's stop there, get a bottle of wine, and stay the night. If we leave at 5:00, we'll be back in the city in plenty of time for both of us in the morning."

Sax's initial impulse was to say no, because she wasn't certain she had the energy to be decent company and she wasn't certain what kind of company Pam might be looking for. They'd known each other casually for over a year, ever since Pam joined the staff at St. Michael's. Recently their conversations had taken on a decidedly flirtatious air, and Pam had pointedly asked her out a few months before. Sax had vacillated over accepting the invitation because she disliked complications, and dating in the conventional sense always got complicated.

Regarding Pam now, trying to glean her intent from her expression, Sax debated how to respond. She had absolutely no reason to go home. In fact, if she did, she would very likely spend the night pacing or searching for something to help dispel her restless energy and her unwelcome emotions. She decided she could worry about Pam's intentions when and if she needed to...or wanted to. Pam Arnold was a very desirable woman.

"That sounds fine. We ought to be able to find a package store that's open. Since you're providing the accommodations, I'll buy the wine."

Forty-five minutes later, a chilled bottle of champagne in a cold-wrap bag resting between the bucket seats, Pam pulled up in front of a moderate-sized rustic cabin overlooking one of the myriad lakes in the Catskill Mountains. She'd chosen the hideaway because it was an easy drive from the city via the thruway but still far enough from popular resorts to be private. She closed the top on the convertible and led the way up to the front porch of the wooden structure, sorting through her key ring as they walked.

"Nice place," Sax remarked as Pam unlocked the door, and she meant it. Through the trees opposite the cabin she could see moonlight shimmering on the smooth surface of the lake, and though lights twinkled along the shoreline, there were no other structures in the immediate proximity. The night was very still and very quiet.

"It's a perfect place to come to read or write or...to have some privacy." Pam pushed open the door and held it for Sax to enter.

The large front room was enclosed on three sides by windows, while a stone fireplace and a double archway, which led into a spacious kitchen, took up most of the fourth. Sax assumed the bedroom was in the rear as well.

"Is there ice?" Sax asked as she walked toward the kitchen.

"All the modern conveniences," Pam said lightly as she followed. "I may like solitude, but rustic camping is not my idea of a good time. There's electricity, heat, and honest-to-God indoor plumbing. All the comforts of home."

Laughing, Sax opened several cabinets above the long kitchen counter and found an array of glassware, including wineglasses. She pulled down two as Pam handed her a metal bucket for ice.

"If you'll take care of this, I'll start a fire. It might be July, but what's a cabin without a fire? Besides, if we leave the windows open, it will cool off before long. By midnight, we'll need a blanket."

By the time Sax had opened the bottle, filled the bucket, and found a tray, Pam had a small log burning nicely and had placed several candles on tables by the sofa. The effect was charming and intimate. Sax handed her a glass of the champagne and sat next to her on the sofa.

"So," Pam said, slipping off her Ferragamos and propping her silk-stockinged feet on the stone coffee table, "let's not talk about the hospital, surgery, departmental politics, or anything remotely related to work."

"All right." Sax smiled as she shrugged out of her suit jacket and laid it over the arm of the sofa. "What does that leave?"

Pam laughed. "We're pathetic. No sports. Let's see...film, literature, art, or plain old-fashioned gossip are acceptable."

"It'll be a struggle," Sax joked, "especially the no sports part, but I think I can manage."

Pam sipped her champagne and studied the woman beside her. She loved to look at her, and it wasn't just because of her physical appeal. There was a brooding sense of mystery about her that was incredibly attractive. Pam liked a challenge in her women, and Saxon Sinclair was certainly that. This was as close as she'd ever gotten to a private moment with her, and she didn't intend to let it pass unexploited. Leaning forward, she rested her fingertips on the back of Sax's neck and softly ran a few strands of black hair through her fingers. "Or I suppose we could skip conversation altogether."

Carefully, Sax set her champagne glass on the small end table by her side. She turned back to find Pam only inches away, her lips slightly parted and her eyes liquid with promise. The statuesque blond was the very definition of sultry. Desire spread through Sax's body as the fingers in her hair slid under her collar and trailed over her neck.

"I have this rule," she remarked softly, her throat tight with the sudden swell of arousal. Usually, she didn't find many reasons to resist when a beautiful woman expressed an interest, but this time she wasn't certain she could let anything sexual happen. Not with Pam, not now.

"I don't think I'm going to like this," Pam whispered hoarsely as she moved closer on the sofa, her breasts brushing along Sax's arm. She traced the edge of Sax's ear lightly with one hand as she slid the other over Sax's abdomen. Muscles twitched under her fingers, and she smiled at the response. She enjoyed seduction, especially when the rewards were so tantalizing.

Sax caught Pam's hand gently as it slid lower toward the waistband of her trousers. "Pam, we have to work together almost every day. Something like this can make that relationship awkward." She drew in a breath as Pam's fingers danced along her fly. Swallowing the involuntary moan, she added, "And I would rather avoid that."

"Saxon," Pam murmured as she pressed her length against Sax's body and kissed the edge of her jaw, then moved her lips closer to the corner of Sax's mouth. "I'm not proposing marriage here."

"I'm devastated to hear that." Sax laughed softly. For a moment, she was captured by the heady scent of Pam's perfume and the subtle hint of desire. Succumbing to the urge that spread hotly through her limbs, she angled her face to accept the kiss.

When they both leaned back to catch their breath, Pam said, "I *am* proposing you spend the night making love with me, but I'm not opposed to going slower, if that's what you really want." Deliberately yet delicately, she drew one finger along the pulse in Sax's neck and traced the faint trail of perspiration down the center of her chest. Practiced fingers worked loose the first button on Sax's shirt. "Though I wouldn't have thought that you were the type to need courting."

"It's not courting I require." Sax's hips lifted automatically as Pam's hand slid inside her shirt and over the top of her breast. *A couple more seconds of this, and it won't matter why I thought this was a bad idea.*

"What is it, then," Pam dipped her head and pressed her lips to the skin she had exposed on Sax's chest, "that you require?"

Anonymity. I want to walk away and owe nothing.

Already hard and wet, she ached to touch the stiff points of Pam's nipples so clearly outlined against the sheer material of her blouse. She wanted skin against her palms and heat beneath her lips. She wanted to hear a woman cry out as she filled her and held that fragile passion in her hands. She wanted a woman to stroke her own aching need, and she wanted to explode against the sweet demanding softness of another's lips. She wanted it badly, so badly that in another minute she'd forget that the woman she held in her mind was not Pam Arnold.

A few weeks before, it had been a dream vision, but even in the dream, she'd known who it was that stirred her desire. One unguarded moment, she'd nearly succumbed to that same woman in the dark, still hallway of the hospital. Instead, she'd let a stranger satisfy the lust Jude Castle had ignited in her that night, but she couldn't let Pam do it now. She knew Pam's face. They were friends. But if Pam kept touching her, she would forget that and she would forget her basic rule of noninvolvement.

"Pam," she gasped abruptly as skillful fingers found her nipple. "Time out...time out...oh, Jesus..." She grabbed Pam's hand and stilled it against her flesh.

"You're serious, aren't you?" Astonished, Pam drew back far enough to look into Sax's face. She knew desire when she saw it, and she recognized the need in those heavy-lidded, hazy blue eyes. "I suppose it would be churlish of me to say that I know you want this."

"Wanting...is not the issue." Sax took a deep breath and willed her heart to stop pounding.

"I don't suppose you'd like to tell me what the issue is?"

"No." *I don't want to explain it to myself.*

"Saxon," Pam whispered, removing her hand reluctantly. "It

usually takes more than a kiss to make me want someone as badly as I want you right now. The only reason I care about your issues is because it's preventing me from having you. I'm a big girl...I'm not worried about tomorrow."

"If it makes you feel any better," Sax said with a weary sigh, "you've pretty much demolished me, too. I can barely think."

"But you're still not going to fuck me, are you?"

Sax laughed, relieved to feel her control returning. "Not tonight."

"God, I hate you," Pam said, running both hands through her long blond hair and sighing. "I can't sleep like this, and we both need some rest." She stood and reached for Sax's hand. "Come on, let's go swimming."

"It's the middle of the night," Sax protested, but she followed obediently as Pam tugged her through the front door.

"Good. Then no one will know we're naked except us."

The night was never truly dark in New York City, because the lights from thousands of buildings and tens of thousands of cars always illuminated the sky in a palette of ghostly pallor. The windows were open, street noises wafted up from below, and a faint breeze cooled the sweat on her skin.

"I'm fine," Jude whispered, cradling the still trembling woman in her arms. She ran her fingers through the other woman's hair, over her shoulders and down her back, resting her hand in the delicate valley just above her hips. The skin was so soft there, so fragile, and it was such a private place—it never ceased to fill her with wonder each time she touched her there. "You were enough."

"Mmm," Lori sighed, brushing her cheek over Jude's breast. "You were wonderful. And as soon as I catch my breath, I want to return the favor."

"It's late, we should get some sleep."

"I'll put you to sleep," Lori insisted, rousing herself and sliding on top of Jude. She insinuated her leg between Jude's thighs, her breath catching quickly as she felt the wet heat against her skin. "God, I love the way you feel."

Jude sensed her own arousal as if from a distance. They'd made love because it was part of the rhythm of their relationship, and her body had responded to the familiarity and the stimulation. But even as she caressed the places she knew so well and drew from Lori cries of pleasure and, finally, sobs of release, she'd felt as if she were watching a favorite film. She recognized the players and the play, and she couldn't help but respond. She was aroused, but still she felt a disconnection that left her feeling hollow, and alone.

Disconcerted, she accepted Lori moving lower over her body. The silken heat of Lori's mouth made her gasp, and she closed her eyes and tried to empty her mind, willing her body to find release. It wasn't something she usually had to work at. She hovered for agonizing minutes on the verge of climaxing, muscles taut and nerves singing— shivering on the brink, straining for the peak. Breath tore from her lungs on strangled sobs and her heart thundered in her ears. She was burning, bleeding, dying—and still the moment eluded her.

Gasping, she meant to tell Lori to stop; she meant to say she couldn't. She didn't mean to allow the images of another place, another face, to surface. She didn't mean those other eyes to hold her, or that stark, intense image to claim her.

But it happened, and she couldn't stop it. She couldn't stop the swift surge of blood that pulsed through her already painfully distended flesh or the wild plummet into orgasm.

"Oh God, oh God, oh God," she whispered, Saxon Sinclair's face shimmering through her mind. *What am I going to do?*

Chapter Sixteen

July 25, 7:38 a.m.

I thought you'd overslept," Melissa teased as Jude sat down beside her in the cafeteria. Jude was never late. When her friend failed to reply, Melissa looked up from her breakfast and regarded her seriously. "You look beat. Rough night?"

"Not exactly." Jude tried to decide whether she even wanted the yogurt she had picked up more out of a sense of responsibility than hunger.

After Lori had fallen quickly asleep beside her the night before, she'd barely slept, lying awake to stare at the ceiling and wonder what was happening to her. Eventually, she'd slipped into a fitful slumber just before dawn, only to be awakened in what felt like minutes by the alarm. She'd rolled over and closed her eyes, trying to decide if she should awaken Lori then and talk to her about what she was feeling.

But what was I feeling? What was I going to say? I've been unfaithful to you with a fantasy vision?

She wasn't even certain that Lori would consider it unfaithful if she'd actually started *seeing* another woman, let alone been guilty of nothing more than some severely erotic fantasies about one. They'd never placed any limits on each other regarding monogamy; for her it had just worked out that way. Seeing Lori was all she had time for, and apparently the same was true for Lori as well. They were monogamous by default.

Still undecided but out of time, she'd pulled herself from bed, more exhausted than if she had been up all night working. She had merely leaned over and dropped a light kiss on Lori's cheek as she left, whispering goodbye and remaining silent about her own troubling thoughts. They both had to work, and she could barely make sense of her own emotions, let alone articulate them to a woman with whom she'd been intimate for months, but who in many ways she hardly knew. Lori deserved more than a rushed explanation at some ungodly hour of the morning that was going to make very little sense to either of them.

"Are you okay?" Melissa persisted, her expression more serious now.

"Yes...no...I don't know." Jude surprised herself at the admission. She smiled ruefully across the table, appreciative of the concern in Melissa's eyes. "It's nothing serious. Relationship stuff."

"What's happening? Does Lori want to move in with you?" Melissa imagined that the attorney had finally pushed for the relationship to become more serious. Jude hadn't seemed likely to do so.

"No, thank God." Jude didn't bother to mask her relief. "In fact, she's never pressured me about that kind of thing. She seems to be pretty happy just the way things are—casual and sort of unstructured."

"So?" It was clear to Melissa that something was bothering Jude, and she couldn't understand why Jude was being so vague. She was one of the most direct people Melissa knew. "Do *you* want to get more serious, then?"

"No." Jude shook her head emphatically. "Not at all. Everything is fine just the way it is."

"Uh-huh. That's obvious."

"I'm just tired," Jude reiterated, forcing an effort at breakfast. *Lori hasn't asked for anything more, and I don't want anything more. So, what's the problem?*

But she knew what the problem was. She couldn't continue to make love to one woman while thinking of another, and she didn't know how to stop thinking about Saxon Sinclair.

July 25, 7:58 a.m.

Pam pulled the convertible to the curb in front of St. Michael's and turned in the seat to study her passenger. "I'd like to see you, Saxon. You know that. Dinner, the theater, a few hours in bed...anything you like. Will you call me when you're ready? If you're ready?"

Sax sighed and met Pam's gaze. She wasn't at all sure why she was resisting. Pam Arnold was alluring and talented and sexy as hell. Losing herself in Pam's arms was likely to give her at least two things she needed—a few hours of rest and a reason not to dream about Jude Castle. Still, she hesitated.

"I'm not exactly relationship material, Pam. And I meant what I said last night about avoiding involvement with anyone at work."

"I'm not looking for a relationship." Pam's eyes traveled the length of Sax's body. "I'm looking for a little diversion and a little pleasure, and I have a feeling that you're exactly what I require." As Sax laughed good-naturedly and stepped from the car, Pam added, "*Call* me."

Standing on the sidewalk watching Pam pull away, Sax wondered if Jude had arrived at the hospital yet and mentally reviewed the morning's schedule. She might not see the filmmaker all day if the admissions were slow and they had no reason to film. Maybe that wasn't such a bad thing. Maybe then the insistent hum of arousal that only got worse whenever Jude was near would dissipate. Maybe.

Personal Project Log — Castle
August 3, 11:35 p.m.
DRM–15,530-17,200

It's only been a month, but already I can see the changes in Deb. She's always been confident, and of course she should be, because she's already finished an entire general surgery residency before coming to St. Michael's. Still, a month ago, she was a brand-new trauma fellow, and now she seems like a seasoned veteran. [Note: Episode title: "Squad Commander."]

Today was one of those days when there was a steady stream of injured...most of them blunt traumas...motor vehicle accidents usually. We'd just get one settled and another would arrive.

I noticed that when new patients rolled into the trauma admitting area, Sax didn't get involved in the assessment as quickly. Sometimes not at all. She still watched everything and supervised everyone in the same totally efficient, totally confident, totally commanding manner...but she let Deb lead

*the team and make all the calls. Still, I could feel Sax there
in the background, watching. There's something comforting
about knowing that she's there and that if anything goes
wrong, you're not alone.*

Jude turned off her recorder and leaned out over the top of the
stone wall edging the rooftop, letting the night wind cool her skin and
thinking about what she had just said. *If anything goes wrong, you're
not alone.* She wondered why that mattered to her. As a child, she had
struggled for independence, especially during the years when much
of her life had revolved around competition and she had chafed at
the restrictions that had been placed upon her. She had finally found
something of her own in filmmaking and had pursued it, both because it
satisfied her intellectually and because it was her banner of freedom.

She enjoyed her friends and her more intimate relationships, but
she had always hesitated to establish any serious ties for fear that she
would no longer be able to control her own life. Being alone had never
bothered her and she usually felt content and fulfilled. With an impatient
shrug, annoyed at her introspection, she chided herself.

*I really should be pleased. It was a busy but not overwhelmingly
hectic day. We got high-quality footage, and it was a good day's work.
Things are going even better than I expected. I don't need to complicate
the situation now.*

"I can leave if you'd rather be alone," a quiet voice said from
behind her.

Jude turned to search the darkness, and a rush of heat rose unbidden
when she recognized the familiar figure. "I'm in *your* space up here. I'll
leave."

"No." Sax stopped by Jude's side. "Stay. Please."

For a few moments, they said nothing, merely standing side by
side in companionable silence, watching the city teem with life far
below.

"Why did you decide to do this...surgery, I mean?" Jude asked,
not expecting Sax to answer. She wasn't even sure why she had asked,
except that she wanted to know.

Perhaps it was because she sensed only honest interest that Sax
answered. "Surgery is one of the few areas in medicine where you know
you've made a difference almost immediately. You don't have to wait
for a drug to work or for a test to be completed. You make a difference

with your hands and your mind. And if it doesn't work, it's on you. You know where you stand in surgery. There are no gray zones."

"That sounds...comforting."

"Yes." Sax detected a note of surprise in her own voice. She hadn't really expected Jude to understand.

"And why trauma surgery?" Jude probed softly. She heard Sax sigh and saw her shrug from the corner of her eye. *This is where she turns around and leaves. She's made it pretty clear that she isn't going to talk to you about herself. Why can't you just let it be?* But she couldn't.

She'd never hungered to know anyone the way she wanted to know Saxon Sinclair. She couldn't explain it, not even to herself. It was more than respect, more than attraction, and more than curiosity. When she looked at her, she saw so many things—dedication, responsibility, anger, stubbornness, passion. Most of all, passion—for what she did and for what she believed. She was too intriguing to walk away from.

When Sax made no comment, she repeated, "Why trauma?"

"Ego is a big part of it," Sax admitted. "It's a personal challenge when a life is on the line and you're the only one there who can change the tide."

"And when you fail?"

"You try to make sure that doesn't happen."

"Everyone tells me that trauma burns you out quickly," Jude commented. "After only a month, I can understand why. It's so intense, and there's so little time to make a decision. So much depends on what you do. You *personally*. Doesn't that take its toll...wear you down?"

"It does for some people." Sax met Jude's gaze. "But it's that pressure—that thrill—that makes it all worth it, too."

Even in near darkness, Jude could see Sax's eyes sparkle. There was a pent-up energy and excitement about her that was nearly palpable. "I bet if you weren't a surgeon you'd be a firefighter or an astronaut or some other high-stress, adrenaline-producing job."

"Maybe," Sax agreed, chuckling. "There's nothing quite like winning."

For a moment, as she watched Sax laugh with her head tilted back and moonlight angling off her profile, Jude forgot what they were discussing. All she could think was how beautiful the surgeon was. It was more than just physical; there was a magnetism and vitality about her that made Jude want to grab on to her and soar wherever that crazy energy would take her. It was a heady, addictive sensation and she was instantly ready to stop thinking altogether and just feel.

"How about you?" Sax asked unexpectedly. "What is it about filmmaking that satisfies you?"

"A million things," Jude answered, her heart still pounding. "In a lot of ways, it's like what you do. It's technically challenging, it's exciting, and there are rewards beyond my own personal satisfaction. Film is a communication medium, and communication is one of the greatest tools for shaping society." She laughed a little self-consciously, pushing her hair back with one hand in a gesture that Sax was coming to recognize. "Not that I think I'm changing the world, but if what I do causes a few people to think about something differently—to think at all—then I've succeeded."

"I understand," Sax said. It was surprising how easy it was to talk to Jude. The moments they'd spent together were some of the most relaxing she could remember. She had spent her life surrounded by intense people, but Jude's quiet intensity was both comforting and compelling. From the very first moment Sax had met her, she had sensed Jude's underlying honesty and commitment. That, perhaps more than anything else, was what she valued about her.

Maybe it was because they were alone in one of the few places where she had ever been able to relax, but she felt oddly peaceful. She didn't really stop to think about what she said next.

"I owe you an apology for my rudeness during the interview. I know you were just doing your job."

"No, you don't need to apologize. When I'm going for a story, I tend to be relentless, because I've learned that oftentimes the only way to get the details that you want is to push. You told me up front what the rules were, and I ignored them."

"I'm sorry, nevertheless," Sax repeated.

"Accepted, then," Jude replied softly.

They were standing very close together, completely alone on the rooftop of the hospital. The night lay heavy and warm around them, cocooning them and making it seem as if they were even more isolated than they actually were. Halogen lights at the far corners of the helipad lit the landing area in a harsh artificial glare, but they stood outside the illumination in shadows.

Neither of them wanted to end the moment; neither of them moved into the light.

CHAPTER SEVENTEEN

August 4, 12:50 a.m.

As it turned out, neither of them had a chance to suggest they go back inside. Sax's beeper went off, making the decision for them.

Trauma alert STAT...trauma admitting. Trauma alert STAT... trauma admitting. Trauma alert STAT...trauma admitting...

Sax shrugged an apology and sprinted away, Jude close on her heels. Not bothering with the elevators, they clattered down the concrete steps of the stairwell to the first floor. By the time they reached trauma admitting, the first of several gunshot victims were being wheeled in from the line of emergency vehicles pulled up behind the trauma admitting bay. Deb was already there, examining the first patients and starting her evaluation; Aaron Townsend was triaging and informing other nurses and residents as to which individuals needed immediate attention; Melissa was on scene with her camera rolling.

"What have we got?" Sax asked as she came through the double doors on the run.

"Gang fight," Deb replied without looking up from the young male she was intubating. "Multiple penetrating injuries—gunshot and stab wounds."

"How many are we getting?" Sax moved to the next patient in line, pulling on gloves as she went.

"I don't know," Deb said distractedly. "The EMTs said there were at least a dozen injured. This guy's got a hole in his belly and needs to go to the OR right now."

"Aaron," Sax called as she lifted the blood-soaked gauze bandage on the second youth's chest, "call in Tyler and the rest of the backup team. We're going to be busy down here for a while." Studying the two-inch laceration between the second and third ribs, she asked the patient, "What's your name?"

"Fuck you," the teenager grunted, twisting to look at the boy on the bed beside him. "You better hope you die, motherfucker, because if you don't, I'm gonna kill you!"

"You've got a punctured lung. You need surgery," Sax informed him impassively.

"I want to go...to...another hospital. I don't...wanna be anywhere near these...pricks." As he spoke, bright red blood frothed from between his lips, and Sax had to force him back to a lying position.

Great. Rival gang members still looking for someone to fight. Perfect. "Save it for some other day. You've got a stab wound in your chest. At the moment, you're not going to be fighting with anyone."

"Just keep...them...away from me," he wheezed weakly just before his eyes rolled upward and he lost consciousness.

For the next few minutes, Sax was busy inserting a chest tube and starting multiple large intravenous lines so that the nurses could hang blood and intravenous fluids. Deb was silently and efficiently doing the same thing as three more critically injured boys were delivered in rapid succession. Several nurses and two more surgical residents were recruited from the intensive care unit to assist in the initial stabilizations.

Jude and Melissa stayed out of the way of arriving stretchers and bustling medical personnel while managing to find a good vantage point from which to film the action. After more than two hundred hours of on-call experience, they had worked out a system that was nearly as seamless as the choreographed resuscitations occurring around them.

By now, Jude knew from the footage they'd been getting that she and Mel were working on the same wavelength. That was what happened when a director and photographer were of one mind. She didn't worry about Mel missing something important, which was a good thing, because she often found herself watching Sax—just to see her work. Trying to observe both Deb and Sax now, she was so caught up in the excitement that she didn't register the sound of a scuffle just outside in the hallway. It was the sound of Aaron's voice, raised in anger and tinged with fear, which finally made her look around.

"Hey!" Aaron exclaimed. "You can't come in—"

A sharp crack like snapping wood and the startled sound of Aaron's stunned cry caught her full attention. She spun toward the entrance of the trauma admitting area.

Three young men shouldered their way inside, all of them blood spattered and wild-eyed. The teenager in the lead had a pistol in his hand, swinging it erratically back and forth as he stared at the people in the room. Aaron was lying on the floor just a few feet away, his eyes closed and a spreading patch of maroon on his scrub shirt.

"You killed my brother, you fuck!" the boy screamed, focusing on the wounded, semicomatose boy that Deb Stein was struggling to save. He raised his gun in a trembling hand, and to Jude's amazement, Deb leaned over her patient in an attempt to shield him.

"No!" Jude shouted, and the gunman hesitated, jerking involuntarily in her direction. She didn't have time to register fear because the next thing she knew, she was flying through the air. Her shoulder struck a counter and her head bounced resoundingly off the floor as she landed. Dimly, she heard several more loud popping sounds, and then there was silence.

❖

"Jude, Jude!"

Jude opened her eyes and looked up into Melissa's frantic stare. "Stop shaking me, damn it. I'm awake."

"Let me examine her, please, Mel." Sax knelt down next to her and placed her hand gently on Jude's shoulder, preventing her from rising. "Jude, just lie still for a minute."

For the second time in her life, after awakening confused and disoriented, Jude stared up into Sax's comforting deep blue gaze, but this time there was something in addition to reassurance and confidence in Sax's eyes. This time there was fear.

"I'm fine," Jude said quickly.

"Let me be the judge of that." Sax flicked a penlight into each eye, watching the brisk, even pupillary constriction and feeling the tightness in her own chest lessen slightly. *No intracranial injury.* "Do you know where you are?" She was having trouble keeping her voice steady. *Jesus, that's never happened to me before.*

"I know exactly where I am. I don't think I was actually unconscious. I just had the wind knocked out of me. What the hell happened?"

"Just a minute." Sax concentrated on getting her voice under control as she pressed her stethoscope to Jude's chest. Once again, she was relieved to hear the sure, steady rhythm. Satisfied that there wasn't any major organ dysfunction, she pressed her fingers slightly to the carotid artery in Jude's neck, finally drawing her first full breath since she had seen the gun pointed in Jude's direction. The pulse tripped rapidly under her fingers, but it was full and strong. Looking directly into Jude's questioning green eyes, she stated with some urgency, "I have to go. Aaron's been shot, and Deb is on her way to the operating room with him. I'm going to let one of the residents finish examining you, just to be sure, but I think everything is fine."

Jude grasped Sax's wrist. "There's blood on your neck. Are you all right?"

"Yes." *Now that I know that you are.*

"Go. I'll see you later."

Personal project log—Castle
August 4, 7:10 a.m.
DRM 20,172–22,350

> *Sax and Deb are still in the operating room working on Aaron. One of the surgery residents came out about an hour ago to give us an update. Apparently, it was a small caliber bullet from a Saturday night special, which is why Aaron is still alive. But it did a lot of local damage in his abdomen, and he lost a lot of blood. They've been working now for over five hours. I keep thinking how tired they must be and I wonder if they even notice. I keep seeing Deb reflexively shielding her patient, someone she doesn't even know, someone who may have been responsible for killing someone else just moments before...I'm not sure I could have done that. I haven't wanted*

to screen the videotape because I don't want to see it again so soon.

The waiting is getting to me now...I can't stand waiting and not knowing. At least if I'm working, I won't have to think about what's happening in there.

"Let's go back to the on-call room and run the tape."

"Sure," Melissa agreed flatly. Anything to break the monotony of watching the slow crawl of the minute hand on the large, plain-faced clock visible in the operating room control center across the hall.

A few moments later, they were ensconced in their familiar location, settled into the routine, replaying Melissa's footage of the previous night. Jude had her recorder out and was dictating notations as the counter on the tape measured out the moments to the critical scene. Her heart rate climbed as they approached the section where the gang members burst into the admitting area.

She wasn't sure how much Mel had been able to get before everything erupted into chaos, but she steeled herself for what she knew was coming. She didn't have much memory for those few moments because everything had happened so quickly. And for a good part of the time, she had apparently been lying on the floor.

"Here we go," Melissa murmured, her voice tense with emotion.

Jude watched as the nightmare rolled. The three young men suddenly appeared almost simultaneously with the sound of the gunshot, and Aaron stumbled back as if he had been kicked.

Miraculously, Melissa had reacted immediately to the sounds of shouting in the hallway and had caught the entire sequence perfectly. There was a dizzying blur of movement as she swung the camera around to follow along the shooter's sightline, and Deb came into view. Jude watched that amazing moment again as the young surgeon threw herself between the weapon and her patient.

"God, Mel, you are so good," Jude said aloud reverently. "You just captured the one scene that's going to mean more for this project than anything else."

"Maybe." Melissa wondered if she had gotten the rest of it.

"Oh, believe me, I'm right," Jude said emphatically. "This is going..."

Her voice trailed off as the camera moved again, and this time

Melissa had pulled the camera back enough to get almost the entire room in her lens. The shooter swung his arm, and Jude saw him point the gun right at her chest. Then Saxon Sinclair stepped directly into the line of fire, grabbed her by the shoulders, and pushed her violently out of the way. It happened so fast Jude hadn't even been aware of it at that moment. Stunned, she watched herself thrown out of the bullet's path as her body caromed off the back counter. Almost simultaneously, four armed security guards entered behind the gang members and rapidly subdued them.

Wordlessly, she pushed rewind. This time she watched Sax's face. For the briefest instant, Sax's stark features had been a study of ferocity and fury.

"I heard gunfire. I remember gunfire," Jude stated numbly. "Did someone shoot?"

"That kid did. About a millisecond after Sinclair knocked you ass over teakettle."

Jude swung her seat away from the tape and stared at her friend. "Why didn't you tell me sooner?"

"I wasn't sure we had it on tape, and..." Melissa shrugged. *I was scared to death that you'd been shot, and I didn't even want to think about it.*

"How did he miss her?" Jude managed, her throat tight. She wasn't even thinking about the danger to herself. The potential danger was meaningless to her now, because she was fine, and, besides, she had no memory of it. But she had a visceral image of Saxon Sinclair saving her life at certain peril of her own. *What if he had shot her instead?* The thought was terrifying.

"Just lucky." Melissa shrugged. "He fired, but I think the bullet went high. Then the hospital police arrived and right behind them the city cops. Within moments, it was over. All I could think about then was you."

"Hey," Jude said softly, aware of the tremor in Mel's voice. She rested her hand gently on the photographer's forearm and squeezed lightly. "Thanks. You're wonderful, Mel."

Melissa nodded wordlessly. She'd seen the way Jude and Sinclair had looked at one another as they both frantically tried to determine if the other was all right. She'd never seen Jude look at anyone that way.

"Yeah, that's me. Wonderful."

August 4, 5:45 p.m.

Jude turned over on the narrow bed and sat up. A soft knock came again at the door. "Just a minute," she called, searching at the foot of the bed for her T-shirt. She pulled it on and tugged her jeans closed as she walked toward the door.

Sax stood outside in the hall in sweat-stained scrubs, looking rumpled and weary. "I'm sorry I didn't come sooner. I wanted to, but I needed to stay with Aaron..."

Extraordinarily relieved to see her, Jude reached out impulsively and grasped her hand, pulling her into the room. She closed the door behind them and said, "Sit down. You must be exhausted."

To Jude's surprise, Sax complied, sinking down on Melissa's unoccupied bed.

"How is he?"

"He's stable," Sax said dully, struggling with fatigue and the aftermath of controlling her emotions for hours. The entire time she had worked to repair the multiple holes blasted through fragile tissues, she had fought not to think about who lay on the table before her. She could not associate the torn and bleeding organs with the man she considered a friend and colleague. She had needed to separate her feelings for Aaron while she battled with death, but it had cost her. She was beyond tired. "If any of a dozen things don't go wrong over the next few days, he should be fine."

"Thank God," Jude said with relief. She noticed a reddened area on Sax's neck and leaned over her, turning the surgeon's face toward the small bedside lamp. "You've got a cut here."

Sax lifted her fingers and laid them gently on Jude's. "It's nothing. One of the instrument trays fell over when you and I ended in a heap on the floor."

"Thank you for that," Jude said, suddenly aware that her hand was still lightly cupping Sax's jaw. In that moment, she sensed Sax stiffen at her touch and they both drew back.

Sax pushed herself to her feet and started toward the door, knowing that she should go, because she'd been up for over thirty-six hours, her emotions were stretched to breaking, and the light touch of Jude's fingers drove her crazy. She couldn't stay here, alone with her like this, but God, she didn't want to say goodbye—not yet.

Maybe it was just because she was too damned tired to think clearly, but she turned at the last moment and regarded Jude steadily. "Do you know who Madeleine Lane is?"

"Of course." The film icon had stopped making movies and pretty much disappeared from public view. Jude had heard occasional rumors about her reasons. "Why?"

"She wants to meet you."

"What?" Jude was perplexed. One of them apparently *did* have a concussion, and she didn't think it was her. "How do you know?"

"She told me."

"I'm not following. When?"

"Tonight. Come on."

Jude stared at the hand Sax extended, still uncomprehending, and then she did the only reasonable thing.

She took it.

Chapter Eighteen

August 4, 6:20 p.m.

Just give me a minute to change," Sax said as she unlocked the door to her on-call room and motioned Jude to follow.

Taking a few awkward steps just inside the threshold, she determinedly looked elsewhere as Sax began shedding her scrub shirt and pants. "Look, I should probably just go home. I didn't even mean to fall asleep this afternoon, and the few hours I had didn't help much. I still feel like I've been dragged through a keyhole. Plus"—she grinned sheepishly, indicating her own rumpled appearance—"I don't have a change of clothes."

Sax rummaged in a drawer built in under her bed and tossed a T-shirt in Jude's direction. Pulling on her own tight black T, she said, "Now you do. I can't help you with the jeans, though, because I don't have a spare pair. You can shower when we get to the house and do laundry if you need to."

"We're really going to do this, aren't we?" Jude's familiar rational life was fast receding, and she was about to step through the looking glass. Probably, this bewilderment was due to fatigue, or maybe it was the result of the emotional assault that had started with the gunmen in the trauma admitting area and had culminated with the agonizing wait to find out if Aaron was going to survive. Whatever it was, she didn't feel like herself, and yet, in a way, she had never felt more alive, nearly exhilarated. Seeing yourself almost shot in slow motion a few times did that to you, apparently. She was too shell-shocked to decide exactly what that meant, but watching the muscles flex in Sax's arms, she didn't care.

"Well, I'm going because right now I need to ride off some of the last twenty-four hours," Sax said, tucking in her shirt and pulling on her boots. "And I'd like you to come."

"All right."

Jude supposed she should ask herself why, but she didn't. And it didn't really matter. She simply wanted to go, and the fact that it didn't make sense just wasn't important. Nothing much had made sense since the moment a bunch of teenagers with lethal weapons had threatened the lives of innocent people who were merely trying to do their jobs.

Come to think of it, not much of anything made sense if she really stopped to think about it. One morning five years ago, she'd nearly died riding the subway to work. Now, almost every day in the trauma bay, she saw individuals whose lives were altered forever by bad luck or whimsy or the ill winds of fate. Probably after a good night's sleep, or maybe half a dozen, she'd feel like her sensible, balanced, grounded self again. But right now, the idea of riding on the back of Saxon Sinclair's motorcycle seemed like the most reasonable thing around.

"I'll be ready in a second," Jude said, turning away and stripping off her T-shirt. When she pulled on the borrowed one, she had a quick thought of how intimate it was to wear someone else's clothes. That musing was a bad idea, because instantly her skin began to tingle, and she knew what was coming next. Maybe if she didn't think about anything, her body would behave.

Thankfully, Sax opened the door and stepped out into the hall. Keeping up with her took Jude's mind off the steady pulse of arousal that had started with the first touch of soft cotton over her breasts. It didn't help a bit that she wasn't wearing a bra.

"Have you ever been on one of these before?" Sax asked, leading Jude through the small doctors' parking lot to her bike in the far corner. She unlocked the helmets from the back and handed one to Jude.

"Not one this big," Jude replied. "Only dirt bikes that we used to fool around on when we were kids at the shore."

"All you have to do is hold on to me and let the rhythm carry you."

As she spoke, Sax swung one leg over the leather seat and motioned for Jude to do the same. The seat was gently curved so that Jude would easily be able to sit behind her and reach around her waist. Sax grew very still as Jude settled against her hips and brought both hands around to gently clasp her stomach. With her arm halted in mid-motion, hand outstretched with the keys dangling from clenched fingers, Sax was suddenly, acutely, almost painfully aware of the firmly muscled thighs pressed against the outside of hers and the soft swell of breasts nestled provocatively against her back. She had to swallow before speaking, because her throat was tight.

"Ready?"

"Yes, I'm fine." Jude's chin was nearly resting on Sax's shoulder. She hoped Sax couldn't feel her heart thudding against the inside of her rib cage, but with only two thin layers of cotton separating their skin, she doubted the flimsy barrier was enough.

They were well out of the city and steadily heading north when the harbingers of a summer thunderstorm amassed out of nowhere. Dusk was at least an hour away, but the heavy clouds that gathered overhead obscured the setting sun, plunging them into premature darkness. Even at the speed they were going, the air practically crackled with static electricity that raised the hair on Jude's arms.

Sax flicked on her turn signal and brought the bike to a stop on the shoulder of the highway. She reached up to pull off her helmet as she put a leg down on either side of the machine. As she half turned on the seat to look at her passenger, her bare arm inadvertently pressed against Jude's breasts. All at once, she felt the firm curve of flesh and the hard peak of nipple, and she nearly shuddered.

Stomach clenching, she said huskily, "I don't think this is going to blow over. Ordinarily, I wouldn't mind, but with you on the bike... I don't want to chance it. We can wait it out here, but the roads will be treacherous right after it rains. We'd probably do better to get inside."

What she didn't add was that she wasn't sure she was up to the challenge of a dark, wet highway in her present state. On the one hand, she was drained—emotionally perhaps more than physically—while at the same time, all she could think about was Jude. The heat of Jude's body was like a furnace against her back, and the unconscious way Jude lightly ran her hands up and down her abdomen was making her so hard she couldn't concentrate. She could have handled the huge bike if her only problem were fatigue, but not when her mind was clouded with lust, too.

"How do you feel about that Motel 6 up ahead?" Jude asked, hoping that the slight tremor in her voice wasn't audible.

She'd been pressed up against Sax's back for what felt like forever—a most pleasant eternity during which the vibration of the machine began to echo the building hum of excitement between her legs. If she wanted to delude herself, she could blame it on the powerful engine throbbing just under her, but she knew that wasn't it. It had taken every ounce of her willpower not to slip her hands under Sax's T-shirt and caress her skin. If she lifted her palms a mere fraction of an inch, she could cradle Sax's breasts in her palms.

Mouth suddenly dry, she added, "We were probably insane to even try this."

"Probably," Sax agreed, and she wasn't thinking about the storm or the danger. Nevertheless, when she glanced up the road to the large and brightly lit motel sign, she couldn't for the life of her think of anything she would rather do more than spend a few hours sheltered from the night's fury with Jude Castle.

While Sax got them a room, Jude waited in the shelter of the short overhang that ran above the narrow cement walkway fronting the dozen motel units. She tried to remember the last time she had done anything as unplanned and out of character as this and couldn't. But watching the wind slant the rain in heavy sheets against the asphalt parking lot while goose bumps grew large on her arms, she couldn't help but feel that some part of her had been waiting for this moment. Whatever strange congruence of forces was at work to bring her to this particular spot on this particular night, she wasn't going to question it. She was alive, and she might very well not have been. In fact, she had never felt so alive.

Turning at the sound of approaching footsteps, she watched Sax draw near, enjoying the sight of her lean muscular body and the way her rain-soaked T-shirt clung to her breasts and stomach. Sax pushed her wild, dark hair out of her eyes with the casual flick of her hand, and Jude was reminded of the skillful, certain competence in those fingers. Another rush of liquid heat streamed from the base of her belly down her legs, and she had to pull her bottom lip between her teeth to hide its quivering.

"I expect these accommodations will be less than four-star," Sax joked as she fitted the key to the lock with hands that trembled slightly. She was intensely aware of Jude standing just behind her, as if she could sense the woman through her skin. Every sensation seemed heightened—her skin prickled with excitement; her blood ran hot through her veins; every atom in her body seemed to vibrate. She was stoked red-hot, on the verge of exploding, and she wondered if it showed.

"If there's heat and hot water," Jude rejoined lightly, grateful to step into the generic motel room out of the lashing storm, "I'll be more than satisfied."

It took only the briefest glance to confirm that it was, indeed, the standard, unadorned, functional fare of any roadside lodge. A double bed, a dresser with a plastic ice bucket, cellophane wrapped cups, and a cable TV edged the room.

"I think at least one of your requirements will be met," Sax remarked as she walked to the opposite side of the room, twisted a dial on the forced air heater, and held her hand above the unit. Facing Jude across fifteen feet of space that suddenly felt much smaller, she remarked softly, "You're drenched and shaking. I think you should shower first. If you drape your clothes over a chair by this blower, they'll dry faster."

"All right." The plan made sense. Jude wondered if she should point out that neither of them had a change of clothes, and then thought she would probably sound foolish. There was no reason two adults couldn't be in the same room together in a state of near undress without losing control of themselves. No reason at all.

She took several steps toward the bathroom and stopped, staring at Sax who had lifted one foot to the single straight-backed chair to pull off her boots. It reminded Jude of the way she had looked that first morning making rounds in the TICU, so damned arrogant and commanding. Her eyes followed the long, taut line of Sax's leg and in the next instant, she flashed on the memory of Sax in the murky light of the bar, back arched as she was about to come. Her head swam with the vision and something tightened deep inside her.

"This isn't going to work," she said breathlessly, her voice nearly unrecognizable to her own ears.

"Oh, yes, it is," Sax responded, her own tone low and dangerous as she straightened. She moved so quickly she was beside Jude in the space of a heartbeat. Then she tugged the borrowed T-shirt from Jude's jeans at the same instant as her mouth came down on the redhead's. A low groan that turned to a ravenous growl escaped her as their lips met.

Sax hadn't a single coherent thought in her mind, only a collage of images, all of them Jude—pensive and quiet as they talked on the rooftop, intense and focused as she worked, helpless and vulnerable in the sights of a gun. Her hands danced over Jude's skin, tracing along the arch of ribs, the tips of her fingers gently following the faint spaces between the fragile bones. She slid upward until her hands closed around Jude's breasts, her thumbs coming to rest on the hardened prominence of her nipples.

"Ohh," Jude moaned as she pressed her lower body against Sax's. Frantically, she tugged Sax's wet T-shirt free from tight jeans as she reclaimed the kiss.

Their tongues met, gliding over and around, as Jude forcefully backed Sax in the direction of the bed with the press of her body. When Sax's legs hit the edge of the mattress and she tumbled backward, Jude went down on top of her. Their legs intertwined, Sax's hands still on Jude's breasts, their mouths still seeking.

Gasping, Jude reared back, breaking their contact to stare wordlessly down into Sax's eyes as she stripped the T-shirt off her torso and threw it onto the floor. Unable to tear her gaze away from Sax's face, inflamed by the desire echoed in those blue eyes, she reached for Sax's shirt, insistently tugging at it until the woman beneath her arched her back from the bed and ripped it off. Then, hair streaming with rainwater and breasts damp with sweat and storm, Jude fell upon her again. Bare upper bodies fused, jean-clad hips thrust, and their mouths met in a clash of hunger and need.

Sax wrapped her arms around Jude's back and tilted her pelvis to the side, rolling Jude over and following in one continuous motion, ending on top of her. She moved away despite Jude's protesting moan and, with shaking hands, groped for the buttons on Jude's jeans. Frantically following her lead, Jude pulled at Sax's fly and slipped one hand inside.

As Jude's fingers worked lower, Sax's vision dimmed and the roaring in her ears escalated to deafening levels. She was desperately afraid she might come the instant Jude found her clitoris, and almost as afraid she would beg if Jude didn't touch her soon. She wanted to come with a ferocity that was driving her insane. Finally, beyond thought, she stood and pushed her jeans down, kicking them away. Jude's eyes were on her, inviting her, urging her to return, as she just as vehemently bared her own flesh. Sax stretched out upon her again and wedged her thigh between Jude's, crying out as Jude's skin slid slickly between her legs.

"I'm coming," Sax groaned helplessly, shuddering as a barrage of sensations gathered between her legs and pummeled toward her spine. "Oh God, I'm coming."

Jude could do nothing but hold her. As she felt the tremors ripple through Sax's body, for a timeless moment, her own heart stilled in her chest. She had never known such sweet, sweet wonder, and had she been able to form thoughts, she would have realized she had never before even dared dream it.

CHAPTER NINETEEN

S till shivering lightly, Sax lay where she had collapsed, her cheek cradled against Jude's chest, listening to the erratic pounding of their hearts. Jude's hands were in her hair, stroking softly down the back of her neck and over her shoulders. The razor edge of her desperate need had been softened by her violent release, but desire smoldered fiercely in her still. Turning her face a fraction, she pressed her lips to the hot, slick skin and pulled a tensely swollen nipple between her teeth, smiling faintly as Jude's hips rose involuntarily under her own.

Wordlessly, she drew her fingertips along the curve of Jude's breast, cupping her hand around the sensitive flesh, drawing Jude deeper into her mouth. At that, Jude moaned faintly, her hands trembling now where they lay on Sax's back. As Sax sucked, biting lightly with no particular rhythm, she shifted enough so that she could explore Jude's body. She'd been too frantic earlier, too blinded by the ferocious hunger, but now she wanted to revel in her. Lightly, she ran her fingers up and down Jude's stomach, over the arch of hip—pressing her thumb into the tender hollow just inside her hipbone, then drawing it along the line of her upper thigh to the outer edges of the soft damp curls at the base of Jude's belly. With each stroke, Jude's legs shook.

"You feel so good," Jude whispered faintly against Sax's ear, her voice thick with urgency. Her body hummed with arousal, honed to laser sharpness by their lovemaking.

Sax lifted her mouth and murmured, "I'm just getting started."

"I'm so...God, I'm so..." Jude shuddered, the ache so intense she could barely think. "Do something—please."

"All right," Sax whispered. Moving her lips swiftly to the opposite breast, she caught the erect nipple sharply between her teeth and bit down.

Jude cried out, arching off the bed. "No...yes...yes..." she choked out, her clitoris twitching sharply. "You'll make...me...come," she warned, wanting to hold on but so close she knew she couldn't.

Sax relented, keeping Jude's nipple in her mouth but merely brushing the tip with her tongue. Curled against Jude's side, with Jude's pulse tripping frantically beneath her cheek, Sax struggled to ignore her own rising excitement. She eased her thigh over Jude's, rubbing her wetness over the soft skin—a torturous pleasure, but some small bit of relief from the escalating pressure nevertheless. Slowly and deliberately, she slid a finger along either side of Jude's stiff, swollen clitoris, then squeezed firmly as she rocked her hand lightly back and forth.

When Jude whimpered, it took all of Sax's restraint not to enter her immediately, not to claim her completely, not to give her what she so clearly needed—that swift, blinding relief. Biting her lip, she ran her thumb feather-light over the sensitive tip, scarcely breathing.

"Please...please...please..." Jude intoned, her head rocking anxiously. She forced her eyes open, but she was too crazed to focus. "I can't...I can't I can't..." She found Sax's wrist and tried to force her hand inside, protesting incoherently when Sax resisted.

Sitting up quickly, Sax straddled Jude's thigh, thrusting hard along the tense muscle, aware of the warning spasms between her own legs but pushing the cry of her flesh from her consciousness. *Jude.* It was Jude she wanted. Watching Jude's face as she touched her, she drew her fingers teasingly along the edges of the hot, full folds, almost frightened by the magnitude of her own desire. God, she wanted to be inside her; she wanted to fill her and drive her hard to the edge and over. She wanted to know her—only her—for those few precious seconds.

"Jude," she whispered softly. "Jude."

Already sensing the first welcome swell of orgasm, Jude heard the call from far away, a strong, gentle voice demanding she follow. Blinking, she gasped as another ripple of excitement rolled through her, but she managed to find the blue eyes, so dark they were almost purple, intense and penetrating, gazing down at her. Helpless, she had no choice but to deliver herself to her confident, unwavering lover.

Deep inside, the pressure crested as Sax filled her, one excruciating fraction of an inch at a time. She opened to accept the pleasure, closed to contain the passion, over and over and over. One sharp cry escaped her as she spasmed hard and fast, but she kept her focus on that commanding face. Then her body clenched almost painfully as Sax pushed deeper, forcing an even greater burst of release.

"Sax!" Jude screamed, her eyes finally closing as she reared off the bed, her stomach muscles contracting with the explosion.

"Jude," Sax whispered again, stunned by her beauty. "Jude."

❖

Jude moved her fingers and felt Sax's clitoris twitch.

Sax moaned faintly.

"Have I missed something?" Jude murmured. They were lying wrapped around one another in the still, dark room, the sheets twisted around their lower legs. She had no memory of falling asleep, or how her hand had come to be where it was.

"Dunno. Depends on what's the last thing you remember." Sax stretched, then placed her palm over Jude's hand, trapping it against her. "God, that's nice."

Jude stroked her lightly, still feeling a little out of body. "Uh... the last thing I remember. Let's see...that would be a mind-shattering orgasm—mine, not yours."

"Well then"—Sax laughed—"you missed a minute or two."

"Damn," Jude increased the pressure and speed a little, pleased when Sax gasped. "Can I have a replay?"

"I'm taken care of for the moment," Sax admitted apologetically, placing a kiss against Jude's neck.

"*That*," Jude pronounced, squeezing her, "does *not* feel taken care of. Or is that your usual state?"

Around you it seems to be. Sax shifted until they were face to face, and kissed her again, this time on the mouth. After a moment, she answered. "I think I need a bit more recovery time. Otherwise, I may need medical care."

"Oh, God—not that!" Laughing, Jude stopped the motion but kept a hand cupped loosely over her. She peered at the small bedside clock and groaned. "It's 3:00 a.m. But I no longer have any idea what day it is."

"Does it matter?"

"No," Jude replied, surprising herself, "it doesn't."

It didn't matter, and that fact was almost as astonishing as finding herself in bed with Saxon Sinclair. She didn't usually fall into bed with women just because the very sight of them turned her bones to jelly, but here they were. It had happened, and God, it was good. For the rest of this crazy night, all she wanted was to fill her hands with Sinclair's flesh, to taste her heat, to drown in her.

Without intending it, she'd moved her fingers lower, and it wasn't until she heard Sax groan close to her ear that she realized she had slipped inside her. "I'm sorry," she whispered quickly, beginning to pull out.

"No, stay," Sax murmured, shuddering faintly, "just...stay. I can't again, though—not yet."

Jude pressed closer until their bodies touched, joined inside and out. She enjoyed the quiet connection almost as much as the wild release they had just shared. "This'll do," she replied sleepily, "for the moment."

Sax chuckled softly as she closed her eyes, welcoming rest, if not sleep.

Turning carefully, so as not to awaken the slumbering woman in her arms, Sax squinted at the clock. She was astonished to see that it was a little after 8:00 a.m. Five hours of deep, uninterrupted sleep was unheard of for her, and she'd never slept with anyone that long in her life. Cautiously, she started to untangle her limbs from Jude's.

Jude protested, tightening her hold. "Where are you going?"

"Shower."

"Why? Are we leaving?" Jude blinked. The hazy morning light was mercifully dulled by the heavy drapes pulled across the single large window.

"Breakfast at Maddy's should not be missed," Sax remarked, leaning back enough to gaze the length of Jude's body. In the clear light of day, she was even more beautiful than the night before, and that had been almost more than Sax could bear.

"I see," Jude said, aware she was being studied. She supposed she should feel self-conscious, or at the very least, perhaps embarrassed by her complete and total loss of control the night before, but she was neither.

Since she had the opportunity, she stared back, confirming with her eyes what she had sensed with her hands and her lips hours before. Sinclair was all taut muscle and smooth flesh. Looking at her, Jude's mouth was abruptly dry and other parts of her were not. She gently turned Sax's face away with a finger on her jaw. "Oh, dear. This could be a problem."

"Hmm? What?" Sax asked absently, as she pushed the sheets lower to see the rest of the woman beside her.

"There's a new...mark...on your neck. I am *so* sorry," Jude confessed, finally nonplussed. She had absolutely no memory of doing that. *I never do that. Oh, hell—what am I saying? I never do* this!

"It's okay. If Maddy notices, she won't mention it. She already knows I'm all grown up," Sax replied, clearly distracted. She traced the incision on Jude's leg, her expression appraising. The scars were still thick, raised and red. There was a slight hollow in the middle of her calf where the muscle had been torn away.

"When did this happen?" she asked.

Jude stiffened slightly; she couldn't help it. No one had ever touched her there. "Five years ago."

"Car accident?" Sax held her gaze.

"No." Jude wanted to say more but her throat was so tight the words didn't come. It wasn't that she couldn't talk about it; it was just that when she did, some small part of the terror returned like an unwelcome visitor. Much, much better now than it had been, but she still had to struggle not to let the involuntary reaction frighten her. With difficulty, she murmured, "Subway crash."

Sax frowned, doing the math. "The one here in Manhattan?"

"Yes."

"That was bad," Sax said sympathetically. *And this looks like it was bad, too.* She hated thinking about Jude injured and in pain. The knowledge of what Jude must have suffered made her stomach clench, and she stroked the damaged skin softly, wishing she could undo the hurt.

"I was lucky," Jude stated. *Lucky to be alive; lucky you were there.* She sat up in bed, pulling the sheet up to her waist. "I remember you— at Bellevue. You were the first person I saw when I opened my eyes."

Sax stared at her, searching for a memory of Jude's face, wondering if she had helped her then, hoping that she had eased her fear. "I don't remember you," she said regretfully after a minute. "I'm sorry."

"There were dozens of injured, and I wasn't the worst." Jude smiled. "I imagine you were a bit busy that day—I wouldn't expect you to remember one patient. Then after the surgery, I was on the orthopedic floor, so you wouldn't have had any reason to know me."

"I still should remember," Sax insisted, running the backs of her fingers softly down Jude's cheek. "I can't imagine forgetting you." *I never will now.*

Jude shivered at the caress, her body tightening. They were very close, lips mere inches apart, leaning toward one another in the heavy silence.

"Do we have time?" she breathed as she watched Sax's eyes shade to purple.

"Yes," Sax said hoarsely, intent on the way Jude's lips parted as her color rose. "Yes."

They moved about gathering their clothes after a perfunctory, purely functional shower—the scarcity of hot water had precluded anything else. Separated for the first time in twelve hours, Jude watched silently as Sax toweled off and reached for her jeans. The physical distance between them brought both a disorienting sense of loss and an abrupt reemergence of reality. The night was gone, the connection they had shared nearly as fleeting as that distant moment at Bellevue when Jude had surrendered to Saxon Sinclair the first time.

"I don't know what to say," Jude admitted softly as she pulled on her T-shirt. *What does this mean? What happens next?*

Sax paused with her fly half buttoned. "Is there something you need to say?"

Jude thought about it. *There should be, shouldn't there? You don't just make love with someone for hours and then simply carry on, do you?* She looked at Sax who was regarding her steadily. Waiting.

"Yes, there is." Jude walked the few feet to Sax and put both hands on her face, cradling her jaw, fingers resting on her cheeks. Then she kissed her—tenderly at first, then more deeply, until Sax's hands came gently to her waist and pulled her near. They stood holding one another for a long moment after their lips parted, breathing each other in.

Then, as if by mutual agreement, they walked to the door and stepped out into the morning.

CHAPTER TWENTY

If it hadn't been for the lingering desire that the night had stirred but barely sated, Jude might have been lulled to sleep by the sun and the steady drone of the engine. But with her arms around Sax's waist and the scent of her so sharp where her cheek lay close to Sax's neck, Jude couldn't do anything but think of her. And thinking of her always seemed to bring a thousand images cascading into her consciousness, probably because before the previous afternoon she had observed Sax so many times on tape—often unawares, when she was most exposed. When she was most intriguing.

Those glimpses of the surgeon were fixed in her mind and powerful enough all by themselves to make her stomach clench, but now she carried the imprint of the woman on her skin, and inside her body. The visceral memory of Sax naked beside her, above her, stole Jude's breath and threatened to demolish her composure. *I need to get a grip or I'm going to embarrass both of us.*

Sax felt Jude clutch her convulsively and shouted into the wind, "Are you all right?"

"Yes," Jude shouted back. *Not really, but I will be as soon as I find where I left my sanity.*

"We'll be there soon." Thinking her passenger was probably just exhausted, Sax rested one gloved hand reassuringly over Jude's where it lay against her stomach. It surprised her to discover that she liked Jude's warm, solid presence behind her on the bike.

Often she rode to escape the residue of her work—to leave behind the frustrations of bureaucracy or to block out a particularly devastating trauma—but sometimes, most times really, she rode because she just couldn't rest. Eventually the rhythm of the highway passing underneath her and the demands of handling the big machine would relax her. Oddly, Jude's nearness accomplished the same thing, although feeling her curved close behind almost as they'd been in bed a few hours before did a bit more than just relax her.

Thankfully, her mind was clearer than it had been the previous night, because the pressure of Jude's breasts against her back brought a smile to her lips and a very lovely picture to mind, but at least she wasn't in danger of driving off the road and killing them both. A little low-level arousal she could handle. She hoped. Where Jude was concerned, it seemed that she had no warning when some totally unexpected surge of...*desire* seemed too civilized a word for what Jude made her feel—hunger, perhaps—would flare and burn wildly through her, vaporizing most of her control, too. Perhaps now that they'd had that one night, the fury would pass. She didn't have time to wonder if she was deluding herself as she slowed in the lane in front of Maddy's and coasted the big bike to a stop.

"We're here," Sax announced, pulling off her helmet and clipping it to the side of the machine.

"Does she know we're coming?" Jude thought to ask a little belatedly, wondering about their reception. She was beginning to think this might all be a joke or a hallucination. How had she come to be out in the middle of nowhere with a woman who made her skin melt? That is, when she wasn't making her too angry to see straight, of course.

"She'll have heard us." Sax laughed, easing her leg over the body of the bike and waiting while Jude climbed off.

Sure enough, as Jude followed her gaze, she spied the unmistakable visage of Madeleine Lane. "Wow. She's still beautiful."

"Yes, she is."

Maddy walked quickly down the flagstone path and through the gate. Standing on tiptoe, she kissed Sax's cheek, then turned to Jude and said warmly, "Hello. I'm Maddy."

Jude tried not to stare, but it wasn't often she got to meet a film legend. Plus, the woman's eyes were the precise shade of deep blue as Sax's and just as sharp. She introduced herself, hoping she didn't sound as awed as she felt.

"I suppose my granddaughter has had you up all night on some adventure or another," Maddy said, squeezing Jude's hand. "She always shows up here worn out and starving."

"Maddy," Sax sighed as Jude blushed.

"Never mind," Maddy said firmly, shepherding them toward the house. "Come inside and have something to eat. You can tell me all about it later."

Taking her grandmother's arm, Sax continued, "Jude is the filmmaker I told you about."

"Wonderful. I am so curious to know what things are like in the business these days." Maddy stopped on the porch. "Saxon, take your guest upstairs and show her where she can freshen up. Breakfast will be ready when you come down."

"Yes, ma'am," Sax said with a laugh as her grandmother left them.

"Madeleine Lane is your *grandmother?*" Jude asked *sotto voce* as they climbed the stairs.

"The one and only."

"Oh my God, what stories she must have to tell."

"I'm sure you'll get to hear them before long." Sax grinned, opening a door on one side of the central hallway. "There's a bathroom adjoining this bedroom. I can bring you some clean clothes, if you don't mind wearing more of mine."

"Oh, please, yes. I feel like I've been in these forever," Jude replied gratefully. *And I like wearing yours.*

"I'll be back in a little while, then."

"All right," Jude said as she watched Sax walk down the hall and open another door. She had a sudden urge to follow her, so instead, she turned resolutely into the guest room.

"Come in," Jude called in response to the soft knock on the door.

"Feeling better?" Sax asked, entering with an armful of clothes. Her hair was wet from the shower, and she wore fresh jeans and a clean T-shirt.

"Much." Jude pulled the top of the towel tighter over the tops of her breasts, acutely aware at that moment of just how little of her the material covered. She'd hoped that when she saw Sax again, some of the unsettling effect the surgeon had on her would have worn off. It hadn't. The woman was still gorgeous.

Sax's eyes flickered down the length of Jude's body before resting once more on her face. "Sorry," she said, noting Jude's blush. "I have you at a disadvantage." She held out the garments from a respectable distance of a few feet away. "The chinos might be a little long, but—"

"If they haven't been slept in, they'll be perfect." Jude grabbed them gratefully and held them to her chest. She stared at Sax and couldn't think of a thing to say. She could think of plenty of things she wanted to *do,* and none of them were possible for more reasons than she even wanted to consider. Not before breakfast, and not with Sax standing right there with a look in her eyes that made Jude's heart rate triple.

"I'll see you downstairs, then," Sax said, her voice oddly strained. *If I can't be in the same room with her without wanting to take her clothes off, we're going to have real problems at the hospital. God, I hope this passes quickly.*

"Yes, fine. I'll be right there."

Jude listened to Sax's footsteps receding down the hall and wanted nothing more in the world but to call her back.

❖

"And of course, you can't reshoot it, can you?" Maddy asked, passing Jude the pitcher of orange juice.

"No." Jude smiled as she emptied the last of the juice into her glass. She was thoroughly enjoying her discussion with Maddy about documentary filmmaking but wondered, with one part of her mind, where Sax had gone off to right after breakfast. "If we miss a moment of the action, it's gone for good. That's part of the reason it's a long-term project, and also why we're filming every chance we can. There's always the possibility that we won't get what we think we're getting, or that there'll be a technical glitch, or that something else will go wrong, and we'll miss the shot."

"Your photographer. Is she stubborn and pigheaded?"

"Aren't they all?"

"All the good ones," Maddy remarked with a sharp nod.

"Actually, Mel is terrific. She's independent, but she's willing to try to understand what I'm thinking, what I'm looking for. I'm spoiled now, and I want her on all my projects."

"Ah, yes, all the great directors form that kind of relationship with their cinematographers—Scorsese and Ballhaus, Kubrick and Alcott, Hitchcock and Burks." With a smile, she added, "But of course, they were well before your time."

"I'm afraid I am nowhere near the league of those people."

"Well, they also had actors who were willing to give them thirty takes until they got exactly what they wanted." Maddy's eyes twinkled. "I don't imagine Saxon is quite that cooperative."

"Ah." Jude colored. "She's got a lot to worry about in the middle of a trauma. How the scene comes out isn't one of her top priorities."

"Oh, well put and very diplomatic," Maddy said, laughing outright. "You needn't defend her to me, and I wasn't being critical. I know my granddaughter. She doesn't let much of anything get in her way."

Jude smiled, too. "No, she doesn't." She glanced at the clock, amazed to find they had been talking for nearly two hours. It was midafternoon already. With a start, she realized that in less than eighteen hours, they were due to be back in the hospital for another day and night of call. "Would you mind if I went to find Sax? I just want to know when she plans to leave."

"Of course not. It was wonderful to hear all about your work. You must come back and show me some of the dailies one of these days."

"I'd love to," Jude replied, thoroughly charmed.

"If you just follow the sound of the hammer, I'm sure you'll come across Saxon," Maddy called as Jude went out through the back screen door. Watching her go, Maddy thought what a strange coincidence it was that the first person Saxon ever brought home with her was a filmmaker. But she imagined it had less to do with that and more with the fact that Jude Castle was intelligent, energetic, and quite beautiful.

Jude found Sax inside a barn, a part of which had been converted into a garage. At least, she assumed that the denim-clad butt, which was all that was visible of the person leaning under the hood of a classic car, belonged to Sax, because she hadn't seen anyone else about the place.

"Sax?"

The surgeon straightened and reached for a nearby grease rag, carefully wiping her hands. She turned, grinning, and leaned against the fender of a gleaming black Rolls. "Maddy tire you out?"

"No, I fell in love with her in about two seconds."

"Most people do."

"She's wonderful, and she was a wonderful actress," Jude enthused, still so excited that she missed the change in Sax's expression. "She retired much too early—at the peak of her career, really. It was a shame, a great—"

She stopped, finally aware that Sax had grown pale. Jude had never seen her even the least bit distressed about anything. Angry, yes. But this wasn't anger—this was pain. "Sax? I'm sorry...what is it?"

"Nothing," Sax replied, her voice carefully neutral. "I just checked in with the hospital. Dennis Kline, my senior staff surgeon, says Aaron is holding his own."

"I'm glad," Jude said softly, meaning it, but also quite aware that Sax had changed the subject. She couldn't press her; she hadn't been invited to share that kind of intimacy. She almost laughed at the irony of that fact—they'd done everything but climb inside each other's skin, but she couldn't ask her what was hurting her. That bothered her more than she would have thought possible.

"Am I crazy, or are we on call again in the morning?" she finally asked.

"We are," Sax replied, relieved to be back on safe ground. "We can go back tonight or early in the morning."

Jude regarded her carefully but she could read nothing in her expression. She couldn't tell for certain if there was an invitation in Sax's words, and even if there was, she realized that she couldn't accept it. She couldn't spend the night here with even the slight possibility that there would be a repeat of the night before. Because she wouldn't be able to say no, and she wasn't at all sure it would be wise to say yes. She needed to get some perspective, she needed to decide what she was going to say to Lori, and she needed to figure out what the hell she was feeling for Saxon Sinclair—she couldn't do any of that if she was anywhere near her.

"Let's go tonight."

"Fine," Sax responded. "Let me finish here, and I'll get cleaned up. If you want to nap for a bit, you can use the room upstairs."

"Aren't you tired?" Jude was aware that she hadn't been invited to stay in the garage while Sax worked.

"I don't sleep much," Sax answered noncommittally.

"I'll probably be upstairs," Jude informed her quietly.

"I'll find you." Sax turned back to the engine. She did not watch as Jude walked away, but she was aware of every step taken, and she was also aware that she already missed her.

CHAPTER TWENTY-ONE

August 6, 6:57 a.m.

S orry I didn't return your calls," Jude said as she joined Mel in the cafeteria. "I got in pretty late." *And I didn't want to talk to anyone.*

They'd left Maddy's in the evening, and the ride back to Manhattan was uneventful. That is, if polite distance could be considered uneventful, especially after they'd been wrapped around each other for over an hour on a motorcycle. Their good nights were equally civil and proper.

"I'll see you tomorrow," Sax said, straddling her bike by the curb, the engine purring beneath her.

"Yes. Thank you for taking me to Maddy's." Jude stood on the sidewalk, her hands in the pockets of the borrowed chinos, her own clothes rolled up under her arm. "I loved talking to her."

"I know she enjoyed it, too." Sax turned her helmet around and around in her hands. She seemed to be waiting. "Well," she pulled on her helmet, "good night, then."

"Good night."

Jude watched her pull away, gunning the engine as she roared off down the street, and berated herself for feeling so let down. *What the hell is wrong with me? What did I expect Sax to say? We slept together. Okay, fine. People do it all the time. It's natural and normal and doesn't have to mean anything beyond the moment.*

She was still mentally chastising herself for expecting something more.

"Jude?"

"Hmm?" Jude asked distractedly. Her mind was still on the image of Sax disappearing into the night, and the loneliness that had followed—a feeling foreign to her. Focusing on Mel, she said, "I'm sorry if you were worried."

"No, it's okay," Mel assured her quickly. "When I didn't hear from you, I figured you wanted a break from all of this for a while."

"Not from you, Mel," Jude corrected firmly, studying her friend over the top of her coffee cup. Mel looked about as worn out as Jude felt, although she'd had six hours of sleep after she'd finally gotten to bed.

For whatever reason, sleep hadn't made her feel any better. That was probably because her dreams, populated by dark faceless figures racing through rain-swept, foreboding landscapes, had been permeated with a sense of danger. *Jesus, talk about classic anxiety dreams. How original.* Annoyed with herself, she mentally shook off the lingering unease.

"You said in your message that you wanted to talk about something. Is there a problem with the project?"

"No," Melissa answered with a shake of her head. Of course that would be Jude's first thought. For all their affection, they rarely talked about anything really personal. Jude never seemed to have the need to do so, and her perfectly neat, orderly life always made Melissa feel as if she were a fuck-up whenever *she* had a problem. Not that Jude ever said that or even suggested it. It was just that, somehow, whenever Melissa compared her own life to Jude's, she felt inadequate.

"It's...uh...not work."

"Is everything all right?"

"Yeah," Melissa replied in a tone that suggested otherwise, poking at the toast on her plate. "I guess so."

"Mel, I can tell that's bullshit. Spit it out."

"Well, it's just that...what happened with Aaron. It kind of shook me up."

"Of course," Jude said softly. "It was horrible. And terrifying."

"I mean," Melissa continued as if she hadn't heard Jude's reply, her gaze slightly unfocused, as if she were reliving the moment, "we've been in tight spots once or twice. Remember that time we thought the tanks were going to start shelling right where we had our cameras set up?"

"I remember."

"But it didn't feel personal then, you know? It almost didn't feel real. It was—like—uh-oh, we're in the wrong place. Better run like hell now. It was exciting in a crazy kind of way."

"Maybe after the fact it was," Jude acknowledged with a grimace. "For a few seconds there, I thought I was going to scream or throw up."

"Yeah, me, too." Melissa smiled wanly. "But ten minutes later, when they just lumbered past and left us with nothing to film, we laughed."

"Nerves."

"Well, I haven't laughed yet. Seeing someone I know almost die like that freaked me out."

"Do you need some time off? I can handle the camera."

"No, it's just that...I might have screwed up."

Melissa looked so miserable that Jude couldn't imagine what she was talking about. "Mel," she said gently, "what happened?"

"After you went to the on-call room to wait for word about Aaron..." If Melissa had been standing, she would have been shuffling her feet. But, as it was, she just rearranged her silverware incessantly.

"Yes?" Jude prompted, now really worried. "Mel, hey, come on. It's me."

In a rush, Melissa blurted, "I was on my way out of the hospital, and I realized I was starving, so I detoured by here to get a late lunch, and I ran into Deb, and we started talking, and then we went out for a drink, and then we went to her place, and then we...ended up in bed."

Nonplussed, Jude stared, her mouth opening and closing but no sound coming out.

"Oh man—I *knew* you'd be upset. I've never fooled around before when we were working," Melissa said hurriedly. "Well, almost never. That one time with the soccer player—but that was after we'd already finished the shoot. Well, I mean we were *almost* done."

"I'm not upset."

"And that one time in Brussels, with the airline attendant, that didn't—" Melissa stopped abruptly and stared. "You're not?"

"No."

"But I know how uptig...um...how strongly you feel about separating work and personal stuff."

"Do I?" Jude asked quietly, thinking about that for a minute as if it were a new concept. Actually, it was more the case that, for her, there *wasn't* any difference. Work *was* personal—more than that, it was her passion—and she didn't want any extraneous diversions like relationships to interfere with it. None had, until recently. "Well, sometimes things just...happen, don't they?"

"They do?" Melissa asked, a note of incredulity in her voice. "Right! They do, absolutely, they do."

Jude slowly and carefully spread cream cheese on her bagel, wondering if it had all been some kind of group psychosis—an emotional time warp, a bizarre twist in the fabric of reality—like a David Lynch movie. That would explain it. But then, if that were the case, it should be over. And every time she thought about waking up beside Saxon Sinclair, her skin grew hot and her stomach did flips. It didn't seem to be over.

"Jude?" Melissa queried in a puzzled tone. "Is that it?"

"I'm really not hungry," Jude announced, pushing her bagel away. She glanced at her friend, who was regarding her with a mixture of curiosity and concern, and sighed. "Are you okay with what happened?"

For the first time, Melissa looked like herself. Shrugging, a rakish grin on her face, she said, "Well, yeah."

"Is Deb?"

"Seems to be."

"Are the two of you going to have any trouble working together?"

"Don't see why we should," Melissa replied seriously.

"Then I don't see a problem." Jude stood to leave. "Just try to save the personal stuff for your own time, okay?"

"Right," Melissa said hurriedly. "It was just—you know—one night. Just one of those crazy things. It's not serious or anything."

"Yes, I know. Just one night. Nothing serious."

"So," Melissa gathered the remains of her breakfast and followed Jude to the tray disposal area, "are *you* okay? With what happened?"

"What do you mean?" Jude retorted sharply.

"With Aaron," Melissa replied. *Why do I feel as if we're speaking two different languages?*

"I'm fine. Come on, let's book a conference room. I want to schedule an on-tape interview with Deb as a follow up to the shooting."

She really just needed to get back to work, back on track. Everything would make sense then, and if it didn't...well, it wouldn't matter. Because she wouldn't have to think about it.

"Good idea," Melissa agreed, delighted to leave the topic of her indiscretion behind. She'd save her questions about what the hell was wrong with Jude for another time.

August 6, 7:51 a.m.

Sax stopped as someone called her name and smiled when she turned to see Pam approaching. "Hi."

"Hi," Pam said warmly. "I just ran into the plastics resident, and he says they're available this afternoon to harvest rib grafts for me. I'd like to take that boy in bed two to the OR if we can get him on the schedule. I've got office hours until noon, but after that, I want to debride that clot from the frontal sinuses so that plastics can plug the holes with bone."

"He's running a fever, Pam." Sax propped one shoulder against the wall outside the double doors of the TICU. "And Kline says his blood pressure's been all over the place since last night. He's not in great shape for surgery."

Pam shrugged and replied with a hint of irritation in her voice. "No guts no glory, Saxon. He's not going to get a lot better with us just standing around waving our hands in the air. If that intradural hematoma turns into an abscess, we won't have to worry about his blood pressure because he'll never wake up at all."

"Go ahead, put him on the schedule," Sax relented, rubbing her eyes briefly. She was tired and that was odd, because she was almost never aware of fatigue no matter how long she went without sleep.

Of course, she'd never gotten to bed at all after dropping Jude off at her apartment. She hadn't been able to stop replaying the events of the night before. Remembering the way it felt to be with Jude, her whole system had kicked into hyperdrive. She'd been ready to climb the walls.

Forcing herself to focus on Pam, she added, "I'll clear him if he's stable for the next few hours. If his pressure bottoms out, though, you'll have to wait."

"Thanks," Pam said, satisfied. Her attention shifted abruptly as she noticed people coming down the hall toward them. "Your fan club has arrived."

"What?" Sax recognized that predatory glint in Pam's eye. She looked back over her shoulder, and her eyes met Jude's. The filmmaker was just a few feet away with Melissa beside her. Sax smiled, suddenly feeling energized. "Good morning."

"Hi," Jude said softly, slowing as she drew near. She was pleased that she managed not to blush, because Sax's gaze was unexpectedly intense. "Is Deb—"

"Inside." Sax gestured toward the unit with a nod.

"Thanks."

"Sure."

Sax followed the two women with her eyes as they walked past and disappeared inside.

"So, how's it going with her?"

"What?" The word virtually erupted from Sax.

"Whoa! Just asking," Pam exclaimed, studying Sax through narrowed eyes. "They're filming downstairs, right? Must be a royal pain in the balls having them underfoot all the time. Although," she added with a suggestive laugh, "the scenery is nice."

Sax worked to hide her annoyance, although she wasn't sure what bothered her more—Pam's curiosity or the way she'd surveyed Jude as she walked by. Pam had a way of appraising women as if they were an exotic food group.

"It's not that big a problem. Jude's accommodated to working with a small crew, and she doesn't interfere with Deb's training."

"Jude. That's that very attractive redhead, right?"

"Yes."

"Nice. Is she gay?"

"Jesus, Pam," Sax exploded angrily. "Don't you ever quit?"

"Why, Saxon, your temper is showing," Pam chided with a laugh. "And everyone says how cool and unflappable you are, too. I'll take that as a yes."

"Why don't you ask *her*?"

"I might," Pam responded thoughtfully, "since I can't seem to tempt you."

"I've got to get back to work," Sax said, ignoring the comment.

"If I don't hear from you, I'll assume that case is on." Pam was all business again.

"Fine."

Pam watched Sax push through the double doors with an impatient shove and wondered exactly what she'd said to make her so angry. Whatever was going on, it had something to do with that enchanting redhead. Perhaps the lovely filmmaker would be interested in dinner. She glanced at her watch and sighed. *Well, that intriguing possibility will have to wait until later in the day, but it certainly is a most pleasant thought.*

CHAPTER TWENTY-TWO

August 6, 1:47 p.m.

L et's do this somewhere less formal," Melissa suggested, surveying the conference room with distaste. "This place looks too much like a boardroom."

"You're right. Too impersonal," Jude agreed. She glanced at Deb. "Got any ideas?"

"How about the roof?"

The roof—Sax's favorite sanctuary. It was difficult preventing images of Sax—sweat drenched and exuberant with a basketball in her hands, pensive and still in the moonlight—from distracting her from her schedule, but Jude managed to chase the memories away with an impatient mental shrug. "Good idea, guys. We can get the skyline and the heliport in the background."

Melissa hefted her camera and the three of them trooped out.

Interview—Dr. Deborah Stein
August 6, 2:00 p.m.

"What were you thinking when those boys came into the trauma admitting area with their guns out?" Jude asked. Out of the corner of her eye, she saw Melissa give her the thumbs-up sign. *Good. Sound and visuals are okay.*

"I didn't think anything at first," Deb admitted. "You learn not to pay attention to peripheral activity when you're operating or in the midst of a crisis. People walk in and out of the operating room, the radio might be playing, the anesthesiologist is talking to a student a few inches away—it doesn't matter—while the pressure's on, you don't hear them or even see them."

With her back to the cement wall at the roof's edge and her strawberry blond hair blowing around in the wind, Deb, Jude thought, still looked like the young athlete the country fell in love with during the Olympics. But there were lines at the corners of her eyes now and something harder in her gaze that had been missing before. *She's getting battle scars.*

"How do you filter those things out?"

Deb shrugged. "You forget everything except the moment. No mortgage worries, no car problems, no relationship issues. Just you and the case." She grinned, and this time her eyes smiled, too. "That's where I was that night—in the zone. I was concentrating on the patient and nothing else registered."

"So you didn't realize for a second what was happening?" Jude remembered vividly the commotion at the door and the shouting and Aaron...

"Not until I heard the shot. That got my attention. I used to shoot pistols in competition when I was a teenager. I know what a gun sounds like."

"Even when it was so completely...out of context?"

"A hospital isn't a church. There's nothing sacred here—only life and death." Deb grimaced. "I've taken care of plenty of felons apprehended during a crime. I've treated patients handcuffed to the bedrails with armed cops standing guard. As soon as I heard the shot, I knew we were in trouble."

"And your reaction? What made you put yourself between the gunman and the boy you were treating? What made you risk your life?" *What made Sax risk hers?*

"Totally automatic," Deb said quickly. "I didn't even think about it."

"But there must have been something behind that response, that desire to shield your patient?"

"I wish I could say there was." Deb looked uncomfortable for the first time. "But I wasn't being heroic. It was just that...he was mine, you know? I was the first one to see him, he was *my* patient; it was my responsibility to see that he didn't die." She shook her head ruefully and her gaze traveled away from Jude to fix on some point in the distance. "Believe me, if I'd had time to think, I don't know what I would have done."

"It was still a very courageous thing to do," Jude said. Apparently, talking about surgery was a lot easier for Deb than exploring those highly emotional few moments.

"Maybe. But I can't take too much credit for it. I told you—I wasn't even thinking."

"But it's what we do when we don't have time to rationalize, or even to reason, that really tells the truth about us, don't you think?"

"Yeah, I do think that," Deb replied softly. "Now, what Sinclair did—*that* was brave. She knew that guy had just shot Aaron. She knew he wanted to shoot my patient. And she knew he was probably going to shoot somebody else, but that didn't stop her from stepping in front of you."

"No," Jude murmured faintly, "it didn't."

"I can tell you this"—Deb was emphatic—"Sinclair knew *exactly* what she was doing. She always does. That's brave."

And you've got a bit of a case of hero worship, Jude thought fondly. But she couldn't help wondering if Sax really had acted intentionally and not out of some basic instinct. *And if she did? What would that mean?*

"You both deserve a lot of credit." It was all Jude could manage as she raised a hand to Melissa to signal that the interview was a wrap.

"Cripes," Deb said, shaking her shoulders as if to loosen them. "That's nerve racking. It's a good thing it was you behind the camera, Cooper."

"Oh yeah?" Melissa was playful. "And why's that?"

"I trusted you to make me look good on the tape."

"Well, it was a challenge, but I managed," Melissa jibed, thinking that the one thing Deb Stein did *not* need was to look any better. She turned the heads of too many women to count as it was, and when the documentary started airing, she'd be inundated with calls for dates. Melissa considered that revelation for a second and decided it was a good thing she *didn't* have any long-term plans with this one. *Yep, good thing, all right.*

Personal Project Log—Castle
August 7, 12:20 a.m.

Apparently, this is one of those aberrations that occur often enough that neither Deb nor Sax seem surprised by it. Specifically, nothing much has happened all night. Well, nothing compared to the way things have been all the other nights on call. Around 8:00 last evening, two people were transported by chopper following a fender bender, but both of them were evaluated, screened with X-rays, and admitted overnight for observation only. No surgery. Then again, at a little after 11:00, a young man was brought in with a broken jaw he got on the losing end of a bar brawl. No other injuries. Plastic surgery was contacted, and they scheduled him to have his jaws wired together in the morning. And that was it.

Deb went off a few minutes ago to get some sleep, and I'm about to follow her example. Still, I have this uncomfortable feeling that I'm going to miss something. Deb said that she would much rather be working if she needed to be on call. It was better, she said, to be up all night in the operating room than trying to sleep while expecting that at any moment she might have to get up again. Work rather than sleep. It's astonishing how your entire life gets turned around in this place.

Jude clicked off her recorder and thought about what she had just said. *Oh yeah—life certainly does get turned around in this place.* Sighing, she let herself into her on-call room.

August 7, 3:13 a.m.

It was the middle of the night, and she couldn't sleep. Melissa was breathing softly in the darkness across the room, clearly sleeping the sleep of the innocent at heart. Or the untroubled of mind. Jude had been trying to occupy herself with plans for the project—writing script in her head and editing sections of tape she had reviewed the day before—anything that might tire her mind and help her to relax. Her usual tricks didn't help. After forty fruitless minutes, she thought she would start cursing aloud. That was when she decided to go in search of company.

One thing she had learned was that, in the hospital, there was always someone up and about. The nurses on night shift were bright and energetic, because for them this was their normal workday. There were usually one or two surgery residents camped out in the OR lounge, either waiting for cases to start or unwinding after one had finished. If it'd been a week earlier, Aaron would have been in the trauma admitting area, reviewing billing forms or checking an order status or simply waiting for the inevitable moment when the phone would ring or the radio would chirp to announce incoming patients. But of course, Aaron wasn't there now.

Even though she knew he wasn't there, Jude glanced automatically into the trauma bay as she walked down the hall toward the elevators. The bright overhead lights were off, but a row of flickering fluorescents under the cabinets on the wall above the long counter where the doctors and nurses did their paperwork was illumination enough for her to see the figure bent over the chessboard.

From the door, Jude asked, "Planning the next campaign?"

Sax turned at the sound of her voice, raising one eyebrow as she answered, "You can never have too much in the way of strategy, don't you agree?"

"Honestly?" Jude succumbed to an exhausted shrug. "I don't know. I never seemed to have any—where chess was concerned." *Or anything else, now that I think of it—except work.*

"No, I imagine that you didn't need one."

Perhaps it was the hour, or the unnatural sense of limbo a night without trauma alerts produced, but Sax couldn't seem to call upon her normal sense of distance as she took in the dark shadows beneath Jude's eyes and the weary slump of her shoulders. Gently, she observed, "You look worn out. Shouldn't you be getting some rest?"

"Can't. I already tried that." Jude noted that Sax looked pretty much as she always did, unruffled and in control. It was infuriating—nothing ever seemed to faze her. "You know, I don't think I ever remember you going to bed at night."

"No?" Sax asked, her voice rising in quiet incredulity.

"I meant when you were here working," Jude replied, blushing, remembering very clearly the two of them sleeping in each other's arms. It surprised her that Sax would refer even obliquely to that night they had spent together. She had assumed that Sax would simply forget it and move on, even though *she* couldn't forget it. Was she wrong in thinking that Sax had forgotten, or at least wanted to?

"Would you like a game?" Sax inquired, gesturing to the board. It wasn't the time or the place to explain about why she was often up around the clock, and she doubted it ever would be.

"Why not?"

"Well, one good reason might be that my ego is fragile, and I can only take losing so many times," Sax remarked dryly. "On the other hand, considering that you're so exhausted you're about to fall down, I'm hopeful that I'll have an advantage."

"I know that's not it," Jude said softly as she approached, remembering the almost courtly way Sax had offered her the borrowed clothes that morning at Maddy's after her shower. It had been both touching and heartbreaking, because all she had wanted was for Sax to reach for her. She had only needed the weakest excuse to let the towel fall. Strange how she was learning to regret not the actions she had taken, but the things she'd left undone. "You're too chivalrous to take advantage."

As if reading Jude's mind, Sax recalled those precarious few moments two days ago when her desire warred with caution. She blushed, and the fact that she did surprised her more than anything she could remember. As Jude crossed the room to her now, she pictured her fresh from the shower, her skin flushed a light rose from the heat and the energy between them, faint beads of water still clinging to the tips of her lashes. *So desirable.* She ached to touch her just as strongly now as she had that day.

"Sometimes I regret that caution," Sax murmured, not even realizing she had spoken aloud.

"Do you?" Jude stood very close by.

"Yes," Sax whispered, glancing up into Jude's green eyes.

The moment held, grew—shimmering in the air around them, incandescent with silent yearning. Jude smiled wistfully and Sax smiled back, a faint curve of mouth that spoke of uncertainty and regret.

"Shall we play?" Jude asked.

"Are you sure?"

"Yes."

Chapter Twenty-Three

August 7, 4:59 a.m.

"Checkmate."

"No."

"Sorry."

Sax pushed back in her chair with a sigh, arched her back to work out the kinks she had acquired in the last two hours, and rubbed her face vigorously with both hands. "Well, that was pathetic."

"Not really," Jude said sincerely. Then, fixing Sax with a pointed stare, she added, "And you know it."

"Okay," Sax amended with a grin, "but it would have been *less* pathetic if I'd won a game."

"You came clos...uh, closer."

"Uh-huh," the surgeon agreed with a grimace. *"Closer* being the operative word. You take no prisoners, Ms. Castle."

"I didn't expect you'd want me to."

"You're right, I don't. I want to be killed cleanly and with as little suffering beforehand as possible."

"I'll remember that," Jude replied with a smile.

She glanced at the clock, already regretting that their private interlude would soon be interrupted by the morning routine. Any minute now, Sax would announce it was time for her to go to the TICU for rounds, and the quiet spell of peaceful communion would be broken. Odd, how relaxed Sax had seemed the last few hours. Of all the things Jude would call the formidable surgeon, relaxed was not one of them. It was nice, very nice, to be alone with her like this.

"Let's get some air," Sax suggested, reluctant to say goodbye. She didn't need to look at a watch to know the time; in fact, she never wore one. She always knew. "The sun's about to come up."

Jude was too surprised at the invitation to answer with more than a quick nod as Sax jumped to her feet. *Where does she get the energy?* Walking quickly to keep pace, Jude resisted the urge to reach out and hold her hand. Just to touch her.

A few minutes later, they stood side by side on the rooftop wall, resting on folded arms, watching the sky threaten to burst into color. It was serene in the way those last few moments of the night can be just before morning breaks and the demands of the day begin.

"What will you do today?" Jude asked. She probably shouldn't ask, but she couldn't help herself. She wanted to know where Sax went—what she did—when she changed into her jeans and walked out the door. *What do you think? Who do you touch?*

"After rounds?" Sax mused, staring straight ahead, caught off guard by the question. "Stop by the office, check in with Naomi. Make sure everything is under control there. If it's not too hot later, maybe go for a run in the park." She turned her head to study Jude. *I'll wish we were on the cycle headed for—anywhere—as long as it's just us. As long as you lean against my back and wrap your arms around me.* "How about you?"

"Mel and I will review some footage. I'll stop by the office, check with my secretary and the production crew. Make sure everything is under control there. If it's not too hot later, maybe go to the gym."

Sax grinned a little ruefully. "That's scary, you know?"

"Yes," Jude agreed solemnly, "it is."

"Can I buy you lunch somewhere?" Sax asked impulsively. Before there was time for an answer, the sun crowned behind Jude's shoulder, and the light against the side of Jude's face made her glow. Softly, without thinking, Sax murmured, "Jesus—you're beautiful."

"The air must be thinner up here on the roof," Jude whispered, watching Sax's gaze flicker over her face, down her body. "Because it seems to do something to your judgment. As in, it disappears."

"Just mine?" Sax asked, the long supple fingers of one hand tracing the edge of Jude's jaw, ending with a fingertip against the corner of her mouth. "Or does that include you, too?"

"It definitely includes me," Jude said huskily, turning her head to catch Sax's finger between her lips. Gently, she bit it.

"Then I...think," Sax gasped, "we'll be safe, if...we...stick together."

"You, Dr. Sinclair," Jude stated ominously, stepping close and placing both hands on the back of Sax's neck, "are absolutely anything... *but*...safe."

Their lips were too close for anything but the kiss that began hungry and rapidly became more. Their bodies fused along every sinewy plane, and their embrace pulled flesh to flesh in a perfectly matched eruption of desire. Jude moaned, or it might have been Sax, as their hands lifted shirts to slide under—stroking skin—and their hips thrust slowly—stoking fire.

"You make me crazy," Sax breathed into Jude's ear. "Like nobody ever. Do you know that?"

"Am I supposed to apologize?" Jude murmured, running her tongue lightly over Sax's neck. "Because I don't intend to." She was having trouble keeping her balance because her thighs were trembling, and some part of her brain registered a dangerous rush of blood into a very concentrated spot between her legs. Her ears began buzzing as Sax's hand slipped upward to cup her breast. With the last fragment of her reasoning mind, she choked out, "You can't do that to me here."

"Why not?" Sax growled against her mouth. "Just give me a minute."

Jude rocked back, her eyes hazy. "Because it won't take a minute."

"Even better."

"Sax," Jude warned, stilling Sax's hand with her own, "if you keep it up, you'll have to carry me down the stairs. I'll never be able to walk."

"*I* can't now," Sax murmured, watching Jude's lips and imagining them on her flesh, easing her torment with knowing strokes. "I'm already too hot, too swollen, and—"

Jude pressed her fingers to Sax's lips. "Stop. Right. There." She felt Sax's smile curve under her fingertips. "Hold that thought..."

"Which one?"

"The one that just made your eyes go purple," Jude breathed.

"That would be the one where your mouth was on me and—"

"Enough," Jude groaned. "I mean it. I'll have a stroke."

"That's okay. I'm a doctor."

"I want you," Jude said very clearly, her gaze locked on Sax's.

"I want you so much I can't think. But even if it's quick, it won't be enough. I won't be able to stop if we start."

"When?" Sax asked urgently. "This morning, this afternoon? Forget lunch, we'll..."

"Sax," Jude said softly, regretfully, "I can't today. Tonight..."

Sax's eyes darkened with something that might have been disappointment, but before Jude could explain, the code beeper blared.

"Son of a bitch," Sax cursed, already moving away, and Jude knew that when she caught up to her, there would be no time for explanations.

The day had dawned with a vengeance.

August 7, 11:47 a.m.

Jude stood naked by the bed, toweling her wet hair as the door to the on-call room opened.

"Oops, sorry," Melissa said, quickly backing away, pulling the door closed.

"It's okay," Jude called. "I'm getting dressed right now."

Slowly, Melissa stepped back inside, grinning sheepishly. "I didn't know, you know."

"And if you had?" Jude snapped crossly. "Aren't we both a bit beyond adolescent peek and grope games, for God's sake?"

Melissa gaped, at a loss for words. There was fury in those green eyes.

Jude threw the towel on the floor and reached for her clothes, pulling on her underwear before glancing at Mel again. When she saw her friend's stricken expression, she stopped, one leg in her jeans, the other still bare. "I'm sorry, Mel. Damn, I really am."

Melissa sat down on the end of the other bed. "You want to tell me what's going on? You've been upset since you got here yesterday morning, but this—I've never seen you like this."

"Are Sinclair and Deb still in the operating room with that gunshot wound?"

"Yes, and you're changing the subject. Or avoiding the question. One of those."

"Not really." Jude smiled reluctantly. "I'm angry because I have a luncheon date with Lori, and I wanted to see Sax before I left, and now I won't be able to."

"Do you want me to give her a message?"

"Yeah." Jude pulled on her shirt. "Tell her I'm crazy about her, and I'm going to lose my mind if I don't get my hands on her soon."

Melissa stared, astounded. Jude's statement was so out of character she couldn't even feel jealous. "Um...which one am I giving that message to? Lori or Sinclair?"

For a long moment Jude was silent, the words she had spoken echoing in her head. Then, knowing with irrefutable clarity that she had meant every one, she sighed with something very close to peace.

"Sax."

"Whoa."

"Uh-huh, that about sums it up," Jude agreed. She crossed the room to sit next to Melissa on the bed.

"How much have I missed?" Mel asked. "Like when, where, and how in the *hell* did you pull this off?"

"Two days ago, a motel, and I have no idea."

"Oh my God. You are my queen." Mel's voice held a touch of awe.

Jude burst out laughing. "Trust me—you don't want me in charge the way I'm feeling right now."

"Which is?"

"Totally unlike myself. Thoroughly irrational, insane—all my nerve endings are raw. I can't think."

Well, it's about fucking time. Melissa chose her words carefully, because the one thing she cared about most was Jude's feelings. "What does Sinclair say to all of this?"

"Nothing."

"Nothing?" Melissa asked incredulously. "You two haven't talked about it?"

"Not exactly, no," Jude replied. "Well, *exactly* no, really. It happened out of the blue, and then we were both—I don't know—afraid of it, maybe? I know I was thrown by how...strongly I felt. How incredibly, unbelievably, ama—"

"I got the picture, Jude," Melissa interrupted dryly.

"I'm sorry, Mel. I don't know how to explain because I've never experienced anything quite so...so...disorienting and unexpected."

Love, Jude. That's love.

Melissa got up and began to pace, working to separate her own underlying disappointment from her desire to be a friend. She'd always known, deep inside, that nothing would ever come of her unrequited passion for Jude, but seeing her now, hearing her talk about Sinclair, she felt the loss just the same.

Refocusing, she asked, "And you're meeting Lori today?"

Jude glanced at her watch and began gathering her things to leave. "In exactly twenty-seven minutes."

"What are you going to say?" Melissa queried.

"The truth, I hope, as soon as I figure out what that is."

Lori put down her fork and signaled the waiter.

"Check, please," she said when he drew near. As she counted out bills, she spoke to Jude without looking up. "Let's walk, and you can tell me what you want to tell me."

Jude set her silverware aside. "Lori—"

"You called and said you wanted to talk," Lori pointed out reasonably as she put the check and the money on the table. "I can tell you're not interested in lunch. It's also the second meal in a row where you haven't eaten, and I'm going to start taking it personally. Let's get out of here."

Jude could only agree, so she followed Lori outside into the midday sun. "We'd better at least find some shade in the park," she suggested as they crossed the street in front of the Plaza Hotel and walked toward Central Park.

"Good idea. So," Lori asked, "what is it?"

Jude intended to tell her as much as she knew herself, and she didn't know any other way except to say it directly. "I've met a woman. We're not involved exactly, but we've slept together." She glanced at Lori's face, not knowing what to expect.

"Go ahead," Lori said softly, her expression serious.

"I...I want to see more of her," Jude continued, her feelings becoming clearer as she spoke. She laughed deprecatingly. "I'm not good at juggling two relationships. Hell, I'm not good with one. I needed you to know about this."

"Why don't we sit down over here." Lori indicated a wooden bench under the shade of a maple as Jude took a deep breath. She stretched an arm along the back of the bench and regarded Jude contemplatively. "I have a feeling I'm not going to like where this is going."

"I know it's...sudden. If I'd had any warning—"

"That's not what I meant," Lori said. "I'm glad you're telling me. I'm just concerned about *why.*"

Jude stared, thoroughly confused.

"Is this the first time you've seen someone else since we've been dating?" Lori asked.

"Yes."

"We never said we'd be monogamous. I've seen other women on occasion the last few months. Not steadily, but now and then. When you've been away or just...busy. I assumed you were doing the same when I didn't see you for a while."

"No, I just didn't," Jude said with a shrug. "Honestly, I really *was* busy, and what we had was fine."

"So, what's changed? Why can't we still see each other? I don't care if you're seeing someone else." Lori laughed briefly and amended, "Well, I care *some*...but if I had expected monogamy, I would have talked to you about it. I love your company, and you know I love you in bed. We don't need to change that."

Jude nodded, because everything Lori said made sense and she understood it perfectly. But she knew—no, she *felt*—that what had previously been enough wasn't now. "This may sound completely ridiculous, because I enjoy seeing you, too, and it's always been... good...between us physically, but I...I just can't. I can't seem to keep her out of my mind."

"Ah." Lori heard the tremor in Jude's voice and knew what she'd left unsaid. "This *is* serious."

"I don't know," Jude confessed. "Maybe not for her, but it certainly is for me. I need to know what's happening. I don't think I'll feel comfortable dating you until I do."

"I can't say I don't care," Lori admitted, resting her fingers on Jude's shoulder. "I'll miss you, Jude. If it turns out differently than you expect, if things...don't go anywhere, will you call me? We have something that works. I'd like to keep it if we can."

"I'm sorry, if I've hurt you."

Lori shook her head. "I never asked you for more than what we had because I wanted to keep things uncomplicated between us. That was my choice." She paused, thinking about what she had just said, wondering if she'd been totally honest with herself. "If you've found something that you can't let go of, don't. Don't give it up."

Touched by the faint sadness in her smile, Jude leaned over and kissed her gently on the lips. "Thank you."

Chapter Twenty-Four

August 7, 5:47 p.m.

I'm sorry, but I can't give you that number."

"Look"—Jude attempted valiantly to contain her temper while reminding herself that it was not Naomi Riley's fault that she couldn't find Sax—"it's important that I talk to her. If you can't give me her number, how about this—could you page her and ask her to return my call?"

"Yes, I can do that. But I have to warn you, it's very possible she's left the city and won't respond."

"What about letting me have her grandmother's number, then?" Jude tried.

"I'm afraid that would not be possible," The tone was distinctly cooler now. "Ms. Castle, it's already after 5:00 p.m. Dr. Sinclair left the hospital shortly after she finished surgery. She was on call last night, and I don't expect her back for at least twenty-four hours, if then. The best I can do for you is to page her."

"All right, I understand." Jude wrote her number down for the unbending secretary. "Please tell her it's important if you reach her."

Two hours later, she was still pacing the confines of her apartment and waiting for the phone to ring. The rational thing would simply be to wait until the next time she was scheduled to be on call with the trauma team and try to find time to talk to Sax then. Forty-eight hours—less than that now. That wasn't very long to wait. Except she knew that she couldn't. All she could think about was the last few moments on the rooftop that morning—the way it had felt to hold Sax and be held by her.

The hunger lingered still. And it wasn't only remembering the physical desire that made her so anxious to see Sax. Those fleeting seconds when pain and disappointment had flickered through Sax's normally guarded eyes tormented her. She couldn't bear for the misunderstanding to continue a moment longer.

It didn't even matter that it didn't make sense, because very little *had* since almost the first moment she'd seen her. Maybe from the first instant she had opened her eyes five years before, alone and in pain, and found something solid to hold on to in Saxon Sinclair's sure, steady gaze. When it had started, where it had started, how it had started— none of that mattered anymore. All she knew was that she wanted her.

When she accepted that Sax was not going to call, Jude marched into her bedroom and threw a few articles of clothing into an overnight bag. On her way out the door, she grabbed her car keys off the hook along with a light jacket and hoped that her sense of direction did not fail her.

❖

Jude tapped hesitantly at the door, holding her breath while searching furiously for a greeting or some kind of explanation that would make sense. Unfortunately, none came to her, and when Maddy opened the door, Jude simply said, "I know it's late, but is she here?"

"Yes," Maddy said, as if it were the most natural thing in the world for her to receive late-night visitors, or for her granddaughter to arrive disheveled and haunted looking, only to disappear immediately into the barn. "She's out back making a racket, and apparently, she's forgotten about supper. I'd be grateful if you could get her inside for a meal."

"I'll try." Jude couldn't imagine what Madeleine Lane thought of her showing up like this. But the smile and warmth in the other woman's voice alleviated some of her anxiety. That, coupled with her relief at actually finding Sax at the end of this ill-planned search, probably accounted for her next unexpected question. "Is she all right?"

"That's a question I don't know how to answer," Maddy said truthfully. "It's very hard to tell with her, but I have a feeling she'll be a lot better now. Why don't you go find her and let her know you're here? You can go through the house and out through the kitchen. I imagine the noise will direct you after that."

"Yes, thank you," Jude said gratefully.

❖

The sounds of hammering led her through the dark and across the yard to the barn where a light shone through the cracks around the side door. She opened it carefully and stepped into the dimly lit interior. Sax was across the room, her back to Jude, nailing a sheet of plywood to the wall.

"Sax?" Jude called.

Still turned away, Sax paused, hammer in hand, her left forearm braced against the wood, a long nail held between thumb and forefinger. Jude's voice, so distinctively rich and smooth, reached out to her like a caress.

"The window blew out in a storm. I'm just covering the gap until I can order a new one."

"Do you need any help?"

"No," Sax answered slowly, driving in the nail and then carefully placing her tools on a wooden bench to her right. She pivoted, her expression wary. "How did you find this place?"

"I have an aptitude for global positioning. I only have to go somewhere once, and I can draw the route on a map."

"That makes sense." Sax rested her hips against the counter behind her and slipped her hands into her pockets. "That probably explains why you're so good at chess. You should be able to predict future moves after only one glimpse at the position of the pieces."

"I seem to have extremely strong visual pathways," Jude conceded, "which is probably why film is such a powerful draw for me."

"You are a fascinating woman...in so many ways," Sax responded softly, almost to herself. Then, she regarded Jude intently. "So, what prompted this?"

"We didn't finish our conversation this morning," Jude said evenly as she crossed the room, watchfully avoiding the open tool chest and stack of lumber piled on the floor. She hoped that she sounded more confident than she felt, because she was anything but sure of her welcome, and Sax, as always, was very difficult to read.

"What conversation was that?" Sax felt the room grow warm. Or maybe it was her.

"The one where you wanted to meet me for lunch, but I wasn't free. I never got to explain why."

"You don't need to explain to me." Sax fought to keep her voice even as Jude stepped to within inches of her. It was hard to think clearly with her this close. In fact, it was getting more difficult all the time to concentrate when Jude was *anywhere* nearby. "A simple no is all that's required. If I made you feel uncomfortable, I'm sorry."

"You know damn well what you made me feel," Jude snapped, her patience at an end. "Even if we hadn't already slept together once, and practically managed it again—fully clothed on top of a roof where anyone could have walked up on us, I might add—I'd still want you to know why I was declining your offer."

"Jude," Sax said wearily, "did you ever consider I might not want to know? I keep thinking I'll stop wanting to touch you every time I see you, but I haven't yet. I keep hoping I'll stop *thinking* about you even when we're not together, but I can't. I keep wishing I'll stop dreaming about you at night, but I still do. So maybe I just didn't want to hear about your girlfriend."

For a second, Jude didn't know what to say. Finally, she asked, "Why didn't you say something about this the night we slept together? I would have told you then that I was seeing someone, but that it wasn't—oh God, I don't know—committed, I guess is the term."

"Because I didn't realize how much I wanted that night to happen until it did," Sax said sharply, pulling her hands from her pockets and then clenching them by her sides. "And then I was so...scared by it, I wasn't sure I wanted it to happen again."

Jude's stomach tightened when she realized that she might be alone in her desire for them to see more of one another, but if that were true, she needed to know, for her sanity. "Why? Why does it scare you?"

"Because you make me forget everything," Sax whispered hoarsely. "You make me forget where I am; you make me forget to be cautious. You make me forget about everything except how warm you feel, and how..." She ran a trembling hand across her face and stared beyond Jude's shoulder into the past. "You make me feel...so much."

"That's not bad, is it?" Jude found Sax's hand and laced her fingers through Sax's, closing the distance between them, moving nearer until their thighs lightly touched. "You make me feel things, too. When I'm with you, I feel like all of me is actually in one place at the same time— whether we're in bed together or just together. I'm not watching myself go through the motions when I'm with you; I *am* myself when I'm with you. All of me. I like the way that feels."

"I'm afraid of what I feel," Sax said desperately. If she hadn't had her back to the workbench she would have stepped away, because feeling Jude against her body made her blood race. And then she couldn't think, and then she couldn't hold on to her control.

"Why? What do you think will happen?"

"I've worked very hard to build a predictable life," Sax said. "Everything works better if I don't feel very much; everything is under control then. You make everything crazy—no, you make *me* crazy."

Jude regarded Sax intently, beginning to suspect that Sax was talking about something more than what was happening between them. She was trembling, and Jude had never ever seen her do that, no matter how stressed, no matter how tired, no matter how pressured.

"Tell me why you're afraid," she said very softly.

"God, you are the most persistent woman I have ever met." Sax laughed a little unsteadily. She couldn't escape, and she couldn't lie to her. So, she took a deep breath, and because she really couldn't think what else to do, she told her story. "Do you know who Benjamin West is?"

"Uh..." Jude stuttered, taken off guard by the question. "As in West Enterprises? International trade consortium, Fortune 500?"

"Yes."

"I know who he is. I mean, who doesn't?"

"He's my father."

Jude stared, confused. "I don't understand."

"My given name is Saxon Sinclair West. The Sinclair is my mother's maiden name—Maddy's real last name, too."

"Of course," Jude murmured, struggling to make sense of the abrupt turn in the conversation. "Lane is Maddy's stage name, isn't it?"

"Yes," Sax replied, "but she's used it for years, even privately, so everyone thinks of her that way. I'm sure most people have forgotten that she was ever Madeleine Sinclair."

"Wait—so you go by your mother's family name now. Why?"

"Because it was legally changed when Maddy became my guardian. I was fifteen years old at the time." Sax swallowed. It was even harder than she had anticipated, but then she'd never said it all out loud before.

Jude tried frantically to recall what she could about the West family dynasty. As far as she knew, Benjamin West was still living, although she couldn't remember if children were ever mentioned in the articles she had read. *Fifteen. She said she was fifteen.* Something struck her about the timing, and she did some rapid mental arithmetic. "When Maddy became your guardian, she stopped acting, didn't she?"

"Yes."

"Why?"

"Because I was...in trouble." Sax closed her eyes for an instant, and when she opened them, they were shimmering with tears.

"Sax." Jude took Sax's other hand in hers, cradling them both lightly in her palms. "You don't have to tell me this. Not unless you want to. It hurts you—I can see that."

Sax rested her forehead briefly to Jude's. "No, it hurts me to keep it a secret."

"Then tell me."

"I can't explain it completely. No one has been able to. When I was a child, they thought I had a learning disability—"

"*You?*" Jude was incredulous. "I'm sorry, I didn't mean to interrupt—but why? I mean, I've seen your CV. I've seen you work. Hell, I've played chess against you."

"My attention span was limited." Sax shrugged, uneasy. "I was very active—hyperactive apparently—and I didn't perform well on standardized tests. Finally, when I was nine, the doctors decided I had an attention deficit disorder and began treating me with medications. The problem was, I actually *didn't* have a neurologic disorder, at least not in the sense of pathological. I *do* seem to have a highly sensitive nervous system—I don't sleep much, and when I do, the REM patterns are unusually accelerated. Specialized psychological assessments eventually demonstrated that I assimilate information faster than normal, so that when I was young, what everyone interpreted as an attention deficit was just boredom."

"How long did it take them to figure this out?" Jude asked. *And just how high* is *your IQ?*

"A long time," Sax confessed, her tone anguished as the still vivid memories resurfaced.

She was sweating, and the room was cool. She looked pale, practically gray, and it was scaring the hell out of Jude. "Maybe we should go inside. You can tell me the rest a little later."

"No, I want to finish."

"All right," Jude acquiesced quickly, hearing the note of desperation. "Of course."

"Well," Sax continued, swiping impatiently at the moisture running into her eyes, "the medications only made me worse. Drugs work well for some kids, the ones who have immature or altered neural pathways, but I didn't—mine weren't abnormal, just different. The older I got, the more problems I had, because the psychotropic drugs were altering my brain chemistry, making me..." Her voice trailed off as she stared at Jude, her misery nearly palpable. "It was a vicious cycle. The more they tried to control me with drugs, the worse I became. Part of it was a physical dependence, part of it was drug toxicity. Finally...I cracked."

Oh, my God. How lonely and confused, how terrified, *you must have been.* Wordlessly, Jude put her arms around Sax and pulled her close, holding her tightly, her own chest aching so badly she couldn't speak.

At length, when she thought she could talk without her voice shaking, she leaned back so she could see Sax's face, but kept her tightly in the circle of her arms. "And then?"

Sax's voice grew a little stronger. "The doctors thought I was having a psychotic break, and my parents had me involuntarily committed. Fortunately, the first thing the psychiatrists do in those circumstances is stop all the medication. Once they did that, I started to come around. As soon as I started to feel normal, I refused to take any drugs at all. There was a huge battle between Maddy and my parents about what to do with me, since I refused to go home. It's not easy to keep something like this quiet when you're a high-profile industry mogul, and my father was very paranoid about any suggestion of mental instability in the family. They agreed to let me go with Maddy."

"Thank God," Jude whispered vehemently.

"It took a long time for me to feel that they weren't going to come and take me away, and it took me even longer to feel as if I could trust myself—trust my life."

"Does anyone know?"

"No," Sax said. "I'm fine. But it could be difficult for me, I suppose, if someone *wanted* to make it difficult. Preston Smith would probably have a field day with the information, but I don't really think about it very much anymore."

"You didn't have to tell me," Jude said, smoothing one hand over Sax's chest, wanting so desperately to comfort her. "I'm glad that you did, though. Are you?"

"Yes," Sax said without hesitation. "I told you because...because you're the first person I've ever wanted to spend more than a night with. Except..."

"Except?" Jude feared that the answer was going to hurt.

Sax laughed, and this time the laughter reached her eyes. "Except maybe now you understand why it worries me that you make me crazy."

"Saxon." Jude leaned close to kiss her, then drew back after a second to whisper, "I might make you feel crazy..." She kissed her again. After a long minute, she managed to add through a throat tight with desire, "I hope I do...good crazy, at least." Sliding her hands over Sax's back, she lifted her eyes to those blue ones and said firmly, "But you are the least crazy person I've ever met."

And then she kissed her once more.

CHAPTER TWENTY-FIVE

Sax wasn't sure how long the kiss lasted. But when she finally became aware of her surroundings again, her legs shook and she had forgotten every single reason why being with Jude Castle was a bad idea.

"You're doing that making me crazy thing again," Sax whispered, brushing the outer rim of Jude's ear with her lips.

"Oh, good," Jude murmured against her neck. "I hoped that would happen."

"You got your wish."

"Is there any way at all that I can *keep* making you crazy?" Jude leaned hard along Sax's length, loving the solid strength of her. "Or should we go back to the house and be sociable? Your grandmother expects me to deliver you for dinner."

Sax slipped her hands under Jude's shirt and ran her fingertips lightly up and down Jude's sides, repeatedly drawing her thumbs along the underside of her breasts. Huskily, she confessed, "The only thing I have an appetite for right now is you."

"Deb says you have incredibly fast hands." Jude pressed even closer, insinuating one of hers between their bodies and cupping Sax through her jeans.

"Does she, now?" Sax swallowed audibly, her eyes going cloudy as Jude's touch made her hard.

"Uh-huh." Jude found the seam of Sax's jeans with her nails and tugged slightly. "That's what she says."

"Well, she's pretty smart," Sax gasped, pushing insistently into Jude's hand, rocking against her palm. She'd be in real trouble if she weren't careful, but it felt too good to stop. And she'd wanted it since the moment they'd parted two nights before. "So, if that's what she says, she must be right."

"Prove it."

Jude squeezed and Sax groaned, closing her fingers around Jude's breasts, gratified to hear her groan, too. She cast a desperate glance around the barn, but couldn't see a single place clean enough or comfortable enough in which to make love. Then, through the archway, she caught sight of the answer. Reaching down between her legs, Sax grasped the hand that was rapidly working her to a fever pitch and lifted it away from her body. Lacing her fingers through Jude's, she said urgently, "Come on."

"What?" Jude asked in befuddled astonishment, her attention still focused on the way her nipples felt between Sax's fingers. She had no choice but to follow, however, because Sax was already pulling her across the room.

"Just wait," Sax muttered as much to herself as to Jude, moving on unsteady legs, ready to go up in flames at any second. She fished a key ring out of the front pocket of her jeans and pointed a remote at the elegant Rolls-Royce sedan.

"You've got to be kidding," Jude exclaimed as the headlights flashed twice and the muted sound of door locks opening reached her ears. "I don't think I made out in the backseat of a car even when I was a teenager. I'm certainly too old for gymnastics now."

"You have no idea what these are like inside." Sax hurriedly opened the trunk and pulled out a large flannel blanket. "For emergencies," she commented while opening the rear door. She leaned in to spread the blanket on the seat. Turning to Jude, she extended a hand. "Would you join me, Ms. Castle?"

Laughing aloud, Jude took the offered hand and slid into the spacious backseat beside Sax. "This is crazy. You know that, right?"

Sax regarded her solemnly. "I told you that." Then, eyes dancing, she fell back against the plush leather seat and pulled Jude onto her lap.

Jude threaded her arms around Sax's neck and curled into her body, meeting her lips with urgent intensity. Beneath her, Sax spread long legs, and Jude pressed into the tight vee between those inviting thighs. Sax lifted her hips to meet her thrusts as their tongues sent promises of pleasure to come.

When their kisses became frantic and the air grew thick with hunger, Jude eased away for an instant, stripped off her shirt, and let it fall behind her. A second later, Sax's mouth was on her breast. She moaned with the quicksilver flash of excitement that streaked from her nipple into the pit of her stomach. Working both hands into Sax's hair, she kept the surgeon's head tightly to her breast.

"Bite me," she whispered urgently, and her breath caught in a soft groan as Sax complied. She closed her eyes, wanting only to surrender to the heat and the fury of needs too long unanswered. "You can't know...what...that does to me," she cried faintly, her cheek nestled against Sax's hair.

"Oh, yes, I can." Sax's voice was deep and sure. "I know"—she bit lightly—"that I could make you"—she bit again—"come"—another bite—"like this..." and once more, harder.

"Don't..." Jude whispered, her voice breaking as she tightened inside. "Not yet."

"No," Sax growled. Gathering Jude into her arms, she shifted quickly on the seat until they were reclining, Jude beneath her, their thighs intertwined. "Not just yet."

She kissed Jude's neck, the angle of her jaw, the corner of her mouth, her lips—hard enough to bruise but backing off just short of pain. She wanted this woman—wanted to possess her, devour her, drive her beyond sanity—she wanted her so much it was nearly paralyzing. Her chest felt like it would explode.

Trembling, aching, she moved her lips slowly down the center of Jude's body, her hands between them working Jude's jeans open. After moving lower still between her legs, Sax whispered, "Lift your hips."

When Jude complied, Sax pulled the fabric down and finally off, momentarily resting her palms on the insides of the bare thighs. With splayed fingers, she pressed firmly, willing Jude to open, and then slowly lowered her mouth to enclose the full clitoris. As she pulled the sensitive tissues gently between her lips, tasting Jude's arousal, Sax moaned and her mind dissolved.

Jude arched under Sax's mouth, every fiber contracting with the exquisite sensation of slick hot pleasure. "Go slowly," she murmured, "it's so good..."

Already lost, Sax followed only the rhythm of Jude's heart beating, flowed only to the sound of her soft moans, knew only the call of her flesh. *Beautiful, beautiful, beautiful...*

When Jude came in her mouth, Sax's mind erupted with white heat, absorbing every fragment of the moment, treasuring each sound and scent and tremor. She whimpered, twitching inside her jeans, as Jude's passion swept along her nerves and ignited her. Her thighs tightened, her stomach clenched, and she came hard on the heels of Jude's release.

❖

"You know," Jude muttered drowsily, "if you keep coming without me even touching you, I'm going to start feeling superfluous."

"Believe me, you're not," Sax assured, shifting on the broad seat to settle Jude more comfortably against her. "Something happens to me when I touch you. I get—"

Jude bit her neck. "I know...crazy."

"Yeah, that."

"Well, then, let's find out what happens when *I do* touch you." Jude flicked open the top button on Sax's fly. "Maybe you'll have better control."

"I don't...think so," Sax warned as Jude slid her hands inside tight jeans. "Uh...everything about my nervous system is fast. I don't have anything to say about it most of the time."

"Try."

"Jude," Sax protested as fingers grasped her firmly, and her head nearly blew off. "Jes...wait. Give me a minute."

"Okay. Fifty-nine, fifty-eight..." Jude intoned, punctuating each count with a quick stroke over Sax's clitoris.

Sax gritted her teeth and tried to remember her on-call schedule for the next three weeks. When that didn't help diminish the rapidly escalating pressure between her legs, she considered the quarterly budget. No luck. "Stop..." she gasped, "for a...second."

Jude relented. Sax's heart was pounding so hard it was almost scary. "Are you all right?"

"Yeah. Oh yeah," Sax managed, backing away from the edge. She took a deep breath. "Just...sometimes, quick reflexes are a problem, you know?"

"Ah—does this have anything to do with not sleeping and all that restless energy you have?" Jude stilled her motion but kept a gentle hold between Sax's thighs. "Is it a physical thing?"

"Probably. It gets away from me, and I don't want it to, not with you." She pressed her lips to Jude's temple, and whispered, "I want to feel it all."

"We can do that," Jude murmured. This she could give her. Gently now, she began again. With a light, steady touch, she soothed Sax even as passion stirred. Easing off when she felt Sax shudder, she led her steadily higher, timing her motion to the cadence of the heartbeat beneath her cheek. "Tell me when you're close."

Wordlessly, Sax nodded, feeling Jude beside her, inside her—standing between her and oblivion, guiding her surely home. "What you're doing...I'll come."

"Are you ready?" Jude asked softly, but she knew the answer. Sax's entire body trembled, every fiber poised to snap. She was already there.

"Ye—"

Speech disappeared in an avalanche of sensation, and Sax turned her face to Jude's shoulder, crying out once, sharply, and then she was gone.

❖

"Do you have any idea what time it is?"

"Eleven-forty," Sax replied.

Jude rolled over, raised her head, and peered at the dashboard in the dim light filtering in from the barn adjacent to the attached garage. After a second, she settled back against Sax's chest. "Remarkable."

"A lot of people can do that." Sax adjusted her back so that the door handle didn't poke her in the shoulder blade.

"Are you always that accurate?"

"Yes."

"Does that have something to do with your...heightened nervous system?"

"Most likely. We get all kinds of cues from our environment that we don't really think about. For me, sensory input is processed and categorized very quickly, automatically, and I don't even pay any attention to it anymore."

"It's not dangerous, is it?" Jude asked quietly, unable to forget Sax's story of being hospitalized. "I mean, you can't get...overloaded... or anything, can you?"

Sax pressed her lips to Jude's forehead and then nuzzled her ear gently. "No. Not as long as my system isn't altered in some way. I'm very sensitive to any kind of drug, but I know that, and I'm careful to avoid them. I don't even take aspirin."

"And sexually? Are you always...uh...primed?"

Sax sat up a little straighter on the seat so she could face Jude. "If you're asking me if my sexual response is indiscriminate, the answer is no. I'll admit it's convenient to be able to relieve physical tension and stress with a quick and easy orgasm. That night you saw me in the bar—"

"That wasn't what I was talking about," Jude said quickly, although she *had* wondered if their physical intimacy meant the same thing to Sax as it did for her. She'd be lying if she said she didn't hope this was more than just a casual romp for the surgeon. Whereas once the vision of Sax being pleasured by an anonymous woman had excited her, now the idea nearly made her insane. She wasn't at all sure that she could handle the thought of anyone else touching her. Still, she recognized that she had no right to make Sax feel uncomfortable about things that had nothing to do with her. "I wasn't talking about your relationship with other women."

"Weren't you?" Sax responded mildly. "Well, I'm going to talk about it anyway. I've never attached very much importance to sex, because it was never emotional for me—it was just biology. That's what you saw that night. It was an orgasm; it was a momentary release; it was an instant of escape. By the time it was over, I had already forgotten it."

She ran her fingertips along the edge of Jude's jaw, lifted Jude's chin in her palm, and held her gaze with fierce intensity. "That's not what this is, Jude. When I'm with you, I feel so much it's hard for me to breathe. When you touch me, you reach all the way inside me. When my hands are on you, I feel like something inside of me is breaking, and it hurts so much I think I'm dying. And I've never been so happy."

Jude was silent a long moment, struggling with emotions so unexpected and so powerful they left her speechless. Never had she wanted anything as much as she wanted Sax's words to be true. The intensity of her longing was frightening, even more so because it made no sense at all. She had never imagined wanting anyone, *needing* anyone, so badly. She was terrified to believe a single word that Sax said, but even more terrified to think that her words might not be true.

Finally, her voice shaking, she said, "I wouldn't mind if I were the only one taxing your nervous system from now on."

"I have a feeling you'll be taxing a lot more than just my nervous system." Sax laughed and pulled her close. Then, her tone completely serious, she added, "I can't imagine anyone making me feel what you do. I don't *want* anyone else to. And I want you all the time—so damn much. You don't have to worry about where I'll be at night."

"I wouldn't ask you, Sax," Jude murmured quietly, "if I weren't mad about you."

Sax grew very still. Jude's words echoed first in her mind, and then filled her heart, and finally touched her soul. "I wouldn't make the promise if I didn't feel the same."

CHAPTER TWENTY-SIX

A single light glowed in the kitchen and several covered dishes rested on the counter. The aroma of baked chicken and apples nearly brought tears to Jude's eyes. The clock said 12:30.

"I am *so* hungry."

"Do you want to eat down here or shall we take something upstairs to our room?" Sax lifted a casserole lid and then sniffed appreciatively.

Jude regarded her speculatively. "Our room?"

"You can't really think I'm going to let you sleep anywhere except with me tonight?" Sax regarded her with an amused expression on her face. "And the Rolls has served its purpose for the evening."

"Uh...I hadn't really thought about us...you know, sleeping together. Here, I mean."

"Why, Ms. Castle, I never would have figured you for shy." Sax laughed, enjoying the blush that stole to Jude's cheeks, and enjoying, too, the residual signs of their recent lovemaking. Jude's hair was disheveled, her shirt untucked, and her lips just short of bruised.

Remembering the way those lips had teased her, tormented her, and finally delivered her, Sax's mouth went dry and her knees grew weak. *Oh, man, I am so, so lost.* Suddenly, she forgot all about dinner. She advanced on Jude, ravenous, and only one thing would assuage the hunger.

"It's just that, if we get into bed together, I fully intend to spend most of the night making love," Jude announced, recognizing the shift in Sax's expression from playful to predatory. She put her palm flat against Sax's chest, holding her off, figuring they had maybe five minutes before they were naked again. If Sax touched her, perhaps less time than that, because her skin was already burning. "Maddy's *your* grandmother. Your choice."

"Her room is on the first floor," Sax rasped, backing Jude against the counter, reaching around her waist to trap her. She kissed her neck. "And all I want is your skin next to mine for the next twenty-four hours. At least."

"Well then," Jude replied huskily, slipping her hands into the back pockets of Sax's jeans and squeezing, "we're going to need nourishment. Immediately. Because I don't plan on waiting very long to have you."

The room, with its large four-poster bed, fireplace, and oak dressers, was very much like the guest room Jude had used only a few days before, but it had a lived-in feel that the other did not. The Oriental carpet was worn by the side of the bed from years of footsteps, and a stack of books and journals rested on the nightstand beneath a reading lamp. The large walk-in closet door was open, and she could see shirts and jeans and more formal suits arranged within.

"This is really where you live, isn't it?"

"Yes," Sax replied, her tone distracted as she hastily unbuttoned her shirt. They'd eaten quickly; she couldn't remember now how anything had tasted. She was wound tight inside, desire coiled so tautly she was in danger of spontaneous combustion.

"When?" Jude was mesmerized by the pulse thudding in Sax's neck. She wanted to put her teeth on that spot—leave another mark. *Her* mark. She barely recognized herself.

"Maddy and I lived in her apartment in Manhattan the first year I was with her, but then she bought this place. This has been my room, my home, ever since." Sax tossed her shirt on a nearby chair and was about to start on her jeans when it finally registered that Jude wasn't moving. Concerned, she asked, "What's wrong?"

"Nothing. I'm just enjoying the view," Jude replied a bit breathlessly. *And the minute we lie down together I'm not going to be able to think about anything except the way you feel. And this matters.* Valiantly, she tried to ignore the buzzing in her head. "What happened after you moved in with Maddy?"

"I finished high school with home study soon after I was released from the hospital," Sax answered, moving to the foot of the bed, naked from the waist up, a faint sheen of desire misting her skin. Jude stood a foot away, leaning against one of the bedposts, still fully clothed. Sax rested her fingers on Jude's bare forearms. "Nine months later, I left for college."

"You were young." A steady pounding between Jude's legs kept time with the beat in Sax's neck. Her vision blurred.

"Yes." Sax lifted a finger, ran it slowly down the center of Jude's throat. "Is this a test?"

Jude swallowed. When she spoke, her voice was strained. "How long did it take you? College and medical school?"

"Four and a half years." Sax watched Jude's pupils dilate. She lifted the shirt slowly over Jude's head. Her hands shook. "Why?"

"Because I want to know who you are," Jude whispered, desperate to bury her face in the soft curve of Sax's shoulder. *Wait, Jude, can't you? Don't touch her yet. Just wait. What is wrong with you?*

"You *do* know." Sax slowly unbuttoned her own fly. "You know what I need right now, don't you?"

"There's a lot you aren't telling me," Jude murmured quietly.

"Not so much. Nothing that really matters," Sax replied gently. Closing the distance between them, she took Jude's hands and placed them inside the waistband of her jeans. Then she looked into smoldering green eyes. "You know more about me than anyone else in the world, except Maddy. And there are some things you know that no one else will ever know."

"I like that," Jude whispered, pushing down on the denim, exposing her.

"Yes." Sax's voice was husky. "So do I."

Late in the night, Jude sensed Sax leaving the bed.

"What's wrong?" she mumbled, sitting up, naked in the moonlight.

"Nothing." Shirt in hand, Sax leaned down to gently kiss her sleepy lover. "I never finished that work in the barn. I got distracted earlier."

"I remember," Jude said softly. "Have you slept?"

"Not yet."

"Lie here with me for five minutes." Jude grasped Sax's hand and urged her back toward the bed. "Then you can go."

"That's a tough order," Sax whispered, stretching out beside her. "But I'll do my best."

The last thing Sax remembered was Jude stroking her face, the comforting warmth of her body, and the sweet tender touch of her mouth. The next thing she knew, she was awakening to sunlight on her skin. Opening her eyes, she found Jude propped on an elbow, watching her. "What time is it?"

"Don't you know?" Jude asked, smiling.

"Actually, no." Sax stretched contentedly. "God, I feel great."

"It's nine o'clock."

"How long have you been awake?"

"About fifteen minutes."

"You have a very pleased smile on your face," Sax observed, slipping her hand into the mass of rich red curls at the base of Jude's neck. She gathered her close and kissed her. "What were you thinking?"

"How much I liked it that you slept all night with me." Jude slid her thigh possessively across Sax's leg. "And that you're so beautiful it makes my heart hurt."

"Jude, I don't know how I managed before you." She watched Jude's eyes grow hazy.

"I know," Jude murmured, feeling walls tumble and doors open all along the hallways of her soul.

They reached for one another at the same time, arms and legs entwining as they joined. They promised constancy with each kiss and pledged devotion with each caress. With their hands, they found each other's need and eased it. With their lips, they sought each other's desire and reveled in it. With their hearts, they heard each other's dreams and answered them. They climbed together, soared together, came together, calling each other's names as passion burned brightly.

"I'm sorry we missed breakfast," Jude said. She poured her first cup of coffee from the pot that Maddy had thoughtfully brewed and left on the counter.

Sax, finally giving in to restlessness, had preceded her downstairs by five minutes and was now nowhere in sight. However, Jude didn't feel the least bit self-conscious, probably because she was just too damn happy to feel shy.

"Don't give it another thought." Maddy smiled up from the kitchen table where she sat reading the morning paper. "There isn't any timetable to keep to when you're here. And like it says at the old-fashioned diners, I serve breakfast twenty-four hours a day."

"I'd like to help."

"There's not much to do, really. And besides, I enjoy it."

"If you're sure..." Jude acquiesced. "Did Sax get her coffee?"

"She took a cup with her out to the barn. She said to tell you she'd be right back. Apparently, there was something she wanted to finish."

Jude laughed. "Well, at least she managed to wait until daylight."

"That's rare for her," Maddy remarked, regarding Jude astutely. She didn't need a script to read this scene. She knew where the two of them had slept. Much more importantly, she knew that her granddaughter *had* slept, and when Sax had appeared in the kitchen, smiling and clear-eyed, Maddy could have wept. "She doesn't usually pay attention to the time."

"So I understand," Jude replied carefully. She didn't want to infringe on Sax's privacy or betray her confidences, but she could see how much Maddy loved her. "She never stops going."

"She's never been able to tell when she's exhausted. She doesn't feel it. She'll run on empty until she drops."

"I'll remember."

"That's fine, then," Maddy said with a nod, briskly rising to begin breakfast. "So...tell me how the film project's going."

"I can do better than that," Jude announced with a smile. "I have a tape in my bag, and I can show you what we're doing."

Maddy turned, her face alive with delight. "Oh, Saxon has done well finding you."

"Thank you," Sax said with a smug grin from the doorway. "I think so, too."

Jude blushed and sent Sax a look that promised she would make her pay for that remark later. When Sax just gave her a supremely self-satisfied smile, Jude was afraid everything she was feeling must show on her face. And as much as she liked Maddy, there were some things Sax's grandmother did *not* need to know.

CHAPTER TWENTY-SEVEN

D o be careful, you two."
       "Absolutely," Sax responded as Jude climbed onto the bike behind her and then encircled her with both arms. It still gave her a pleasant jolt every time Jude did that. Covering one of Jude's hands with her own where it had settled possessively in the bend of her thigh, she grinned at her grandmother. "We'll be fine."

"Yes, I can see that." To Maddy's knowledge, her granddaughter had never had a relationship of consequence, but given Saxon's volatile nature, she very much doubted that she was inexperienced. But what was happening with Jude seemed to be something different altogether. It was clear to Maddy that they were both seriously smitten. She'd observed the way the two of them had looked at each other all day, and even though *they* didn't seem entirely aware of it yet, it was still a lovely thing to see. "I'll expect you both to visit again soon."

"We'll be back the day after tomorrow to pick up Jude's car," Sax said. Jude had wanted to ride back with Sax on the motorcycle, which was fine with her; she didn't want them to part quite so soon.

"I wasn't talking about a pit stop, Saxon. I had something more civilized in mind."

"Don't worry, Maddy," Jude said, smiling at the woman for whom she was quickly developing real affection. "I'll make sure of it."

For Jude, the afternoon had passed in easy conversation with Maddy, while Sax busied herself with a number of odd jobs around the grounds. When it had gotten too hot for Sax to work, she'd joined them, and they talked of current films and other news. Finally, after dinner, she and Sax had reluctantly prepared to leave.

"Good, because Saxon tends to lose track of such simple things as time, and weeks between visits is too long." Although this time she would worry less about Saxon's well-being while she was gone, knowing that Jude would be nearby.

"Maddy," Sax said ruefully. "You're going to give Jude a bad impression."

"Nothing she doesn't already know, I'm sure," Maddy said sharply. As she leaned forward to kiss Sax on the cheek, she stroked her arm absently, thinking how much she loved the happiness glinting in her granddaughter's normally guarded eyes. "I love you."

"I love you, too," Sax replied firmly, disengaging the kickstand with the heel of her boot. "We'll see you soon."

Maddy waved once as she watched Sax wheel the large motorcycle around in the center of the lane. As the engine roared and the powerful machine leapt into motion, she saw Jude tighten her hold on Sax, leaning against her, at once protected *and* sheltering. Maddy had often wondered if ever a person would come along who could match Saxon for drive and strength and tenderness. Jude did all that, and more. *Oh, what a marvelous pair they make.*

Sax pulled to the side of the road as they entered Manhattan. It was a little after 9:00 p.m.

"Where to?" she asked, turning on the seat to look at Jude. She knew what she wanted, but she was a little reluctant to make assumptions.

The last thirty-six hours had been like a dream. After Jude had declined her offer for lunch the day before, she had driven to Maddy's in a fury of temper and pain, certain that Jude's refusal had been because she was seriously involved with another woman. Sax had wanted her so much, but it wasn't just the physical frustration that had made her wild with rejection and aching loneliness; when they were together, she was happy. More than happy, she was soothed in some primal part of herself that never truly rested. Once that longing had been unleashed, it tormented her, her heart crying out for the peace that only Jude seemed able to bring.

Then, miraculously, Jude had come to her and claimed her—every inch of her, body and soul.

Now, as she contemplated their separation, the night loomed longer and lonelier than any she could recall. More barren even than those desolate nights when she had lain awake in the still, hushed dark of the hospital praying that Maddy would come for her. Maddy had ended her isolation then, but as the years had passed, her needs had changed, and Maddy could no longer banish her demons. But Jude had. *Jude had.* And she wondered, now, how she would make it through the night alone.

Jude sensed Sax waiting for an answer, but she had already taken enough risks. She'd followed her to Maddy's and practically—hell, not practically—*wantonly* seduced her. She'd made clear her desires. Deliberately, she countered, "What do *you* want to do?"

Sax glanced down once at Jude's hand still resting on her thigh, considering whether she could afford to let these feelings loose. She wasn't certain she could contain them, wasn't certain she could ever stop the wanting if she set it free. She looked into Jude's eyes, knowing she had been headed for this moment since the first day they had met. "At 6:30 tomorrow morning, I have to go to work. Then, for thirty hours or so, my life won't be my own. Until then, I want to be with you."

"You know the way to my place." Jude didn't realize she'd been holding her breath.

Ten minutes later, they pulled up in front. Once inside the door, Sax dropped her bag on the floor and waited while Jude walked around turning on lights in an apartment that was a perfect reflection of its occupant.

"What?" Jude asked hesitantly, watching Sax look around with a faint smile on her face.

"It's you," Sax observed, glancing at the array of recording and other electronic equipment fitted into the niches of an antique apothecary bench along the far wall. Beneath the warmth of color manifest in the paintings on the walls, the textured fabrics of rugs and throws, and the lush greenery of living foliage, there was a sense of order and utility. Sensuality and reason, creativity and intent, form and function—the artist revealed.

"It's passionate and purposeful," Sax continued, moving deeper into the room, indicating the space with a sweep of her arm. "You work here, and you live here, and they're the same thing for you, aren't they?"

Jude stared at the woman in the tight black T-shirt and faded black jeans, a handsome, dangerous stranger who knew things she shouldn't and touched her in ways no one ever had. "You scare me."

Sax cocked her head, stood still, studied Jude's eyes. Green—they were deep, deep green verging on black. They looked like that when she was aroused or angry, and now, Sax knew, when she was frightened. "I think it's too late for safety."

"So do I," Jude murmured, walking to within inches of her. "What do you want?" she asked again. *How long will it be before I can stand this close to you and not want my hands on your skin?*

Sax searched desperately for some way to explain how Jude had changed everything. "I want to do to you what you do to me," she said fervently.

"What?" Jude's voice was low and husky. "What is it you want?"

Sax put a gentle hand on Jude's cheek. "I want to abide in your secret places and catch your tears before they fall."

"I should make you leave," Jude breathed. *You can't know what you're asking. You can't.*

"Why?"

"You could hurt me."

"I won't."

"You can't know that."

"Yes. I can."

"What if I don't want you in those places?"

"Then you should make me leave." Sax dropped her hand. Eyes riveted on Jude's, she waited.

Jude ran her fingers lightly over Sax's face, tracing her eyebrows, the steep slope of her cheekbones, the rich curve of her lips. "It's too late."

"Yes. For me, too."

For a moment, they didn't speak, they didn't move. Then Jude took Sax's hand and led her across the room and through a doorway. Once inside her bedroom, Jude lit a candle by her bedside. They undressed wordlessly, unhurriedly—eyes locked on one another as each slowly revealed herself in measured, mesmerizing glimpses, denim and cotton falling from candlelit flesh. When they were naked, Jude turned down the covers and slid between the sheets, beckoning to Sax.

Sax stretched out on her side facing Jude, her palm lightly resting on the arch of Jude's hip. Amazed at how much she desired her, Sax was surprised even more by how exciting it was to wait. She was wet, she was hard, and she wished the wanting never to end.

"You know, I hated to leave Maddy's," Jude whispered in the flickering light, raising a hand to brush along the curve of Sax's breast. There was a wistful, almost sad note in her voice.

"Why?" Sax leaned forward enough to press her lips to the hollow below Jude's collarbone. "We can go back."

Jude wondered if she was foolish to say these things out loud, yet she was unable to stop. "Because I was afraid something would change when we got back to the city."

Instinctively, Sax moved her hand to Jude's back, pulling her closer until their breasts met and melded. Her body hummed, electrified. She held Jude, giving her the chance to speak, wanting her to know it was safe to tell her anything.

"I was afraid you'd disappear." It took all Jude's strength to say those words, because admitting how very much she wanted Sax was terrifying. She slipped her fingers into Sax's hair, pulled her head near, and sought her mouth. *You are real; I can touch you.*

"I won't disappear," Sax said deliberately when Jude released her. "I couldn't." She ignored the thunder of arousal as Jude's hand stole lower over her stomach, fingers seeking to claim her. She caught Jude's wrist before those sensitive fingers could touch her, because she knew she would be beyond words then. Raising the hand to her lips, she kissed the palm tenderly and placed it over her own heart. "Do you feel that?"

"Yes," Jude whispered, her eyes searching Sax's face. In the yellow glow of the candle, her blue eyes were black.

"It's yours."

"Why hasn't someone else claimed it before this?" Jude's throat was tight with desire and tears. "It's so precious."

"No one ever wanted it before," Sax murmured, her lips caressing the fine hair at Jude's temple. Carefully, she skimmed her palm up the inside of Jude's leg to the vee between her thighs, catching her breath at the slick, welcoming heat.

"I can't believe that," Jude said throatily. Her hand still rested on Sax's chest. "You're handsome and brilliant and sexy as hell."

"And arrogant and stubborn and secretive," Sax added with a tremulous laugh. God, she wanted to take her, just take her. Her arm trembled with the effort it took to go slowly.

"Yes, true," Jude agreed softly. She turned onto her back, drawing Sax with her. "But it balances out...in the end."

"I'll remind you of that one of these days when I've aggravated you too much." Leaning on one elbow, Sax was stroking languorously now, fingers gliding over engorged flesh, parting her gently.

"Good idea," Jude agreed. Her voice shook. She was losing focus.

"Jude," Sax said tenderly when she caught the faint whisper of uncertainty, "you make it safe for me to be myself. I am not afraid when I'm with you."

Slowly, watching Jude's countenance dissolve as her lids fluttered, Sax moved inside her.

"Thank you," Jude whispered, laying her head where her hand had just been, against Sax's heart. With closed eyes, listening to the sure, steady beat, she yielded all her secrets.

CHAPTER TWENTY-EIGHT

Personal Project Log—Castle
August 31, 9:45 a.m.

[Note: Episode title: "Call to Battle."] Holiday weekends are even more difficult than normal, because when people party, they get into trouble. Trouble comes in many forms—bar brawls, car accidents, domestic disturbances, robberies, gang altercations. What it means in practical terms for the trauma team is that there is more work, fewer people to do it because of vacation schedules, and a general sense of stress and anxiety about what might be coming next.

I should qualify that statement—Sinclair and Stein don't seem particularly worried. The two of them are almost unnaturally calm, as if they know that they'll deal with whatever fate may deliver. Confidence? Self-assurance? Maybe just simple experience, at least on Sinclair's part.

The rest of the staff are keyed up—from the nurses to the ancillary personal to the security guards at the front doors—you can see it in their faces and hear it in their voices. Excitement mixed with dread, like the kind of ambivalent anticipation you feel looking at one of those ridiculously large amusement park rides, wondering if you'll vomit or laugh halfway down.

Labor Day weekend is the end of summer, and underneath the gaiety is a thread of anger and sadness.

Today's Saturday, the first full day of the long weekend, and the team just finished rounds in the TICU a few minutes ago. Stein and Sinclair are already in the operating room doing emergency exploratory surgery on a patient who was shot three days ago. Apparently, she is having episodic spiking fevers and they suspect an abscess somewhere in her abdomen. Because Sax and Deb are also the admitting surgeons for the day, the backup team—all of whom have been here since six o'clock yesterday morning—has to stay until this surgery is over and the two of them are free.

Jude turned off her recorder and randomly selected a tape from the pile on the desk. She slid it into the VCR and pushed play, then leaned back in the swivel desk chair and propped her feet on the wastepaper basket. It only took a few minutes to recognize the scene as the one in which Sax and Deb had been working on a New York City police officer who had been injured in a high-speed crash while pursuing a suspected dope dealer up the West Side Highway. Parts of the tape were dizzyingly shaky because Mel had been jostled by the clutch of police crowding into the trauma bay trying to find out how their fallen comrade was faring.

She muted the volume. Not interested in the conversations, she was only interested in the dark-haired surgeon whose face was a study in fierce concentration and whose hands moved like magic over the landscape of flesh and bone.

As she watched, images unexpectedly fused and blurred; her memory transcended time. Sax leaning over the officer became Sax leaning over *her* in the trauma bay at Bellevue. And then suddenly, it was Sax leaning over her in bed last night—hands playing over her skin with unerring certainty, finding all her tender places, making her molten, making her scream, making her come.

She caught her breath at the swift stab of pleasure that accompanied the memory. Watching the tape had been a bad idea. She'd only wanted to see Sax's face for an instant, because she missed her, and now she ached in a way she knew was going to torment her for hours.

"Jude?" a curious voice behind her inquired. "You okay?"

Swinging around, she grinned ruefully at Melissa. "Yeah. Fine... just woolgathering. Waiting for Deb and Sax to finish up."

"And the silent movie?" Melissa pulled over a chair and nodded toward the tape that still ran on the monitor.

"Oh...that. Nothing. I was just..." She stopped, unable to think of an explanation that wasn't ridiculous, as if the truth weren't ridiculous enough. Sighing, she admitted, "I wanted to look at her."

Melissa followed Jude's gaze and watched Sax and Deb work for a few seconds. It was good footage. They were captivating women. But Jude looked more than captivated; she looked stunned.

"You really are nuts about her, aren't you?" she asked with a touch of awe.

"Seems like," Jude acknowledged. She glanced self-consciously at her photographer. "Crazy, huh?"

"Not as long as it's mutual," Melissa replied carefully, mindful of the fragile line between caring and intruding. "Is it?"

Jude smiled, recalling Sax in the shower that morning, head thrown back, eyes closed, fingers laced through Jude's hair, moaning Jude's name.

"Yeah. Uh-huh. Certainly seems so."

September 2, 1:00 p.m.
DRM 15,860

We're on the roof waiting for South Star to bring in two patients found unconscious in a burning crack house. Preliminary reports indicate burns and inhalation injuries. As I look around, Nancy Stevenson—Aaron's replacement—a respiratory technician, a med tech, and Sinclair and Stein are standing in a cluster, faces turned to the sky, poised to move. You can almost feel the tension rippling in the air. It's not as hot today as it has been, and there's a breeze. In the distance, I can hear the rotor blades thumping. There are stretchers with equipment piled onto them awaiting the wounded. No one is talking. The silence is eerie.

"The blades aren't that low, but watch your head, okay?" Sax advised as Jude stepped up beside her.

"Understood." Jude kept an eye on Melissa, who was filming as they all moved forward in anticipation of the chopper's arrival. She had to be sure that her photographer was clear of the landing site as the helicopter descended. Looking up into the sky, she held her breath, waiting for the drama to begin.

"It's odd how all sense of time, everything actually, disappears when the injured arrive," she observed almost to herself.

There was a terrible pain in her leg...she found herself staring into a huge silver disk with a hot white bulb in its center. A silhouette took shape in her field of vision; backlit by the bright light...features began to emerge. A face bending near—blue eyes, so dark they were almost purple, intense and penetrating—black hair, thick and unruly...

Remembering, Jude shivered lightly in the warm air. "Everything recedes into shadow except the space around the patient, and that's like a spotlight in the center of a darkened stage."

Sax glanced at Jude, struck by the pensive tone in her voice. They hadn't had much time alone together since the weekend had begun. The sun on Jude's burnished copper hair glinted like shimmering firelight, reminding her that when they'd last awakened together, those glorious tresses had been scattered across her chest and Jude's face had been nestled in the crook of her neck. Jude had fallen asleep after shuddering to a climax in Sax's embrace while Sax had lain awake, more than content to rest with the soothing sound of Jude's soft breathing whispering in her ear. Finally, she had truly slept, and it had been a sleep without dreams or anxiety.

She moved a step closer, her arm brushing Jude's. "Time *is* suspended. There is only the now. No past, no future, no hopes, no dreams. Only the reality of life and death. If you spend enough time on call, you'll forget there *is* any other world."

"That's frightening," Jude said quietly. *I don't want to forget what I feel when you touch me. I don't want you to forget what I make you feel.*

"But very effective. It's difficult to be efficient and focused if you're worrying about a dinner date or a birthday party. Everything about the training is oriented toward isolating us on some level from everyone else, even if it's never truly acknowledged."

"Here comes the chopper," Jude observed with a sigh. Knowing that their brief moment together was about to end, she was both excited by what was about to happen and saddened that, in the midst of such exhilaration, she and Sax would be distanced even further.

"I still know you're here, Jude," Sax murmured as the helicopter grew larger against the backdrop of blue. "I still feel you on my skin."

"You say things that make my heart stop." Jude breathed shakily, staring at her in amazement. Sax stood with her face in profile, a smile lifting the corner of her mouth. "And at the damnedest times—like now, when I can't touch you—and it's sure to make me wild. You're so damn impossible to predict, it drives me crazy."

"No, I'm not." Sax's grin widened. "Just because I understand the game doesn't mean I choose to play. I won't let this come between us. I'll *always* know where you are."

"Sax..." Jude began, but her words were drowned out by the descent of the helicopter, and Sax was already racing forward, one hand guiding a stretcher. Jude watched her go, and even though she knew Sax's mind was now entirely focused on the wounded men being lowered from the helicopter onto the waiting gurneys, she felt the connection between them. What they had shared in the night would not end with the coming of the dawn or fade in the harsh, bright light of life on the front lines.

"Are you getting it?" Jude shouted as she rested one hand on Melissa's shoulder and steered her to an open space where the sight line was better for the camera. She maneuvered the photographer and her camera around the group of medical personnel who started administering to the injured almost before they had been lowered from the helicopter.

"Of course I'm getting it." Melissa never looked away from her viewfinder. She trusted Jude to make sure she didn't lose the top of her head to one of the rotor blades, because if she missed the shot, she'd lose her entire head to Jude's temper. "Just keep me in the clear, and I'll get you what you want."

"Roger that," Jude called, riding high as everything in her life came together almost as if it had been scripted—she was doing the work she loved and watching the woman she lov... *Oh, no. Do not go there. No, no, no. Not now. No way.*

She kept well back as Sax swung the gurney around, Deb steering the second one, and the whole group headed down the ramp toward the elevators at a run. Sprinting to keep pace, Jude tried not to think about how mind-shatteringly sexy Sax looked.

❖

September 2, 1:27 p.m.

En route to the trauma admitting area, both men had already received pain medication and loading doses of antibiotics. One had been intubated by the paramedics, and the breathing tube extending from his trachea had been connected to a respirator. Sinclair and Stein bent over him, discussing the plan of action in low, measured tones. Jude and Melissa edged closer to capture both the picture and the sound.

"What's his pO_2?" Sax asked.

"Lousy. Eighty-four on a hundred percent oxygen," Deb replied, glancing at a computer printout she had just collected from a nearby terminal. "His carbon dioxide level is high despite being ventilated, too."

"What do you think?"

Deb studied the young man who didn't appear to be much older than his late teens, lying naked on the stretcher connected to a plethora of monitors and intravenous lines. Much more remarkable than this array, however, was the circumferential rubbery scar tissue encircling his chest that indicated a full thickness burn. The rest of his body was fairly untouched, and it appeared as if his shirt had caught fire, probably from his crack pipe.

"I think the burn scar is constricting his chest movement and preventing efficient ventilation. If we can't expand his chest, we can't fully aerate his lungs and it doesn't matter what we pump into him, he's not going to breathe well," Deb summarized.

Sax nodded in evident satisfaction. "Agreed. Your recommendation?"

"He needs scar release—escharotomies—right now."

"Here or upstairs in the OR?" Sax rested back against the counter, arms folded over her chest, her tone conversational, as if she were discussing the latest sports scores. Her eyes, however, belied her nonchalance. They were fixed on Deb's face so intently that Jude thought perhaps Sax could actually *see* what Deb was thinking.

She's marvelous, Jude thought. *She's always watching Deb—evaluating her, testing her, guiding her—and all the while she's allowing her to grow and become independent.*

"Breathe, Jude," Melissa murmured in Jude's ear. "It's going to be a very long day, and you're going to need all your strength. Maybe you should just let me film and you try not to look at her. It seems to do something serious to your system—like shut it down."

"Shut up, Mel, or I'll be forced to hurt you," Jude whispered back, but she couldn't hide her guilty grin. God, she loved to look at Sax and couldn't imagine that ever changing.

Deb Stein shrugged her shoulders and came to a decision. "I think we can do it right here. The burn scar is insensate so he won't feel it, plus he's got narcotics on board even if there is some discomfort. We need to stabilize his cardiopulmonary status before we do anything else, so we might as well get to it."

"Go ahead," Sax said, moving out of the way so that Deb could open the instrument packs and prepare the area where she would make the incisions. "It's your show."

After stepping back next to Jude, Sax asked quietly, "You okay?"

"Yes," Jude replied. "Is he going to live?"

"Probably. He's young and we got him early. We'll know better in a few days." Craning her neck to see over Deb's shoulder, she instructed, "Put that lateral incision a little more anterior, Stein. And don't go too deep or he'll bleed all over the place."

Jude watched Deb work, aware that Sax, despite her casual demeanor, was completely focused.

"You free for lunch?" Sax asked after a moment, her gaze following the sweep of the scalpel blade in Deb's hand.

"Yes."

"I'll treat you to the street carts out front."

"Wonderful." Jude caught Sax's grin and thought she'd never had such a perfect invitation.

CHAPTER TWENTY-NINE

September 3, 5:48 a.m.

Jude came awake with a jolt, startled from sleep by the sound of shouts and running in the hall outside the on-call room.

Across the room, Melissa sat up and reached for her jeans. "Fuck. Aren't we supposed to be off call in an hour?" she grumped as she fumbled into her clothes. "What's going on?"

"I don't know." Jude jumped from her bed and stepped into her chinos. As she was pulling on her boots, there was a sharp knock on the door.

Sax's voice called, "Jude?"

Jude crossed to the door in a matter of seconds. Melissa crowded behind her. "What is it? What's happened?" she asked almost before she swung it open.

"A tanker overturned in the tunnel. It's blocking the exit on this side, and there's a huge chain reaction pileup behind it underground. Mass casualties—that's all I know at the moment. I'm taking the first response team out there now. Deb is organizing the second team. I'll let you know as soon as I get—"

"Mel, get the portable video cameras and all the tape you can carry," Jude interrupted urgently as she kept pace with Sax, who was already hurrying down the hall. Interpreting Sax's quick frown to mean that she was concerned about delays, she added, "Don't worry, we won't hold you up. We'll get our gear, join Deb's team, and meet you there."

"Jude." Sax had too many things on her mind to be circumspect.

"It's going to be a mess out there. We'll be first on the scene because we're practically right on top of it. I'm not even certain yet that the tunnel is structurally secure." She didn't need to elaborate that if the stretch of highway carved out of bedrock under the Hudson River collapsed, the casualty count would soar.

"Let's go find out," Jude answered impatiently, electrified by the opportunity to be one of the first photojournalists on the scene. These were the moments of human tragedy and human greatness. These were the moments she lived to immortalize.

No. Sax wanted to tell her to stay behind; she wanted to tell her it would be chaos and insanity out there; she wanted to tell her that she couldn't work worrying about her. Yet she couldn't say anything, even though her stomach clenched with apprehension, because she knew if the situation were reversed, nothing would keep her from doing what she had to do. Instead, she grabbed Jude's hand and squeezed it briefly.

"Fine, but I probably won't see much of you. Just...be careful, okay?"

"Okay," Jude responded instantly, unconcerned about her own welfare. Suddenly, however, she realized that as the leader of the first response team, *Sax* could be in danger. The initial moments in situations like these were always so unpredictable. The tanker could blow; the tunnel could flood; vehicles could explode. *God.* Tugging on Sax's arm, she halted her mid-stride and pulled her around until they faced one another. "Don't be a hero, understand? I couldn't..."

Sax smiled, lifting a hand to rest her fingertips on Jude's cheek. Unmindful of hospital personnel moving around them in the hallway, she closed the distance between them until their bodies nearly touched. Softly, her eyes holding Jude's, she assured her, "I wouldn't think of it. Just you be careful, too."

Before Jude could respond, Sax kissed her swiftly and then was gone.

September 3, 6:08 a.m.

"Look at this mess," Deb exclaimed as the three of them stood on the sidewalk in front of the hospital, surveying a scene out of a disaster movie. "We'll get there faster on foot. Let's go."

Street traffic was completely gridlocked. People were standing outside their cars, trying to see the cause of the holdup, shouting at one another. Scores of police were hastily erecting barricades and working to divert traffic. Emergency vehicles, sirens blaring, were making painfully slow progress in the crush of stalled or immobilized trucks and cars and were forced at some points to detour onto the sidewalks. The noise level made conversation almost impossible.

"What about the rest of the team?" Jude indicated the ambulance edging out into traffic from the emergency entrance of the hospital farther up the block.

"They'll catch up." Deb was already moving. Melissa, with her camera braced on her shoulder, was beside the young surgeon, tape rolling. Jude fell into step with them, the decision clearly made.

It wasn't hard to tell where they needed to go. The tunnel was only a few blocks away, and even if they hadn't known that, they could have navigated by the reflection of flashing emergency lights against the undersurface of the gray dawn clouds or followed the sound of screaming sirens.

As she ran, the second camera tucked under her arm, Jude wondered if Sax and her team were already at the crash site. "How many cars are trapped?" she asked, hastily clipping her network badge to her multipocket khaki vest.

"At least twenty." Deb was in scrubs, a stethoscope dangling precariously from her neck and a handful of rubber tourniquets streaming from her pockets. "According to the first radio report, there are as many as a hundred injured, but you know how inaccurate that can be." Abruptly, she stopped short and Jude nearly collided with her.

Melissa drew alongside, breathing hard from the added effort of carrying the extra gear. She didn't look tired, though; with her blond hair poking out from under her baseball cap and her baby blue eyes sparkling with excitement, she looked exhilarated.

"Holy cripes," she gasped when she saw what awaited them.

They all stared, speechless, their mission forgotten for a moment. The four lanes leading from the mouth of the tunnel into Manhattan were completely blocked with dozens of emergency medical and police vehicles, many parked haphazardly with their light bars flashing. A huge fire engine nearly blocked the mouth of the tunnel—firefighters clambered over it, unrolling thick hoses, disappearing with them into the billows of black smoke that poured out, engulfing them in acrid air and ash. It was impossible to see very far inside the tunnel through the dense clouds. Already a dozen or more injured men and women had found their way out and were now staggering aimlessly about in the midst of the pandemonium.

Jude stood rooted to the spot, staring into the face of her nightmare. She knew exactly what it was like inside that tunnel. She knew the sounds, and the sights, and the smell—twisted metal, broken shards of glass; the pungent odor of electrical fire and burning rubber; confused shouts; screaming. She knew the pain and the fear and the helplessness, too. She wanted to run—from the memories, from the reality, from the terror that surged into her chest with all the force it had on that morning five years before. *I can't go in there.*

"I need to set up a command post and a triage center," Deb shouted, suddenly finding her voice and mercifully jolting Jude back to the present. She pointed to the several emergency medical vehicles that were closest to the tunnel ramp. "That looks like the best place."

"What about Sax?" Jude was running next to Deb again, barely avoiding collisions with firefighters and police officers and emergency paramedics, all of whom seemed to be running as well. "Where is she?"

She didn't go in there. Of course she didn't. Why would she do that? No one would do that. That would be insane.

"Don't know. She probably went inside to assess the number of injured. There must be people trapped in vehicles in there, too."

A new rush of fear seized Jude by the throat, and for a moment, she couldn't breathe. *Sax is not inside that tunnel in the midst of smoke and fire and God knows what else. She said she would be careful. She said she wouldn't be a hero. She promised!* Glancing frantically about, she searched for Sax's distinctive figure in the churning mass of people. Now that they were closer, she could see paramedics emerging from the tunnel—some carried stretchers with injured, a few led those who could walk, and others shouted for assistance.

In a voice that sounded startlingly calm to her own ears, she directed, "Mel, you stay with Deb. I'm going inside."

"No way," Melissa objected, looking up from her viewfinder. She'd begun filming in earnest as soon as they'd gotten close. "This story is in there. I'm coming with you."

"We don't have time to argue about this," Jude said sharply, her temper flaring with a mixture of worry about Sax's whereabouts and her own terror of walking into that dark hole in the ground. "We need footage of Deb for the documentary."

"We'll have plenty of time to get that later. Right now, we need to be where the action is. You know damn well it's inside that tunnel," Melissa insisted. *"You* stay with Deb and let me go in."

Jude wanted to agree. Everything she feared was in there. And so was everything she cared about. If it had just been the story, she might have given in to the nausea that clawed at her throat, turning her blood to ice, and sent Melissa in alone. Maybe. But Sax was in there, too. She couldn't just stand outside and wait. She needed to go in, for herself and everything that mattered.

"We'll go together." She grabbed the sleeve of Melissa's jeans jacket. "Come on, before they get organized and try to keep the press out."

"Stay close, will you," Melissa shouted as they ran. "I don't want to lose you in there."

"Don't worry. I'll be right on your back—just like always."

"Today, I won't mind," Melissa said fervently.

They made a hard right around a barricade the police were setting up to prevent unauthorized people from going into the tunnel. Someone shouted, "Hey, you can't go in there!"

Melissa and Jude ignored the voices calling them back, and within moments, they were obscured from sight by the dense curtain of roiling smoke and plumes of fire.

CHAPTER THIRTY

September 3, 6:37 a.m.

The main overhead lights were out. The rescue teams had not yet rigged the portable arc lights, and the only illumination in the tunnel came from the safety lights at ground level, which were working sporadically at best. Entire sections were nonfunctional, casting the underground highway in patches of murky yellow and foreboding shadow.

Fortunately, the air was still breathable despite the noxious smoke pouring from around the overturned truck. Firefighters were already hosing it down with flame retardant foam as Jude and Melissa skirted the throng of workers at the entrance.

"Follow those guys," Jude shouted above the din. She pointed to emergency medical personnel, identifiable by their tackle boxes of medical equipment, who were inching their way past the rubble at the mouth of the tunnel to reach the stranded motorists deeper inside.

After climbing over bits of concrete and debris from the wreckage, they emerged on the other side of the tanker and got their first view of the real scope of the disaster. Cars were piled up as far as they could see, several overturned and burning, and the first rescue workers on the scene were rushing from vehicle to vehicle, assessing the status of the occupants. Victims were sitting or lying beside many of the wrecks, some being attended to by paramedics while others waited, confused and disoriented, for someone to lead them out. Here and there, EMTs were starting IVs and intubating the more seriously injured.

"Do you see Sax?" Jude asked urgently.

The faces of many of the rescue workers were already smudged with smoke and grime. In the murky light that flickered and flared as electrical circuits burnt out and small fires began, everyone had the eerie appearance of figures in a waking dream. Until she was right up next to someone, Jude couldn't even be certain if they were male or female. Most of the emergency workers were garbed in some form of hospital apparel, and only the firefighters in their heavy asbestos coats were easily recognizable.

"Do you see anyone from St. Michael's?" Jude repeated.

"No," Melissa replied grimly, trying not to think about the extent of the carnage. "Let's just keep going and see how far this goes. They must be somewhere close by. Eventually, we've got to run into them."

"Look at the ground," Jude remarked hollowly. The water on the floor of the tunnel was already six inches deep. There were tons of rock and water above their heads, and she wondered how long the damaged infrastructure could sustain the tremendous pressure without flooding or collapsing completely. She glanced ahead and could see only darkness beyond the first thirty feet. Every instinct in her body screamed for her to leave. She craved daylight and fresh air with an exigency that bordered on frantic. She bit her lip, refusing to let her fear show, desperate to stave off the wave of dizziness and surge of nausea that threatened to bring her to her knees. She tasted her own blood.

"What do you think?" Melissa stared at the water slowly eddying around her boots. "Turn back or look for them?"

"Keep going." Jude reached into one of the cargo pockets of her vest, found her halogen flashlight, and switched it on to supplement the diminished lighting.

As they passed the wreckage of the deadly early-morning commute, she spied a few motionless forms inside crushed vehicles, lying in the awkward poses only death could confer. Fortunately, most of the victims she saw appeared to be alive, although many would require assistance getting out of the tunnel. The fact that the rush-hour congestion had already begun by the time the accident occurred meant that traffic had been moving fairly slowly. She prayed that would mean fewer fatalities despite the large number of people who seemed to be injured.

"Over there!" Melissa pointed in the direction of several demolished vehicles facing north in the southbound lane. "Isn't that Nancy?"

Jude squinted into the gloom and felt a surge of relief as she recognized the head trauma nurse. "Yes! Sax must be with her." She didn't wait for Mel's reply but hurried as quickly as she could between the jumble of vehicles toward the team from St. Michael's.

As she drew near, she saw Sax leaning through the door of an overturned four-wheel-drive vehicle. Her heart jumped, and her first instinct was to run to her. All she wanted was to touch her, just touch her, and feel the solid certainty of her body. Instead, she forced herself to slow down and take a deep breath. "Just keep the focus on Sax, Mel. She'll be recognizable to every viewer. We can't get anything better than this."

Moving carefully around open instrument packs and tackle boxes filled with drugs, Jude edged closer to the car until she *was* nearly touching Sax's shoulder. When she peered into the vehicle, she saw a man trapped by the collapsed steering column.

"Nancy, get another flashlight in here, will you?" Sax ordered tersely without looking around. "I need to tie off this bleeder, and I can't see a damn thing."

"I've got one right here, Nancy," Jude said, holding hers aloft and pointing it into the interior of the front seat. The car was on its side, and the bucket seats were angled nearly perpendicular to the ground. The unconscious middle-aged man was suspended in midair by a spear of metal penetrating his shoulder.

Sax glanced up quickly at the sound of Jude's voice. "It's treacherous down here. I'd be happier if you were doing your thing outside somewhere."

"Ditto," Jude replied. "But here we are. Can I do anything besides hold this light?"

"You think you can pass instruments to me? That'll free Nancy up to check other victims." Sax turned her attention back to the deep gaping gash in the man's upper arm. "Seeing as you're staying and all."

"I can manage. If I don't know what it is, just describe it to me." Jude allowed herself one brief caress along Sax's shoulder. "And I missed you, too."

"All right, Ms. Castle," Sax replied, registering the touch and smiling to herself. "You're hired. Hand me a hemostat."

Melissa got as close as she could and, for the next eight minutes, she documented some of the most exciting footage she had ever shot. Sinclair worked without a single break in her concentration or the slightest hesitation in the swift, smooth rhythm of her hands as she clamped and sutured and tied, controlling the bleeding, and then extricated the impaled motorist so that the paramedics could lift him out onto a backboard.

"Okay." Sax rested back on her heels as her patient was taken away. She wiped her forehead with her bare arm, managing only to smear the sweat, smoke, and blood splatters around. Glancing at Jude, she smiled dolefully. "A success, I hope. Let's pack up this gear and keep going. Nancy will be triaging, so keep an eye out for her. If there's anyone that needs acute surgical attention, she'll call for me. Otherwise, we'll just direct the paramedics to the ones that need to be evacuated first."

"Understood," Jude replied, hastily rearranging supplies in the drug box.

Thirty minutes later, they were nearly at the end of the line of involved vehicles. Rescue workers were approaching from the New Jersey side of the tunnel, although several vehicles burning out of control at that end had hindered their progress. Others worked steadily behind them, transporting the injured to safety as quickly as possible. It seemed to Jude that the water level had risen several more inches.

"Looks like most everyone is out," Sax said as the EMTs moved a woman with a fractured leg onto a stretcher.

"Things don't look too stable down here," Jude observed. "I think we should consider getting out ourselves."

"I think you're right. Let's head back."

They had nearly reached the beginning of the pileup, just behind the tanker, when they ran into Deb coming in. Speaking rapidly, her stress apparent, she said, "The structural engineers are afraid part of the ceiling is about to give way. We're double-checking to make sure all of the injured are clear."

"All clear back there," Sax indicated the area behind them with a jerk of her head. "Who's running the show outside?"

"Kirkland showed up." Deb gestured toward one of the attending surgeons from Sax's department. "I just left long enough to do this final canvass." She didn't mention that she had gone in against the orders of the police because she knew that the three of them were still inside. "Let's get..."

A low rumbling that rapidly built to a roar drowned out her words. The ground beneath them seemed to lift and undulate as if shaken by some giant hand. The four women struggled to keep their footing as bits of concrete and tile began to rain down.

"This section is collapsing," Sax shouted. She grabbed Jude and Mel by the shoulders and pushed them in Deb's direction. "Run!"

They and the few remaining paramedics still in the tunnel sprinted toward daylight, a distance of fifty yards that seemed like fifteen miles, as chunks of debris fell faster. Even Melissa finally gave up filming and simply cradled her camera against her chest, put her head down, and ran. One by one, they vaulted over the final barrier of twisted metal and chunks of concrete while close behind, clouds of pulverized stone bore down upon them.

Jude had just cleared the tunnel mouth when she realized that Sax was no longer by her side. Barely able to see through the billowing dust, she reached out and caught Mel's sleeve.

"Did Sax pass you?" she screamed over the roar of destruction freight-training in the tunnel.

"No! She's right behind—" Mel looked over Jude's shoulder, her expression one of dawning horror. "Oh God. She's still in there."

Jude wasn't aware of making the decision to turn back before she found herself plunging into the darkness. "Go back," she screamed as Mel caught up to her.

"No way."

"There!" Jude exclaimed, pointing to a swatch of blue next to the overturned truck, just barely visible under a powdering of stone and ash.

Sax lay facedown, a trickle of blood streaming down her neck. A four-inch gash on the back of her head bubbled with blood, bone visible at the base.

Jude fell to her knees next to her unconscious lover, ignoring the shards of glass, metal, and jagged rock that tore holes in her jeans. Tentatively, she reached toward Sax. She was afraid to touch her. She had no idea what death felt like, and she was afraid that she might find out. Her fingers hovered just above Sax's shoulder, the shoulder she had caressed not long before. *This can't be. She isn't supposed to get hurt. She's the one that makes everything else all right.*

"Can we move her?" Melissa yelled, her fear making her voice shrill.

"I don't know," Jude said harshly.

"We've got to!" Melissa watched huge slabs of concrete slide from the walls onto the roadbed. "We don't have any time."

Suddenly, Deb's voice calmly instructed, "Let me in there, Jude." She slid her fingers under Sax's jaw, checking for a pulse. "It's a good thing I saw you two lunatics running back this way." After a few seconds, she raised her head and met Jude's gaze. "She's alive."

"She's not moving. Her head..." Jude's voice was rising rapidly, and she felt things begin to break apart inside. She clenched her fists so tightly that the nails dug into her skin. "Deb...what about her neck..."

"I know, Jude. But we have to get her out of here. I'll stabilize her neck and shoulders if you two can lift her body. Can you do that?"

"Yes. Yes, of course."

Melissa and Jude slung their camera straps over their shoulders and reached for Sax. With Deb directing, they maneuvered the trauma surgeon's unresponsive body clear of the tunnel, onto a stretcher, and into the nearest unoccupied EMT van. The three then piled into the back as well.

Deb quickly executed the routine resuscitation maneuvers. As she wrapped a tourniquet around Sax's upper arm, she yelled to the driver, "St. Michael's. And call ahead for the neurosurgeon. Let them know we're bringing in Dr. Sinclair. You got that? Tell them Dr. Sinclair is down."

Jude knelt by the stretcher, completely unaware of what Deb was saying or doing. If there was a world beyond this six-by-six-foot space, she had no sense of it. Everything that mattered to her was just inches away in the form of the dark-haired woman who lay so frighteningly still.

CHAPTER THIRTY-ONE

September 3, 8:21 a.m.

A s the double doors of the ambulance swung open, Pam Arnold
climbed up onto the rear running board and peered into the
interior. She hadn't truly believed the frantic, garbled radio transmission,
but as soon as she'd heard it, she'd hurried down to see for herself.
She'd even left her resident alone in the trauma bay to continue with
the evaluation of a firefighter who'd fallen from an extension ladder.
Blinking from the glare of the vehicle's ceiling lights, she surveyed a
scene she would not soon forget. For a few seconds, trying to absorb the
reality before her, she forgot why she had been called.

The trauma fellow, her back braced for balance against the partition
that separated the transport section from the cab, was attaching EKG
leads to the chief of the trauma division, who lay unresponsive on the
stretcher, naked from the waist up, an IV running into her left arm and
a stiff cervical collar immobilizing her neck. The film person—the
redhead—was on her knees next to the gurney with Saxon's left hand
clasped between both of hers. She turned at the sound of the doors
opening, and the look she gave Pam was wild—not with hysteria,
though that would have been understandable, but with a kind of
ferocious protectiveness. In the far corner of the small space, a grimy,
bedraggled blond in a ratty baseball cap held a camera at eye level.

Pam shook her head. *This is not happening. Saxon Sinclair is* not
lying on that stretcher. In the next instant, she squared her shoulders

and narrowed her gaze, totally focused on the patient. As she stepped inside, she asked brusquely, "Is she stable?"

"Vital signs are rock solid," Deb answered steadily, pulling the sheet up to cover Sax's breasts while watching the blood pressure monitor. "Pupils are equal and reactive but sluggish."

"No respiratory problems?" Pam leaned down to flick her penlight into first one, then the other, of Sax's eyes. She edged aside a few inches to allow the EMTs to pack up the monitors so they could remove the stretcher from the ambulance.

"Nope—she's breathing fine all on her own. She never lost her pulse or pressure."

"Was she ever conscious in the field?"

"No, she's been unresponsive since we found her," Deb said a bit dispiritedly, "but I think we're dealing with just the closed head injury."

"What about the blood?" Pam nodded toward the stain on the sheets and the streaks down Sax's neck, lifting and flexing Sax's limbs. "Good tone, no hyperreflexia," she muttered.

"Her head is cut—something hit her." Jude winced as she stood up. Her legs were sore from the lacerations she'd not noticed earlier, and her muscles were cramped from kneeling on the rough corrugated floor of the ambulance.

"Stein?" Pam glanced from Jude back to the trauma resident for confirmation as the paramedics slid the gurney from the truck. At Deb's nod of assent, Pam said, "I want to get her right to the CT scanner. They're holding it for us. You good with that?"

"Yes. I'll go with you, just in case there's a problem." Deb climbed out, Jude and Melissa right behind her.

Hurrying alongside the wheeled stretcher being steered by the paramedics, Pam was about to suggest that the civilians wait in trauma admitting, but one look at the redhead's face made her change her mind. Mentally sighing, she figured it couldn't be any more of a zoo than it was already going to be, considering who the patient was. Besides, it didn't look like anything short of a nuclear blast could budge the woman from Sinclair's side.

"What's your name?" Pam asked as they commandeered an elevator.

Distractedly, Jude replied, "Jude Castle." Her eyes never left Sax's face, scouring for some kind of movement. *Sax, wake up, for God's sake. Just open your eyes. Just...just come back.* She smoothed the backs of her fingers over Sax's cheek. "Can you tell anything yet?"

The eyes she finally lifted to Pam's were dark with anguish. Pam had seen the look a thousand times. She would have given her the stock answer—*too soon to tell, I'll know more later*—not because she didn't care, but because she couldn't share every single person's pain and still be able to work. But it was Saxon Sinclair lying there, and this woman so obviously loved her.

"There's no sign of focal injury—no paralysis or anything else to suggest major brain damage," Pam said gently. "That's good. That means there's probably no surgical problem that's causing pressure on one part of the brain. The CT scan will tell us that for sure."

"Then she'll wake up soon? She'll be all right?"

Pam hesitated. "Look..."

"Please," Jude said.

"If it's just a concussion, she'll have a megaheadache and nothing else to show for all of this," Pam acquiesced with a sigh, hoping she hadn't just shot herself in the foot by breaking her own rule never to prognosticate. Glancing at Melissa, she said pointedly, "I'd prefer not to have this conversation on tape."

"Sorry." Melissa quickly terminated the tape as they disembarked. "It's automatic. You're welcome to see it and we'll erase—"

"Fine, fine," Pam said absently, her mind already back on her patient. She stopped at the double doors to the CT suite. "You two will have to wait out here. As soon as I see the scans, I'll let you know. Has anyone called her family?"

"Oh God," Jude gasped. "Maddy—I don't even know her number."

"I'll leave that to you," Pam said.

And then the neurosurgeon was gone, and so was Sax. The heavy windowless doors swung shut, and Jude was left standing in the stark, harshly lit hallway, wondering how everything had changed so quickly.

"Jude?" Melissa asked. "Who's Maddy?"

"Her grandmother," Jude said dully. "I need to call her. I'll check Sax's on-call room. There should be something in her wallet..."

"She'll be okay, you know." Melissa tried to sound positive. Man, she felt inadequate. She'd never needed to comfort Jude before. She couldn't ever remember her being really upset even, not personally, not about the kinds of things that people usually got upset about—a love affair gone south or a professional setback—nothing that had ever hit her somewhere deep like this. Jude was always in control; Jude always managed to stay a safe distance away from all the upheaval that plagued most people's lives. "Jude, these people are not going to let anything happen to her. She's...hell, she's..."

"She's just flesh and blood, Mel," Jude said bleakly, "and she's vulnerable, just like all of us." She passed a trembling hand over her face, then seemed to pull herself together with conscious effort. "Come on—let's go see if we can get a key to her on-call room."

September 3, 9:11 a.m.

As she opened the door and stepped into the room, Jude thought about the first morning they had met—Sax standing a few feet away, peeling off her faded jeans, looking unconcerned and wholly oblivious to just how damned attractive she was. *And totally unaware of the effect she was having on me.* Jude realized now that she'd been hooked from that moment. First her body, then her mind, and now...so much more. Everything. There was a small kernel of panic growing in the pit of her stomach, and she had to work very hard to not give it credence. *She's going to be fine. You're not going to lose her now.*

"Her jacket's on the chair," Melissa said, watching Jude cautiously. Her friend was standing still, her expression distant, her entire body rigid with tension. "Want me to look?"

"No." Jude forced herself to concentrate on what needed to be done. "I'll do it."

After crossing the room to the chair, she lifted the black leather jacket, caressing her palm over the surface worn smooth by years of use. She thought of the times she had rested her cheek against it while pressed against Sax on the motorcycle. She wanted to rub her face on it, to search for some lingering hint of the heat of Sax's body or a breath of her scent, but she felt the pockets instead, finally locating the wallet in the inner left.

In the billfold, she found Sax's driver's license in a clear plastic slot with several other cards behind it. She slid them out and shuffled through them, noting a medical license, a health insurance card, a donor card, and finally a card with *In Case of Emergency* typed on it. Maddy's name and number were there.

"She even looks good in her license photo," Melissa remarked, peering over Jude's shoulder, trying to distract her friend from her worry. "That's not fair. Nobody looks good in those."

"Mel," Jude's voice almost crackled with tension, "do you think we need to bring this...donor card?"

"Jeez, no," Melissa said sharply, watching Jude's hands tremble. "Put it back. She's probably awake by now."

"Yes, of course, you're right. I'll call Maddy from radiology and let her know what's happened. The CT scan must be done by now."

They were almost to radiology when they heard the overhead PA system blare.

Code Blue...Radiology STAT...Code Blue...Radiology STAT... Code Blue...

They looked at one another, stunned, and then ran.

September 3, 9:36 a.m.

"She's seizing," Deb announced breathlessly as she careened through the doors of the CT room, nearly plowing into Jude and Melissa on the other side. "Fuck. Where do they keep the crash carts around here?"

"What happened?" Jude cried, her fear building as she realized that Deb looked scared. "Deb?"

"I don't know. We were moving her out of the CT scanner, and she started...shaking...sort of." As she spoke, she grabbed a red cart on wheels and began pulling it behind her. "The code team should be here in a second—I've got to get back in there."

Deb pushed the doors open with her shoulder, and Jude and Melissa followed her inside, never even stopping to discuss it. Pam was bent over the stretcher, lifting Sax's eyelid with one finger and peering intently at her pupils.

"It's the damnedest thing," she muttered to no one in particular. "It looks like REM, but it isn't. Not like anything I've ever seen before."

Straightening, she frowned at Jude and Melissa, who looked to be protecting Sax's flank on the other side of the bed. She dismissed their presence as one factor she could not control. "We'd better Dilantinize her, just in case this is some kind of brain stem instability," she said to Deb. "Can you find a loading dose on the crash cart somewhere?"

"I'll have it mixed in a minute," Deb replied tersely, breaking open a vial and drawing the medication into a syringe.

"That's an antiseizure drug, right?" Jude touched her palm to Sax's jaw and softly stroked her face. Sax was shivering all over while her lids fluttered rapidly. Someone answered her question in the affirmative, but Jude couldn't process the information. It was as if every cell in her mind and body had a single focus, as if her entire system was on overload and innately tuned into Sax's, fighting for her survival.

Pam checked Sax's vital signs on the portable monitors. She waved away the members of the code team who had just barreled through the doors ready to start CPR. "Hold off—her signs are all stable." *What the hell is this?*

Jude thought she felt Sax's cheek press into her palm. In her mind, she heard Sax's voice. *I'm very sensitive to any kind of drug. I know that now. I'm careful to avoid them. I don't even take aspirin.*

She turned to the neurosurgeon with urgency. "Can I speak to you, please?"

"I can't tell you anything right now," Pam said sharply. "In a few—"

"It's about Sax. It's important. I think that the Dilantin could hurt her."

Pam looked quickly from the monitors to Jude, her eyes narrowing. "Do you know something about her medical history? For God's sake..."

"I didn't realize—"

"Never mind. Just tell me now." Pam took Jude's arm and led her away from the bed. Over her shoulder, she directed, "Stein, hold the Dilantin but watch her vitals carefully. If her pO2 drops, push it." Facing Jude, she said, "Go ahead."

Jude rapidly related what Sax had told her about the misdiagnoses in her childhood, the problems she'd had as a result of the drug therapy, the unusual REM patterns that no one could explain, and her altered neurologic responses. Desperately, she finished, "I just thought the usual meds might not work or that they might hurt her."

"You might be right," Pam agreed, hiding her surprise and her intense curiosity about what Jude had just told her. Saxon Sinclair was an astounding woman in more ways than one, and she would dearly love the chance to learn more about this aspect of her life. The fact that the very private surgeon had chosen to share such confidences with the redhead suggested to Pam more powerfully than anything else could that she wouldn't be getting to know Saxon quite so intimately.

"We need an EEG before we do anything else," she informed the several medical personnel waiting for instructions. "Dr. Sinclair doesn't seem to be in any kind of trouble, at least not at the moment. Let's move her to trauma admitting, Deb. We'll get a bedside EEG there."

As Deb nodded and moved to wheel the gurney out of the room, Jude stepped over and reached for Sax's hand. Linking her fingers through Sax's, she said firmly, "I'm coming, too."

"Could anyone stop you?" Deb asked with a faint grin.

Jude's heart twisted a little as she realized how much Deb reminded her of Sax at that moment, but she managed to smile back. "Not in this lifetime."

CHAPTER THIRTY-TWO

September 3, 10:23 a.m.

A typical EEG...WAIT...look at this...accelerated or...NO...focal anomaly...seizure activity...no it isn't...more like REM...cycles unusual...what the HELL...

Sax fought to open her eyes despite the piercing glare and found herself staring into a huge silver disk suspended above her head, a hot white bulb in its center. *Oh God.* Waking up...just like before. *Alone.* She recognized the lights...the smell. *Hospital.* Her chest tightened. She tried to move her arms, tried to lift her legs. *Restrained.* She struggled, moaned at the swift surge of pain. A silhouette took shape in her field of vision, backlit by the bright light. She tried unsuccessfully to focus.

"Please..."

Gentle hands touched her cheek; a soft voice spoke. "You're in the hospital. You're going to be all right."

Lies. They tell you lies; they give you drugs; they make you lose yourself. She shuddered. She closed her eyes. *Please.*

"Can you hear me? You're safe."

Lies. Tender fingers brushed her forehead. *They lie.*

"Sax..." Gentle pleading now. "Wake up, please."

She *knew* that voice; she *knew* that touch.

Frantically, she tried again to focus. Features began to emerge from the shadows, giving her something to cling to in the sea of confusion and pain. A face bending near—green eyes, caring and reassuring. Dark red hair, shimmering with gold, a perfect face. The look in those eyes—strong and steady and sure. Tightening her fingers on the hand holding hers, she asked desperately, "Jude?"

"Yes, right here," Jude soothed, seeing the bewilderment in Sax's eyes. *She's trembling. She's terrified.* "I'm right here." Reluctantly, because she had to, she looked away for a second, calling to the doctors still bent over the EEG tracing, "She's awake."

"Don't go," Sax implored, struggling to sit up. She wasn't sure where she was. She wasn't sure what was happening. *They can hurt me...no...Jude is here. This is now, not then. Jude.* "Don't go," she pleaded again.

"Of course not," Jude said, one hand on Sax's shoulder, caressing her. Sax's obvious fear was tearing at her. Her chest ached with the need to comfort her, but she knew it wasn't her sympathy Sax needed. It was her resolve. "Sax, you're at St. Michael's. Everything is all right."

Pam moved to the head of the bed opposite Jude. "Welcome back," she said with a fond smile, but her eyes were searching Sax clinically—examining, assessing. "Do you know who I am?"

Sax studied the tall, lithe figure, her initial panic subsiding, second by second, as she realized that she *did* know who this woman was. Even more importantly, she knew who she *herself* was. "Pam Arnold. Neurosurgeon. And I'm Saxon Sinclair." She turned her head as far as the restraining collar would allow. "And this is my trauma unit."

"Excellent," Pam affirmed with a nod, hoping that her intense relief didn't show. She had so not wanted to put a drill to Sax's skull.

Sax looked from Pam to Jude, aware for the first time that Jude's face was smeared with soot and streaked with sweat...or was it tears? "What happened? Are you hurt?" She tried again to sit up. The two women by the bedside answered simultaneously.

"No, I'm fine. Lie still." Jude pressed one palm to Sax's shoulder.

"You got cracked on the head and sustained a significant concussion, but no serious long-term damage," Pam stated.

"You're sure you're not hurt?" Sax asked again, searching Jude's face.

"I am just fine." Jude smiled, the burden of fear she had labored under for the last sixty minutes finally relenting. "Everyone is."

Satisfied, Sax lifted her left arm to the extent that the arm board taped around it would allow and saw the plastic catheter in her vein.

"Did you give me anything?" She looked at Pam, her face losing the last of its color. *Not again. God, not again.*

"No. Nothing," Pam assured her swiftly. At Sax's look of surprise, she confessed, "You have Ms. Castle to thank for that."

"Thank you," Sax murmured, glancing to Jude and linking still shaky fingers more tightly through hers. She took a deep breath, gradually feeling more settled. Time to move on. "Pam, can you get this damn thing off my neck?"

"Yes, your spine is clear on the CT." Pam released the Velcro straps on the molded cervical collar and removed it. "Do you need something for pain? Let me finish my exam, and I'll order some morphine."

"I'm fine," Sax lied. Her disorientation, while lessening dramatically, had unfortunately been replaced by a throbbing headache—a trade she was happy to accept. She pulled at the strap that ran across her chest pinning her to the narrow table. "Let me up."

"As soon as Stein closes that laceration on your head, we'll get you upstairs to a room." Pam began checking reflexes and motor tone.

"No."

"I'm sorry?"

Sax's expression was implacable. "I'm not going to be admitted."

"Saxon, this isn't negotiable." Pam knew she had an edge to her voice now. *Perfect. Lovely. Just what I need—a power struggle in the middle of a goddamned mass casualty alert.*

"I'm sure you have something better to do than argue with me," Sax said reasonably, as if reading Pam's mind. "I'll sign the Against Medical Advice form if you insist, but I'm not staying."

"Now look—"

"Can I talk to her for a minute...alone?" Jude interrupted calmly. Sax's voice was strong and her eyes were clear, but she was pale as the sheets and the hand that lay in Jude's palm shook. It was clear to Jude that she was in pain.

"Be my guest," Pam replied in clipped, angry tones. "I'm going to check on my *other* patients." She glanced at Jude, who was softly stroking Sax's arm, and added curtly, "Talk some sense into her."

"As if I could," Jude said with a smile. Before Sax could make any kind of argument, she leaned down until her lips nearly touched Sax's ear and whispered, "Do you have any idea how much I love you?"

Sax carefully turned her head until their eyes met, their lips barely inches apart. Jude's irises were so many swirling shades of green, she almost got lost in them. She forgot what she had meant to say. "How much?" she asked softly instead, just because she wanted to hear her say it.

"So much I can't even imagine being without you." She'd said it. It was the truth, and the truth of it was amazingly simple to accept. *I love you. Yes.* "I was scared to death out there when we found you. I can't go through that again."

"Oh, that's not fair," Sax murmured, desperate to hold her. She reached across with her unrestrained right hand and stroked Jude's cheek, traced her fingers along her jaw, then rested her thumb against the corner of her mouth. "I love you. I'd do anything for you."

"Then stay here," Jude said softly, leaning closer, lightly kissing her forehead.

"I'm scared."

Jude's heart twisted, because she knew what that admission cost. "I'll stay with you."

Sax turned her face away, struggling with old terrors, wanting to embrace new trusts. She felt Jude's touch, knew she was not alone. She drew on that strength, relied on that constancy, as she searched for reason and fought to conquer fear. "Okay. But just overnight."

"Deal."

September 3, 8:45 p.m.

Sax awoke drenched in sweat. Rivers of it soaked her hair, the hospital gown, the sheets. The room was dim, illuminated by a faint light from the bathroom. *Nighttime.*

Pushing the covers aside, she carefully shifted toward the side of the bed. The movement didn't seem to produce any adverse effects. *Headache—nearly gone. Nausea—minimal. Vision—clear. Excellent.*

"What are you doing?" Jude asked from the chair a few feet away where she had been dozing.

"I need a shower."

"I don't think you're supposed to get up." Jude went to Sax's side and brushed the hair from her forehead. It was wet, but Sax's skin was warm, not clammy.

"I'm fine." Sax sat up slowly. *No dizziness. Good.*

"What's going on, then? You're soaked."

"It happens to me sometimes. It's probably just the tail end of the trauma. Like when a fever breaks, I guess." She reached for Jude's hand. "Don't worry."

"Is Pam going to flay me when she discovers I've let you get up?" Jude asked only half teasingly. The neurosurgeon's last words to her had been, "Make sure she stays put."

"With any luck, we'll be gone before she shows up." Sax took two steps, felt fine, then a few more. *All systems go.*

"Sax, you have me at a disadvantage here. I don't want you to hurt yourself. Tell me you're not being stubborn and foolish."

Sax met her eyes. "I need about two days before I can drive or work, but I'm okay. I can rest at Maddy's a lot better than I can here. I won't take chances. I promise."

"Then let me give you a hand."

"Deal."

"These weren't designed for two," Jude observed, bumping her elbow against the shower wall as she carefully worked the lather into Sax's hair.

Sax pressed her hips into Jude's pelvis, observing mischievously, "Maybe they were."

"Stop," Jude breathed, enjoying a little too much the slick feel of Sax's skin against her thigh. She'd been so scared that she would lose her, and now she was so damn glad to have her back. *God, it feels good. Too good.* "There are so many reasons why we can't do this here, I can't even count."

"Mmm, I know." Sax ran her fingers along the edge of Jude's breast, watching her nipple harden. "What were they again?"

"Do that for another second, and I'll forget, so...*stop.*"

"Jude," Sax said quietly, her hands resting on Jude's waist, her expression suddenly serious. "Thank you for this morning. For being there, for talking to Pam about the meds."

"Sax—" Jude started to protest, her palms on Sax's shoulders, their breasts lightly touching, their eyes holding one another.

"No, wait...I'm not done," Sax interrupted, smiling faintly, wanting to say the words. "You took care of me, and I...I needed that. I needed *you*. So I...just..."

"Sax, I love you," Jude said. Firmly. Clearly. Tenderly. "I need you."

Sax closed her eyes, rested her forehead on Jude's. "God, I love you."

"Good," Jude whispered and kissed her. *So very good*.

After a moment, Sax moved her mouth to Jude's ear and murmured, "I can't remember why we weren't supposed to do this."

A sharp knock resounded loudly on the bathroom door, clearly audible even above the pounding of the running water.

"That would be one," Jude said dryly. She turned the knobs to off and slid the curtain back. "Yes?"

"Sinclair better be in there," Pam Arnold warned from the other side of the door.

"Uh, could you give us a minute?" Jude called.

"No."

"We need to get dressed."

"I'm not hearing this," Pam's voice announced ominously. "I'm really not. Five minutes."

When they emerged, Sax was in the jeans and T-shirt Jude had retrieved earlier from her on-call room, and Jude wore the clean clothes Melissa had delivered from her apartment. They found Pam waiting in the room's only chair, legs crossed, looking elegant and decidedly cool.

"You agreed to stay overnight. It's 9:30 p.m." She fixed Sax with a piercing stare.

"I'm fine," Sax replied.

Before Pam could snarl a response, the door opened and Deb Stein entered, followed closely by Melissa.

"Hey, boss," Deb called, smiling with delight. "You're up!"

"Hi," Melissa added.

"Wonderful. Now we can have a party," Pam growled, rising to her feet. "You two," she addressed the newcomers. "Out."

As they looked from her to Sax and Jude in confusion, the door opened yet again.

"Whoa," Melissa blurted before she could stop herself as a woman stepped inside.

"Maddy," Sax exclaimed. "I thought Jude told you on the phone not to come."

"I know that, Saxon." Maddy smiled at Mel, who was staring unabashedly at her. "But you can't drive that motorcycle, and I was certain that you would be about ready to leave by now."

"How did you get here? Tell me you didn't drive the Rolls," Sax cried.

"There's a very nice policeman right out in front of the hospital who is watching it," Maddy explained, her eyes twinkling. Saxon appeared fine, just as Jude had said, but she felt better seeing for herself. She knew what being a patient would do to her granddaughter.

"Oh my God," Sax moaned. "I have to go see to it right now."

"Wait a minute." Pam was very nearly shouting.

"Ah, let me make introductions," Jude said quickly before the scene could deteriorate further. As she went around the room getting everyone acquainted, even Pam began to relax.

"Madeleine Lane," Melissa said reverently. "You're Sax's grandmother. Whoa."

"And you're Jude's DP. Lovely work," Maddy said.

Melissa blushed and was, for once, speechless.

"So," Maddy fixed Pam with an assessing stare, "may I take her home? Jude will be there to see that she behaves."

"Maddy," Sax groaned.

"She does seem fine," Pam admitted reluctantly. "I'm not entirely comfortable with the idea, however."

"How about if Deb comes along?" Jude suggested.

"*Check*," Sax whispered to Jude, too low for anyone else to hear. She watched with pleasure as Jude deftly moved the pieces with surgical precision.

"Yes," Maddy agreed. She looked from Mel to Deb. "And you are welcome, too, Melissa. I've lots of room."

"Well..." Mel replied hesitantly, looking at Deb with a question in her eyes.

"It's fine with me," Deb answered with a quick grin at Mel.

Jude moved a little closer to Sax, resting a hand on her back. "Do those arrangements satisfy?"

A wisp of a smile softened Pam's face. "It would seem I've been outmaneuvered. I concede defeat."

"And *mate*," Jude whispered, firmly taking Sax's hand.

Epilogue

Twelve months later

W"ho is it?" Sax called, her scrub shirt half off over her head. "It's me." A deep male voice replied from the hallway outside her on-call room.

Hastily, she pulled down her shirt, quickly crossed to the door, and peered out. She was annoyed to see that, clearly, *he* was on schedule. He looked dashing in black tie, every blond hair in place as always.

"What do you want?" she snapped. "It's already 6:20."

Raising an eyebrow at her obvious state of unreadiness, Aaron said, "I know precisely what time it is. I was just checking to see if *you* were ready."

"No, Aaron, I'm not ready. Do I look ready? Are you planning to help me get dressed? Because if you're not, would you please go away and leave me alone?"

Aaron Townsend was enjoying Sinclair's nervousness. It wasn't often—make that never—that he got to see her even the least bit off her stride. Nervous was just not a word that applied. "Well, if you want me to, I could probably accommodate you."

"Just because I might *once* have said I missed you, I've forgotten that by now. Don't push, or you could be back doing float work on the medical floor."

"Deb just left," he continued, walking into Sax's on-call room and completely ignoring her empty threats. "She looked truly outstanding. Nice ride, too."

Sax raised an eyebrow. "Let me guess. Black Rolls? Mint condition..."

"Uh-huh."

"Please, please, tell me that my grandmother wasn't driving."

"Nah. Some scruffy little blond." When Sax moaned, he laughed and took pity on her. "No, really, a gorgeous chauffeur's driving—tall brunette with cheekbones like Jodie Foster. And Deb's date looks great, too. Melissa's hot."

"The three of them, together, out on the town with the Rolls. It's terrifying." Sax put a hand on his chest and shoved. "Now, get out."

"Where are your clothes?" He still hadn't moved.

"The tailor is dropping them off." Exasperated, she added, "I mean it. Goodbye." She gestured toward the hallway and began nudging him in that direction.

"What time is she picking you up?"

"Twenty minutes, and I still have to shower. So will you please get lost?"

"Yes, Doctor," he said mockingly and stepped back out into the hall. "I'll see you there."

"Yeah, yeah," she muttered, closing the door resoundingly behind him and finally shedding her shirt. She had untied her pants and was about to step out of them when a knock came again. "I'm not kidding," she shouted from her side of the door. "Disappear, as in vanish, unless you intend to come in here and help me off with the rest of my clothes."

For a moment, there was total silence, and then Jude spoke from the hall. "I'm trying to decide who you think might be standing out here. The only one I can reasonably come up with is Pam Arnold, and if that's the case, I'm coming in there to kill you."

Sax pulled the door open for a second time. "What are you doing here? It's not time yet. Is it?"

Jude didn't reply. She leaned against the door frame, shielding her lover from the view of passersby in the hallway, and stared. Sax was standing a few feet away, nearly naked, her scrub pants halfway off her hips, her chest and stomach bare. Despite the fact that Jude had seen her step naked from the shower that morning, and by now she should probably be used to it, the sight of Sax undressed never failed to drive every other thought from her mind. Her palms actually tingled with the urge to touch her.

Finally she managed, "Who were you expecting?"

"No one. Aaron was just here a minute ago bothering me."

"And you invited him to help you get undressed? That's an interesting twist," Jude remarked with a grin. "Something I need to know?"

Sax grinned back. "Not to worry. It was a threat."

"Not to me." Jude crossed the threshold, tossed the garments she was carrying over one arm onto a nearby chair, and kicked the door closed behind her. In one continuous motion, she closed the distance between them until her breasts were against Sax's and her hands were buried in her hair. She pulled Sax even closer, then swallowed Sax's gasp of surprise before slipping her tongue into her lover's mouth. *Always so good.*

When Sax managed to draw a breath, she rasped, "Are you crazy? We have to be there in forty-five minutes. We're not even dressed. Don't...I mean it...*don't* touch me..." And then they were kissing again, and Sax was not resisting.

Coupled, fused, joined by hands and mouth and lips, they slowly moved across the room, never breaking the kiss. When they reached the door to the bathroom, Jude finally lifted her head and whispered, "We can be late."

"No, we can't," Sax groaned desperately. "Your documentary is one of the selections. This is the New York Film Festival, for God's sake. We can't be late for the premiere."

"I can't sit through four hours of speeches thinking about your hands on me," Jude insisted, pushing Sax into the room and against the small sink, then insinuating one thigh between her legs. She watched Sax's eyes grow hazy and knew that she had won. Gripping the sink on either side of Sax's body to hold her in place, she lowered her head and caught a nipple between her teeth.

Sax gave a sharp cry, arching her back as a swift jolt drilled through her spine and sparked fire between her legs. "Oh. Please...if you start..."

"I've already started."

Sax knew she wouldn't last, and she damn well wasn't going to be alone. Adroitly, she worked the zipper down on Jude's slacks and in the same motion slipped her hand in. "Oh yeah—you're ready," she gasped as they both shed clothing.

"I was ready at the door," Jude murmured, moving her lips to

Sax's neck, her teeth to the skin just below her ear. "All it took was seeing you naked."

"Jesus." Sax felt her head about to explode. Each of Jude's sharp cries made her twitch, and as she thrust, Jude rocked. They were synchronized, leading and following, rising and falling together.

Raising her head, Jude's eyes met Sax's. "I'm going to..."

"Yes."

"Now..."

"Yes...now..."

Sax shuddered, Jude shivered, and they held tightly to one another until they could breathe again.

Finally, Sax gathered herself enough to ask, "Did you happen to bring my tux?"

"Of course," Jude said with a shaky laugh. "I brought both of them."

"I love you," Sax whispered.

"I'm so glad."

Sax nuzzled her ear. "You're going to win, you know."

Jude took her hand, thinking of the past year, and tugged her toward the shower. "I already have."

About the Author

Radclyffe is a retired surgeon and full-time author-publisher with over twenty-five lesbian novels and anthologies in print, including the 2005 Lambda Literary Award winners *Erotic Interludes 2: Stolen Moments* ed. with Stacia Seaman and *Distant Shores, Silent Thunder*, a romance. She has selections in multiple anthologies including *Call of the Dark, The Perfect Valentine, Wild Nights, Best Lesbian Erotica 2006, After Midnight, Caught Looking: Erotic Tales of Voyeurs and Exhibitionists, First-Timers, Ultimate Undies: Erotic Stories About Lingerie and Underwear*, and *Naughty Spanking Stories 2*. She is the recipient of the 2003 and 2004 Alice B. Readers' award for her body of work and is also the president of Bold Strokes Books, a lesbian publishing company.

Her forthcoming works include the fourth in the Provincetown Tales, *Storms of Change* (October 2006), *Erotic Interludes 4: Extreme Passions* ed. with Stacia Seaman (October 2006), and the romance *When Dreams Tremble* (January 2007).

Look for information about these works at www.boldstrokesbooks. com.

Books Available From Bold Strokes Books

Sleep of Reason by Rose Beecham. Nothing is at it seems when Detective Jude Devine finds herself caught up in a small-town soap opera. And her rocky relationship with forensic pathologist Dr. Mercy Westmoreland just got a lot harder. (1-933110-53-8)

Passion's Bright Fury by Radclyffe. When a trauma surgeon and a filmmaker become reluctant allies on the battleground between life and death, passion strikes without warning. (1-933110-54-6)

Broken Wings by L-J Baker. When Rye Woods, a fairy, meets the beautiful dryad Flora Withe, her libido, as squashed and hidden as her wings, reawakens along with her heart. (1-933110-55-4)

Combust the Sun by Andrews & Austin. A Richfield and Rivers mystery set in L.A. Murder among the stars. (1-933110-52-X)

Of Drag Kings and the Wheel of Fate by Susan Smith. A blind date in a drag club leads to an unlikely romance. (1-933110-51-1)

Tristaine Rises by Cate Culpepper. Brenna, Jesstin, and the Amazons of Tristaine face their greatest challenge for survival. (1-933110-50-3)

Too Close to Touch by Georgia Beers. Kylie O'Brien believes in true love and is willing to wait for it. It doesn't matter one damn bit that Gretchen, her new and off-limits boss, has a voice as rich and smooth as melted chocolate. It absolutely doesn't... (1-933110-47-3)

100th Generation by Justine Saracen. Ancient curses, modern-day villains, and a most intriguing woman who keeps appearing when least expected lead archeologist Valerie Foret on the adventure of her life. (1-933110-48-1)

Battle for Tristaine by Cate Culpepper. While Brenna struggles to find her place in the clan and the love between her and Jess grows, Tristaine is threatened with destruction. Second in the Tristaine series. (1-933110-49-X)

The Traitor and the Chalice by Jane Fletcher. Without allies to help them, Tevi and Jemeryl will have to risk all in the race to uncover the traitor and retrieve the chalice. The Lyremouth Chronicles Book Two. (1-933110-43-0)

Promising Hearts by Radclyffe. Dr. Vance Phelps lost everything in the War Between the States and arrives in New Hope, Montana, with no hope of happiness and no desire for anything except forgetting—until she meets Mae, a frontier madam. (1-933110-44-9)

Carly's Sound by Ali Vali. Poppy Valente and Julia Johnson form a bond of friendship that lays the foundation for something more, until Poppy's past comes back to haunt her—literally. A poignant romance about love and renewal. (1-933110-45-7)

Unexpected Sparks by Gina L. Dartt. Falling in love is complicated enough without adding murder to the mix. Kate Shannon's growing feelings for much younger Nikki Harris are challenging enough without the mystery of a fatal fire that Kate can't ignore. (1-933110-46-5)

Whitewater Rendezvous by Kim Baldwin. Two women on a wilderness kayak adventure—Chaz Herrick, a laid-back outdoorswoman, and Megan Maxwell, a workaholic news executive—discover that true love may be nothing at all like they imagined. (1-933110-38-4)

Erotic Interludes 3: Lessons in Love ed. by Radclyffe and Stacia Seaman. Sign on for a class in love…the best lesbian erotica writers take us to "school." (1-9331100-39-2)

Punk Like Me by JD Glass. Twenty-one-year-old Nina writes lyrics and plays guitar in the rock band Adam's Rib, and she doesn't always play by the rules. And oh yeah—she has a way with the girls. (1-933110-40-6)

Coffee Sonata by Gun Brooke. Four women whose lives unexpectedly intersect in a small town by the sea share one thing in common—they all have secrets. (1-933110-41-4)

The Clinic: Tristaine Book One by Cate Culpepper. Brenna, a prison medic, finds herself deeply conflicted by her growing feelings for her patient, Jesstin, a wild and rebellious warrior reputed to be descended from ancient Amazons. (1-933110-42-2)

Forever Found by JLee Meyer. Can time, tragedy, and shattered trust destroy a love that seemed destined? When chance reunites two childhood friends separated by tragedy, the past resurfaces to determine the shape of their future. (1-933110-37-6)

Sword of the Guardian by Merry Shannon. Princess Shasta's bold new bodyguard has a secret that could change both of their lives. *He* is actually a *she*. A passionate romance filled with courtly intrigue, chivalry, and devotion. (1-933110-36-8)

Wild Abandon by Ronica Black. From their first tumultuous meeting, Dr. Chandler Brogan and Officer Sarah Monroe are drawn together by their common obsessions—sex, speed, and danger. (1-933110-35-X)

Turn Back Time by Radclyffe. Pearce Rifkin and Wynter Thompson have nothing in common but a shared passion for surgery. They clash at every opportunity, especially when matters of the heart are suddenly at stake. (1-933110-34-1)

Chance by Grace Lennox. At twenty-six, Chance Delaney decides her life isn't working so she swaps it for a different one. What follows is the sexy, funny, touching story of two women who, in finding themselves, also find one another. (1-933110-31-7)

The Exile and the Sorcerer by Jane Fletcher. First in the Lyremouth Chronicles. Tevi, wounded and adrift, arrives in the courtyard of a shy young sorcerer. Together they face monsters, magic, and the challenge of loving despite their differences. (1-933110-32-5)

A Matter of Trust by Radclyffe. JT Sloan is a cybersleuth who doesn't like attachments. Michael Lassiter is leaving her husband, and she needs Sloan's expertise to safeguard her company. It should just be business—but it turns into much more. (1-933110-33-3)

Sweet Creek by Lee Lynch. A celebration of the enduring nature of love, friendship, and community in the quirky, heart-warming lesbian community of Waterfall Falls. (1-933110-29-5)

The Devil Inside by Ali Vali. Derby Cain Casey, head of a New Orleans crime organization, runs the family business with guts and grit, and no one crosses her. No one, that is, until Emma Verde claims her heart and turns her world upside down. (1-933110-30-9)

Grave Silence by Rose Beecham. Detective Jude Devine's investigation of a series of ritual murders is complicated by her torrid affair with the golden girl of Southwestern forensic pathology, Dr. Mercy Westmoreland. (1-933110-25-2)

Honor Reclaimed by Radclyffe. In the aftermath of 9/11, Secret Service Agent Cameron Roberts and Blair Powell close ranks with a trusted few to find the would-be assassins who nearly claimed Blair's life. (1-933110-18-X)

Honor Bound by Radclyffe. Secret Service Agent Cameron Roberts and Blair Powell face political intrigue, a clandestine threat to Blair's safety, and the seemingly irreconcilable personal differences that force them ever farther apart. (1-933110-20-1)

Protector of the Realm: Supreme Constellations Book One by Gun Brooke. A space adventure filled with suspense and a daring intergalactic romance featuring Commodore Rae Jacelon and the stunning, but decidedly lethal, Kellen O'Dal. (1-933110-26-0)

Innocent Hearts by Radclyffe. In a wild and unforgiving land, two women learn about love, passion, and the wonders of the heart. (1-933110-21-X)

The Temple at Landfall by Jane Fletcher. An imprinter, one of Celaeno's most revered servants of the Goddess, is also a prisoner to the faith—until a Ranger frees her by claiming her heart. The Celaeno series. (1-933110-27-9)

Force of Nature by Kim Baldwin. From tornados to forest fires, the forces of nature conspire to bring Gable McCoy and Erin Richards close to danger, and closer to each other. (1-933110-23-6)

In Too Deep by Ronica Black. Undercover homicide cop Erin McKenzie tracks a femme fatale who just might be a real killer…with love and danger hot on her heels. (1-933110-17-1)

Stolen Moments: Erotic Interludes 2 by Stacia Seaman and Radclyffe, eds. Love on the run, in the office, in the shadows…Fast, furious, and almost too hot to handle. (1-933110-16-3)

Course of Action by Gun Brooke. Actress Carolyn Black desperately wants the starring role in an upcoming film produced by Annelie Peterson. Just how far will she go for the dream part of a lifetime? (1-933110-22-8)

Rangers at Roadsend by Jane Fletcher. Sergeant Chip Coppelli has learned to spot trouble coming, and that is exactly what she sees in her new recruit, Katryn Nagata. The Celaeno series. (1-933110-28-7)

Justice Served by Radclyffe. Lieutenant Rebecca Frye and her lover, Dr. Catherine Rawlings, embark on a deadly game of hide-and-seek with an underworld kingpin who traffics in human souls. (1-933110-15-5)

Distant Shores, Silent Thunder by Radclyffe. Dr. Tory King—along with the women who love her—is forced to examine the boundaries of love, friendship, and the ties that transcend time. (1-933110-08-2)

Hunter's Pursuit by Kim Baldwin. A raging blizzard, a mountain hideaway, and a killer-for-hire set a scene for disaster—or desire—when Katarzyna Demetrious rescues a beautiful stranger. (1-933110-09-0)

The Walls of Westernfort by Jane Fletcher. All Temple Guard Natasha Ionadis wants is to serve the Goddess—until she falls in love with one of the rebels she is sworn to destroy. The Celaeno series. (1-933110-24-4)

Change Of Pace: *Erotic Interludes* by Radclyffe. Twenty-five hot-wired encounters guaranteed to spark more than just your imagination. Erotica as you've always dreamed of it. (1-933110-07-4)

Honor Guards by Radclyffe. In a wild flight for their lives, the president's daughter and those who are sworn to protect her wage a desperate struggle for survival. (1-933110-01-5)

Fated Love by Radclyffe. Amidst the chaos and drama of a busy emergency room, two women must contend not only with the fragile nature of life, but also with the irresistible forces of fate. (1-933110-05-8)

Justice in the Shadows by Radclyffe. In a shadow world of secrets and lies, Detective Sergeant Rebecca Frye and her lover, Dr. Catherine Rawlings, join forces in the elusive search for justice. (1-933110-03-1)

shadowland by Radclyffe. In a world on the far edge of desire, two women are drawn together by power, passion, and dark pleasures. An erotic romance. (1-933110-11-2)

Love's Masquerade by Radclyffe. Plunged into the indistinguishable realms of fiction, fantasy, and hidden desires, Auden Frost is forced to question all she believes about the nature of love. (1-933110-14-7)

Love & Honor by Radclyffe. The president's daughter and her lover are faced with difficult choices as they battle a tangled web of Washington intrigue for...love and honor. (1-933110-10-4)

Beyond the Breakwater by Radclyffe. One Provincetown summer, three women learn the true meaning of love, friendship, and family. (1-933110-06-6)

Tomorrow's Promise by Radclyffe. One timeless summer, two very different women discover the power of passion to heal and the promise of hope that only love can bestow. (1-933110-12-0)

Love's Tender Warriors by Radclyffe. Two women who have accepted loneliness as a way of life learn that love is worth fighting for and a battle they cannot afford to lose. (1-933110-02-3)

Love's Melody Lost by Radclyffe. A secretive artist with a haunted past and a young woman escaping a life that has proved to be a lie find their destinies entwined. (1-933110-00-7)

Safe Harbor by Radclyffe. A mysterious newcomer, a reclusive doctor, and a troubled gay teenager learn about love, friendship, and trust during one tumultuous summer in Provincetown. (1-933110-13-9)

Above All, Honor by Radclyffe. Secret Service Agent Cameron Roberts fights her desire for the one woman she can't have—Blair Powell, the daughter of the president of the United States. (1-933110-04-X)